T0163538

Trust no one:

The Jay-Razor story

Deon Hayes

iUniverse, Inc.
New York   Bloomington

Copyright © 2009 by Deon Hayes

All rights reserved. No part of this book may be used
or reproduced by any means, graphic, electronic, or
mechanical, including photocopying, recording, taping or
by any information storage retrieval system without the
written permission of the publisher except in the case of brief
quotations embodied in critical articles and reviews.

iUniverse books may be ordered through booksellers or by contacting:
iUniverse
1663 Liberty Drive
Bloomington, IN 47403
www.iuniverse.com
1-800-Authors (1-800-288-4677)

Because of the dynamic nature of the Internet, any Web addresses or
links contained in this book may have changed since publication and may
no longer be valid. The views expressed in this work are solely those of
the author and do not necessarily reflect the views of the publisher, and
the publisher hereby disclaims any responsibility for them.

ISBN: 978-1-4401-5028-9 (sc)
ISBN: 978-1-4401-5029-6 (ebook)

Printed in the United States of America

iUniverse rev. date: 03/01/2010

Chapter 1

He packed all he had into a small duffle bag he stole from another boy, and two-hundred dollars. He opens the window and looks down two stories. In the distance, he can see the pick up truck approaching. He prays it parks in the same spot it does every third night. It pulls into that very spot, Jason's excited.

Just then, the same person gets out of the truck. Jay time's it. They do a night check on the boy's every fifteen minutes. The laundry guy loads the back of the truck in ten minutes, with the dirty laundry. Then goes back in, two minutes after the count clears. Gets his coffee then back to the truck, and he drives away.

This means, Jay has to close the window and lay back down in his bed. Just as he does, they flick the light on, and count him. It's just been him for the last three days. His last roommate committed suicide, after he had been raped in the day room while there was a code 99 called, on another block.

Once they turned his light off Jay got up. As he looked down, he could see the guy had loaded the back of the pick-up truck. He slowly opened the window, and let his bag drop first.

Then he climbs onto the window ledge and jumped, once he landed safely in the truck. He quickly covered himself with the dirty laundry bags. And waited for the truck to drive off. Jay had talked to the guy quite often, so he knew the guy's route. He would drive about five miles down the street, where there's a truck stop. He would stop and get something to eat. That's when Jay would sneak into another truck. Jay feels the truck come to a stop. Then he hears the door slam. He waits a few minutes, when he thinks it is clear, he makes his move.

He quickly climbs out of the truck. He grabs his bag, and looks around. He sees the bus stop, and decides to catch the bus instead he goes inside and buy a one-way ticket to D.C. and goes back outside to wait. He sits on the bench, as he goes into deep thought about his first time he was adopted he was adopted twice, and brought back, both times. The first time he was nine years old. The family were the Millers they had a daughter who was two years older then Jason she wore the nicest clothes, and the family treated her like a little princess.

Once Jason arrived things started missing like jewelry, money etc It was hard for them to believe, but they know it could be no one but Jason. One day Jason's new father was missing one-hundred dollars from his wallet. He knew it was there before he got into the shower. Then another incident, were his mom's necklace came up missing as well. But once Dad's watch disappeared, he had had it. And in order to make it official, his sister put her Dad's watch in Jason's top drawer. So when his Mom opened it to put his laundry away she would see it.

She called Jason and asked him where he got it from. He said he never saw it before. That was the first time.

The second time was with the Browns. Jason was thirteen years old. There was Tim, their fourteen-year-old son, and their five-year-old daughter Kate Lynn.

Tim and Jason played baseball everyday and today was no different. Jason's in the house he grabs the bat and ball to go and meet his brother out back to play. He goes out back, and walks around looking for Tim. As he walks pass the shed, he hears noises coming from inside. He steps closer and hears a little kid voice. Jason opens the door to find his little sister naked, giving head to his new older brother. Jason becomes enraged. He tells his sister to get dressed, as he drags Tim out of the shed and starts to beat him with the bat. His parents heard the screaming, and came running out of the house. Thou Jason had explained, what had happened. The Browns did not believe him. He was taken back again, that was the second time.

Jason was a little guy, he stood only 4' 10" at age fourteen. Because he was small, he learned how to keep a razor in his mouth for protection from the bigger kids in the foster home. They got patted down for weapons from time to time so Jason learned to eat, talk and do just about anything, with that razor in his mouth. One day while they were on a field trip, two of the kids tried to take him behind a bush to rape him. Jason cut the one boy across the top of his hand, and till this day, he has no feeling in that hand the other boy left with no scars. But has a lot more respect for Jason then he had.

They never tried, to cross his path again. This all went through Jason's mind as he looked out the bus window. As it passed field after field Jason reached into his bag and pulled out his walkman. He put his headphones on, and pushed play. His favorite rapper 'Redman' came through, the headphones. He bopped his head to the music, as he thought of how his life was about to change for the better.

While Jason was in deep thought, he falls asleep. Forty minutes later, the bus comes to a stop. A few people get on, and it takes off again. A girl gets on and looks down the aisles. There are seats, but she sits next to Jason. As Jason feels someone sit next to him, he grabs his bag and turns. He is then tapped on the shoulder.

"Excuse me? Hi, my name's Pamela, but everyone calls me Pam and your name?" She asked while extending her hand.

"Jason! How are you Pam?" He replied, as he shook her hand.

"Fine, now that I'm leaving this town".

"Oh yeah! So where are you, going?" he questioned.

"As far, as my money will take me!" She reasoned.

"Ha! I know that story, all too well."

"Yeah! Why, Where are you going?"

"Same place babe, same place." He stated, nodding his head.

"Well are you going to meet someone, or what?"

" Kinda, I'm going to meet my destiny".

"Well, I don't want to stop you, from getting your rest. So I'll just read my book". Pam reasoned.

"Oh no! You're not bothering me. It's just nice friendly, conversation. I don't mind cause, who knows, what lays ahead for either one of us. Hey what are you reading?"

"Just this new book 'Flawless' I just got. It's from this new author Deon Hayes, he's good".

"Yeah! So you read a lot, huh?"

"Whenever I get a chance. There's nothing like a good book, to help you relax. So you can get your head right".

"I'll keep that in mind" He spat.

"Hey, I don't have that much money to get a room, and I know you just met me but, is there any way we could share a room, when we get to D.C?" Pam questioned.

"Look! I know we just met and where busting it up and all, but I don't think that would be a good idea. Cause on the real! Trusting people, is not one of my strong points. Tell you what thou, if I gave you fifty dollars, would that help?" Jay offered.

Pam turns cold.

Never mind, I thought we were cool? she said not looking at him.

At this, Jason put his headphones back on and pushed play. Five minutes later, she taps him on the shoulder.

"Okay look, can I still take you up on that offer?"

Jason takes off his headphones.

"Look, I got to ask you this! What's your hustle?" Jay spat.

"What do you mean?" She shot back.

"I mean how do you plan to get money, once we hit D.C.? Cause I roll dolo, you can't roll wit me, unless your shit is 110%. That means if you slipping 10%, your shit is still 100% feel me?" Jay reasoned.

"I like that! That's some food for thought right there, for that ass!" She replies.

"Okay! I feel you. You need me to prove myself to you. Than that's what I'll do". She spat.

They, just sit and talk awhile longer, until their bus pulls, into D.C. they grab their bags, and get off. Pam walks with Jason to the motel. As he checks in he gets his room key.

"Okay so your, in room #24. I'll see you in a little while".

Jason hands her fifty dollars. And she steps off.

Jason thought to himself. Well that's that! I will not be seeing her again. That's how the streets are. People talk the talk, but seldom walk the walk. Get what they can, and it's a rap. He seen it happen before.

Jason opens the door, and turns on the light. He's standing in the door way, then it hits him. He's free. And everything in this little room is his, as long as he pays for it. And, he can really sleep, with no worries. He closes the door, and jumps on the bed. He just lays there, and collects his thoughts. Ten minutes later, he gets up and empties out his bag. He has two pair of pants, two T-shirts. And one hoodie, that he had on, and his walkman. He took off his clothes, and went to take a shower. As he's in the shower, he thinks about the group home again, and how he couldn't just relax in the shower. Like he is now. This is the best feeling, Jason has had, in some time.

He stepped out of the shower, with the towel wrapped around his waist. He heard a knock at the door. He walked over, and peeked out of the window. To his surprise, he saw Pam, standing out front holding two bags.

"Hold on!" He yelled. He threw on his sweat pants, and a T-shirt and then went back to the door. He opens the door. Pam comes in with this huge smile on her face.

"What's gotten into you!" He questioned. She starts to lay out pants. Two pair of Roc-a–Wear jeans, one pair of Sean John. A couple T-shirts, and three hoodies.

"So how's that!" Pam replies.

"What's this?"

"There your new clothes! For this new town". A huge smile goes across Jason's face.

"What do you mean my new clothes!? I don't have the money, to pay you for all of this!"

"Jason! Friends don't need to pay friends back. You needed me to prove myself to you, and I did. That's my hustle, I'm a booster. All I want to do, is have a place to chill tonight. Now, am I good for that?" She inquired.

Jason still in awe. Not knowing what to do, because no one ever got him anything. Except when Mrs. Miller took him out shopping. But, as soon as he was taken back, all the other kids stole it all. But he never had Roc-A-Wear or Sean John. He couldn't stop thanking her. He hugged her tight. And at that very instant, they bonded.

"Okay, okay! So I can stay? Don't go getting all mushy on me". She stated.

" It's not that! It's just. I really only ever had one true friend. And when he got adopted he sent me a new pair of sneakers. And we wrote and kept in touch. Other than that! No I never trusted anyone enough, to call a friend".

"Well Jay! Those days are over, out with the old ways, in with the new. Hey! There's a nice little Ice

Cream Shop, across the street. You like ice cream, right?" Pam asks.

"Of course! Let's go?" He replied.

"Hold on a sec! In case you didn't notice, I still need to get dressed." He grabs his new clothes and goes to the bathroom and changes. Pam sits in the chair in the far corner and waits. Pam talks to Jason through the door.

So, I bet you had no idea you would see me again huh?

Well that thought had crossed my mind, the minute you left. As he comes out of the bathroom.

"Wow! You clean up good". Pam states excitedly.

"Thanks but what I look like before, a junkie?" They both laugh together aloud.

"No, I'm not saying that! Come on, lets get outta here". Jason grabs some money. They leave and he locks up.

"Hey thanks again for the clothes".

" Jason, you thanked me like ten times already, forget about it!"

She grabs his hand, and they cross the street.

"Hey, I need a haircut let's go in here?"

"Jay, you do not need a hair cut, trust me, your straight". She inquired.

"Well, let's go into that deli, I need change and some gum".

They walk into the deli, Jason sees the young girl behind the counter. And goes to work.

Good afternoon! Can I help you? The girl asked.

Yes you can, can I have that cherry chapstick right there.

He said pointing behind the girl as she turned to get it, he quickly snatched a pack of gum off the counter and stuck it in his pocket. As he pulled out his fresh $50 bill,

Do you have anything smaller? She asked.

"No I don't." He replied, lying.

She starts to ring him up. As he bends down, to act like he's tying his sneaker he comes back up. And hands her a ten she make change for the fifty, as she counts it back to him. Pam's eye's lit up.

Once outside the store.

"So you're a flimflam artist?"she spat.

"No! You seen that, huh? That's just one hustle, stick around, you'll see." As Jason hands her a twenty.

"What's this for?"

"Were friends, right?"

"Sure, but you don't have to give me your money Jay".

" Look, never turn down free money, cause it don't come often".

" Jay, there's no such thing, as "free money"." She answered.

"That's true! That is so very true. But take it any way as a friendly jester".

"Thanks! So where are we going?"

" Let's just walk and get to know the neighborhood, If were gonna be here for a while".

"Sounds good to me, I like how you walk".

"What do you mean, you like how I walk. How do I walk different from anyone else?"

"You walk smooth with a little hop stroll thing, going on".

"Hey! If you say so".

They step across the street to the Billiards Jay walks in first. He takes a deep breath.

"Awe! I love the smell of the chalk in a pool hall".

"Oh yeah, you know how to shoot?"

"Oh yeah! I live to play this game". He replies.

They go and get some balls as they pick a table.

"Why you pick the table over here?"

"Cause over here, we can see everything as it happens, and if we had to dip out, there's the exit" .He stated pointing.

"Jay I don't know if your scared, or just smart as hell" Pam says.

"Well I must be smart as hell. Cause there's not to many things, that I'm scared of believe that!" He stated.

They continue to play awhile longer they notice this couple who just got a table next to their's, Jay watches the guy take a few shots.

"Wow! Now he's good". The guy sees Jay looking at him he goes over and introduces himself.

"Hi! How are you? I'm Jason, Jason Sauve".

"Hello, I'm Jay and this is my girl, Pam".

"Hi Pam, nice to meet you. This is my girl, Jen. Hey would you like to shoot a few games with me?"

"No doubt! I could definitely learn a few things, from you".

"Cool, I'll rack, you break. What kinda soda, you two drinking?"

"Cream! Pam answers".

Jay replies "coke"

"Jen, go and get a couple sodas for us please babe?" He orders.

"Of course! I'll be right back".

Jen walks off and Pam follows to help her carry them back.

"You from around here Jason?" Jay asks.

"No, no, I'm just passing through, I just got here today".

"You, and you're girl?"

That's not really my girl I just met her.

"Damn player! You work fast". At this, they gave each other daps.

"How about you Jay? What's your story?"

"Oh! You and I, are one of the same".

"You know what, I'm feeling a connection with you already. Let me take you up under my wing young boy. For these few days, I'm here. Is that cool with you? As he finish racking, Jay breaks. The girls come back with the drinks. Pam comes over, laughing.

"Jason! We gotta hang out with them. This girl is crazy! That guy over there, started flirting with us, she told him. I'd give you my number if you pay for our drinks. He went to pull out some money, she said me, my girl friend, and our boy friends and he did".

"Hey that's my favorite price free!" They all started laughing, except Jay.

The girls excused themselves and went to play the arcade games. Jason and Jay continued to talk.

"Hey! I seen that look that came across your face when she said flirting, Does this girl, got you open?"

"No! We just met, I mean she's cool and all but-"

"Hold up youngster! I asked you a simple question. And you gave me a nervous answer. What's up with that? Look, if your truly are out here in these streets, by yourself. Take this advise over everything, I want to teach you. Just cause your in these streets, don't wear your heart on your shoulders".

" rule #1 Jealousy is a weak emotion, Do what you gotta do to get it out of your system if you don't, it will destroy you. Rule #2 Women come, and women go, But know one thing, no matter how much you do for a women, how much you love, a women. Always respect, when they say it's over, I mean try to understand her. And if you do really love a women, fight to keep her. But if she ever tells you no matter what you do. I don't want to be with you, any more, respect that, and step off. Never hit a woman, and never try to keep a woman where she doesn't want, to be. That should go without saying. You feel me?" Jason spat.

"Hey, I feel everything you're telling me. But hold that thought, I gotta go to the bathroom".

" Cool, I'll watch your stuff".

"Thanks". Jay steps off, and goes to the bathroom. About ten minutes pass, and Jason thought nothing of it at first. Then he notice, the guys at the front counter that were flirting with the girls were gone.

At this, Jason act like he was going to the candy machine, as he stepped next to the bathroom, where he heard a loud bang, as he pushed the door open he saw two guys holding Jay's arms while the other one kept hitting him. As the guy hitting him saw Jason,

"Hey buddy! If you don't want any trouble, turn around and walk out now".

"Hey look, I just want to go to the bathroom". He went as they hit Jay two more times. Jason put his gun on the shoulder of the guy hitting Jay,

"Excuse me can I get in on this?" Jason inquired.

"Now this, is what's gonna happen. I'm gonna hand my man, the heat right here. You two, hold your friends arms". Jason lays into him, with all he's got. The guy falls over, in serious pain. "That's it! That's all your good for, is one punch? Damn!! That's a shame". Jay hands Jason back the gun, as he kicks the guy in the face. His blood spills out on the dirty floor, of the pool hall's bathroom. Jason and Jay, exit the bathroom, and go back to the table.

Damn! Man, that what's up. You didn't have to do

that. But thanks, that felt good, to have someone have my back like that.

"No problem! Young boy, I got you".

" Hey, that sure is a nice piece of chrome you got there". Jay stated, referring to the gun.

"Oh! You like that, huh? That's my little guarantee. I never go outta town without a guarantee, of getting back feel me?" They both laugh together, as they give each other dap.

The girls come back over.

"What's the joke? We wanna laugh too".

"Hey, grab your stuff. We about to bounce up outta here, we had a little run in with the locals. We don't want them to have to much time to call for back up, so let's skate. Hey babe, where's a good place around here, for us to get some thing to eat, my treat of course".

"Come on Jason!, You already done enough for me. I can't, let you treat us".

"Hey, I insist please! Let me, do this? Jen, show us where it's at baby".

She takes them, just around the corner, from the mall. There's a small Italian restaurant.

"Damn Jen! You read me like a book, I love Italian food". He stated.

" Well, I'm glad I made this choice". They go into the restaurant, the host walks up to them

"Welcome four?" The hostess inquired.

"Yes, non- smoking please, thank you".

"Follow me please". Jason follows the host, everyone follows behind Jason. Jay just sits back soaks up Jason's ora. He loved the way Jason, just had this way about him. He was like a tough guy, school boy type, all wrapped up in one.

Once seated, Jason and Jay excused themselves. They went into the bathroom.

"Jay now that you in these streets, you gonna trade that razor, in for some chrome?"

"Man! I would love to, but the truth is, I can't afford it right this minute".

"Youngster, after we finish up here. Were gonna swing by my spot, and I'll see, what I can throw you feel me?"

" No doubt! Damn Jason. You really know how to help, a little nigga out boy, I tell ya. And trust me, I really appreciate all of this, no doubt".

"No problem, I'm here for you dogg. Now let's go out here and have fun with these women, and get our eat on". Jason replied.

At the table, their talk comes to a brief stop. When Jason tells Jen, he's only gonna be in town for three days.

"What do you mean, three days?" She inquired.

"Look, Jen I told you this when I met you the other day. Right off the bus, I'm a drifter. This is what I need to do. A promise I made to myself. I mean, it may sound selfish but that's that. But we can all hang out, until I've gotta roll, If that's cool wit, you all? Come on, don't everybody go getting all bent out of shape on me. Like we all known each other forever! Interesting people, will be in and out of each one of our lives, just make damn sure you get the best lesson, from them. If there's one to be learned and with every interesting person, there usually is". He reasoned.

After they all finished eating...

Jason paid the bill and tip as they all left the restaurant. They all walked down the street to the motel Jason was staying in. They all just sat in the room and all talked freely. Like they've known each other forever.

" Hey Jen! You and Pam feel like walking down the hall, to get some sodas and ice?" Jason questioned.

"Sure! Come on Pam that's his way of saying they need a little time alone". The girls leave, Jason pulls a flat bag out from under the bed. As he unfolds it, its all guns. Jay's eye's, light up.

"Wow! Now that's a nice small arsenal, you got there"

"Well, don't just stand there pick one!" Jason ordered.

"Any one?"

"Yeah Jay! Hurry, the women will be back soon".

At this, Jay grab a 8mm American arms.

"I'll take this one right here!" Once Jay clutched the gun. He fell in love with it, he knew his razor could never protect him, like his new found power. Jason gave him some bullets, and he put it away. The women came back in.

They all sat and talked, well into the night. They

made plans, to meet up the following day. As Jay thanked Jason and Jen.

Jay and Pam left and went back to their room, hand in hand.

The following day…

Jason knocks on the door. Of the room Jay and Pam were staying. As he calls out

"Yo! Jay, you up or what?" Pam comes to the door in her robe.

"He's still sleep, you want me to wake him?" Pam asks.

" Damn! Its 10:00am in the morning, and you two still in bed? It is a new day baby, yeah wake em', tell em' up and at em'. Jen and I will be down the street, at the diner cool?"

"Okay, we will be there shortly".

"Good I will be waiting". Pam closes the door and goes to wake Jay.

"Jay! Get up, so we can meet with Jason and Jen. Their at the diner, down the street".

"That's who was just at the door?" Jay said, half sleep wiping the cold from his eyes.

"Yeah, come on I'm hungry!" Pam Stated.

Jay jumps in the shower. Pam comes in the bathroom, and starts to brush her teeth.

"Hey, are you going to hit that store, and get them clothes for them boys up the street. So we can have some more money?"

She answers. "Yeah!" With a mouth full of toothpaste.

"Good we need to make some fast money, cause we're running low". Jay reasoned.

Jay gets out of the shower. He sees Pam still at the sink, he closes the curtains and reaches for his towel. He wraps it around his waist, as he steps out.

"What was that for?" She asked.

"What?"

"You know Jay, are you a virgin?"

"Are you asking me, am I gay?"

"What's the two, have to do with one another? Why would you think I would think you, were gay?" Pam questioned, stepping towards him.

"Well, I'm 17yrs old, and I was in foster homes, they don't just let us sleep with the girls, you know. And the only ones having sex, on the boys side, was the boys being raped". He spat

"Well, to answer your question kinda". He answered.

"What's kinda?" She replies.

"Well do we have to talk about this now?"

Pam repeats. "What's kinda?"

" Well I had oral sex. I mean I sucked on some breast and I gave the same girl a hickey. She sucked me, you know. But intercourse no! How about you?"

" No".

"That it, just no, not close nothing?" He answered.

 "No". she stated.

"Come on let's go". She throws Jay his hoodie, and they leave.

Chapter 2

At the diner… "Hey you two! Over here". Jason waves them towards their table. As they near the table, Jason stands up and gives Jay dap "what's up partner? How's it going Pam?"

"It's all good Jason!" Pam replied.

"Well that's good to hear, so everybody ready to order or what?"

" Jason, give them some time, Damn! They just sat down. Not everyone's a morning person, cause you are".

"Your right, your right, I'm sorry you two, take your time please but hurry-up". He stated as They all shared a laugh.

Just then…

A guy walks in, Jason recognize. Jason stands up, and calls him over. The guy walks towards, their table.

" Hey Jason, wwhatss uup?" He said, with a strong stutter.

" Look, this is the friend I told you about. Jay this is my old head, they call him poppa rose".

"Please to meet yyou young mman."

"Same here". As Jason excuse himself, and walks away with the guy.

Jen goes, to tell the story about poppa rose-

" You guys, want to hear a funny story? How that guy, got the name poppa rose? Well he was married, to the old lady down the street that runs the cleaners. Well one day, she came home early and found him in the bed, with a younger woman about 18yrs old. Having sex with rose peddles all over the place".

Pam cuts her off. "So, what's so funny about that! It sounds romantic, if it was his wife, and not the girl". Pam stated.

"That's not it, he was on the bed on all fours. And she had a strap-on and was fucking him!"

" WHAT!! Are you, serious?"

" As a heart attack! No lie, I heard she was fucking him like nobody's business! That's some shit huh?"

"No doubt, some nasty shit".

"She first walked in, and heard screaming she didn't recognize, I guess she never heard her husband scream when he gets fucked".

" Stop! That's nasty, your making me sick". Jay said as he looked out the window.

"So what's Jason's business with him?"

Jen answered. "Well the old man, has quite a few connections".

"Did Jason, know him before he got here?"

"Hey, I known Jason, maybe 5 hours, before you two".

" Are you serious?" Pam asked as she looked her up and down.

"Yes! He blew in town I saw him get off the bus, what can I say I see what I want, and I go for it. Apparently Jason's the same way cause, we been together, sense he stepped off that bus".

" This has been the best two days of my life. And I've seriously been thinking, about asking him can I leave with him". She stated.

"Humm, I don't think he's gonna feel that". Jay answered.

"Why you say that Jay! Has he said something to you?"

"No! It's just he comes across as someone really determined to do what he sets out to do and that's that, you feel me?"

"Jay's right Jen Pam chimed in, when he took us all to dinner he said that he's leaving in a few days, he said that with no hesitation".

"I know but, what makes you two so sure, he can't be persuaded?"

"We never said he couldn't be, we were just giving you our opinion".

"Don't think I don't appreciate that, cause I do. It's just I got to hear Jason say it himself".

" Hey everybody I'm back! Sorry to keep ya'll waiting. What's the conversation about? You want to hear me, say what? I heard that part."

Jason inquired.

"Nothing, we'll talk later just, you and I".

" Cool! So what's up Jay? Listen, that guy I was just talking to, Is gonna hook you up with a few things.

I told him to throw your way, feel me? nothing much, but he's got the hook-up and he owes me this, but sense I'm gonna bounce, up outta here tomorrow can't let a favor go to waste, feel me?"

" Sweet, thanks! Yeah I'm feeling you. You're a real cool dude Jason trust me, I'll remember this".

"All it's nothing young boy that's what friends are for. And on these mean streets you gotta take the good with the bad. And I don't want no one to say, Jason Sauve, ain't shit. I always like to leave in good standing, with people, cause a friend will last forever. But an enemy will kill you quick believe that!" Jason reasoned.

"But look on the real, how long do you all plan on staying, in this town?"

" I don't know, why Jason?"

" Cause, Poppa Rose just told me this story about this kid Reese, that went up a few years, on a conspiracy charge, him and his boy was at a party were his boy got stabbed up. Reese started fighting with the other guy who stabbed his boy. After he knocked the boy out, he turn to see where his boy got off to. When he went outside, the people on the lawn, said he got in the car and left. Couple hours later his boy pulls back up, Reese jumped in the car and they rode until they found the other boy. And he shot em'. They said Reese's boy was so coked up, from snorting all night, that after he had been stabbed he drove himself to the hospital, got bandage up. And came back, and even thou his boy shot the kid, Reese was in the car when the police came, his boy dropped dead. He wasn't suppose to leave the hospital but, he sign himself out.

Well, Reese is getting out next week, and I don't think you want to be around here when he gets out. Cause they say he's talking about taking over the town, and all this "King of New York" shit. So just leave theses people, to live out their fantasy themselves, feel me? I'm not saying run, but if you decide to stay, trust me, I got you covered?" Jason spat.

"Look, we'll talk some more later. But for now, let's order, and eat and be merry". Jason waves over a waitress. Everyone orders, she leaves Jen ask,

" So Jason! Are you looking for some company out there all alone, on the road?"

"Tell you what Jen, I'm feeling you like that, on the real but theses streets are mean and there definitely not a place, I want anyone I care about on".

" But I"- he cuts her off

" I'm not finished yet! If you want to come visit me in the next state over. I have no problem with that, but as far as us traveling together, no way. I'm sorry if it sounds mean, but that's the way it is".

he puts his hand on her chin, and lift up her head, as he kiss her. " Is that cool"?

" Hey, sure Jason If that's all I can get, I'll take it".

" Oh trust me, in the famous words of' biggie'

tonight, were gonna party and bullshit, and party and bullshit"….

Everyone laughs as their drinks come, they sit and talk more. Then their food comes. They eat.

" So you think it's best, that Pam and I leave huh?"

" Hey, look I'm just looking out for your best interest, feel me? But like I said, we'll talk later"-

"So, Jason how do you stay in such, great shape?" pam asked.

"Ha-ha, well I'm a member of World Gym. And just about every state has one. So I swing through, and do my thing". Jason answers.

Kathy, the local "crack head" walks into the diner. And walks over to Jason.

"Hey Jason! Can I talk to you, for a minute?"

" Hey Kathy! What's up?"They step over to the side, just far enough away from the table, so is that no one can hear their conversation. A few hand movements later, Jason's back at the table.

"Jason, what was that all about"? Jen questions.

"The cops, are at the hotel I'm in. Someone was breaking into rooms".

"Jason! Why do you talk to that stankin' crack head?" Jen said with an attitude.

" Cause, people like that! Keep me informed with the streets. And that's what you need, out here, Is people to have your back, crack heads, dope feins etc". Jason stated as he looked her up and down, then continued.

Stop judging people, please! It's very unbecoming".

"So Jay, what kinda books do you read, I mean what are your interests?"

" Me, well I like Donald Goines, K'wan, Deon Hayes, Brandon Massey etc". He turns, an cracks a smile at Pam. "Those are just a few of the author's, I read but there's this other guy called, the Dreamer. He writes Poetry, he's hot too".

"So what books of Donald Goines, did you read. Cause I read few of his".

" Daddy cool, Crime Partners, Whore Son".

"Okay yeah! I like that one a lot, and this other guy Deon Hayes?"

"Oh he's new, but he got this book "Flawless" it's hot. Get that".

" I will, no doubt hey if you all will excuse me, I want to get back to the hotel just in case one of the rooms were mine, that got broke into feel me?"

" Hey! Can I come along"? Jen asked.

"Of course Jen, I wouldn't have it no other way". Jason replied.

Jason takes care of the bill, as he leaves with Jen.

"Hey, you look so fresh, in your white tee. Do you know who started the white tee thing?" Jen questioned.

" No doubt! "New York" It's like this, you got ten dudes chillin' on the corner. Shooting dice, hustling whatever, all wearing Air force one's and either some Roc-a-wear jeans, state Property, or Sean John, some thing pops off cops jumps out on you. The chase is on, you run around the corner. There's ten to fifteen, more people wearing the same thing. 'Camouflage', from the cops. It's a hood thing baby, you wouldn't understand". Jason explained.

"Wow! I would have never thought of that, that's smart".

"Yeah, the hoods funny like that, some times". As they continue down the side walk these two kids say hi to Jason.

"That's really funny".

" What's that?"

"Them two kids, I've known them for years. And they don't even know my name, and I live here. You've been here for 2 days. And it's like the whole town knows you, what's up with that?" Jen asked.

" Listen to this advise I'm about to give you, there's more room for love on the outside don't keep it bottled up inside, let it out".

just then…

A kid rides by in a hoopdie, he's leaning to one side his systems banging "Jada kiss's" "animal" Jason screams

"Okay, that's my shit! Damn it's nice as hell, out here".

"Yes, it is isn't it?" Jen replies.

They reach the motel, Jason goes up to the front. As he reaches the office, and talks to the woman. His room, was not one that was broken into. As he thanks God. And gives a sigh of relief.

"That's what's up, I can breath easy now". Jason reasoned.

"That's good baby let's go in". Jen stated.

" After you sweetheart". Jen walks in,

"Who's that lying on the bed?" Jen asked, pointing at the stranger.

Jason, grabs his gun. As he pushes Jen to the side. He then puts the gun to the mans head, as he smacks the shit out of him.

The man wakes up.

" What the fuck!" He screams while rubbing his head.

But he looks more surprised, when he sees the gun in his face.

" Hey man I-" He started to talk as Jason waved him silent.

Jason grabs him, by his shirt and pulls him, to his feet.

"Now I'm doing the talking, what are you looking for in my room? And if I were you, I would chose my words wisely. So let's have it?" Jason stated with venom dripping from his words.

"Young man, please don't shoot me! I wasn't looking, to steel any thing. If you look around, you will see. I haven't been through anything, I'm out on parole.

And I couldn't find a job, and I ate at the dinner down the street. You know, the old "dine and ditch"? Well they must of knew, that's what I was gonna do, so they called the cops. And when I ran out. I was chased by the cops, and I didn't want to go back to jail. Not in the summer, so I ran up here, and started checking all the doors. Until I came across one, that was open".

Jason turns around to Jen.

"You left my door, unlocked?"

"I'm sorry Jay! I thought you locked it. I just pulled it shut".

"I tell you what, old timer. Cause your story sound legit. Stand outside there, with my girl. While I'll check my room over now if you telling the truth! I'll break you off, a little something to hold you up for a while. But if your lying, don't run cause this .45 I'm holding, is a lot faster than you, believe that! You feel me?"

"Hey youngster, you would do that for me?"

"If you're a man of your word, then we have no problem". Jason reasoned.

Jen and the old dude, step outside of the room. As Jason closes the door. And checks under the bed, and unrolls his gun blanket. Everything's there. As he goes, to the middle drawer and pulls it out and checks behind it. His money stash is there. Then one more spot, he moves the chair, in the corner his other money spot. Everything's cool. He peels off, three hundred dollar bills, as he puts the drawer back and steps outside. He shakes the mans hand.

"You're a man of your word, I like that". Jason stated as they shook hands. He hands him the money.

"Thanks young blood, I really appreciate this". He smiled at Jen, and walked away.

Jay and Pam stop by while Jen and Jason was packing for Jason to leave, they were to leave that night.

" Hey! You two women want to hang out for a while, I need to talk to my man Jay alone". Jason hands Jen some money, and tells them to go shopping.

"Jay, let's take a walk".

"Cool I'm with that, where too?" Jay questioned.

"That starbucks across the street".

They go out and cross the street and into Starbucks.

"Hello! How are you guys this afternoon?" The woman behind the counter spat.

"We're good! Thank you". Jason ordered a small cappuccino, Jay ordered a regular coffee. As they paid for their order and sat down. "So Jay, have you giving any thought to what I said?"

"No doubt! Where out of here two days, from now". Jay replied.

"That's what I'm talking about! Good move. Look Jay trust me, we'll be seeing each other again mark my word. Things in life happen like that, but always remember If any problem should occur in your life. Stand back, and look at all the possible angles before you react. Everything in life should be thought out, before act upon feel me? Anything, can be handled in anger. But for every action, is a reaction. Never let your mind go wild without the benefit of intellect".

He continued,

"Handle everything of importance. On a level, and

cool head. If at all possible, got it?" Jason stated, as he schooled his younger protégée

"Listen Jason, no one has ever taken the time to give two shits about me. Let alone spill knowledge on me like you, but trust me when I tell you, you're a great teacher. And I'm gonna miss you dude, and that's on the real, you're the realist cat I've ever met. And I truly would like to run back into you, on the road. In the near future".

Jason loads up the trunk of Jen's Acura. A smile goes across her face, as if to still not believe, that she's going. They jump into the car, and their gone.

———————

Night comes... Jay's in the hotel thinking of his next move, Pam comes in. She has a bag with her.

"Hey I see somebody's, been busy getting money".

"Jay, you know we gotta get this money, before we leave. And once we touch down, in the next town. Trust me, I'm on it". As she goes over to where he's standing, she throws her arm around his neck. And goes in slow, to kiss Jay he's nervous. Being he never kissed a girl before, but after they kissed, and she pulled away, he found himself, wanting more.

She pushed him back onto the bed, she began to undress him. She pulled down his underwear. Jay began to blush, a girl has never seen him naked before. Pam began slowly jerking him off, until he was hard.

once he reached that point .She took off her clothes, and mounted him she went up and down a few times as Jay climaxed.

He would forever remember. The time, the place, and the girl, who took his virginity, that day. Wow! he thought to himself. She kissed him, and laid down next to him.

"So! Jason's gone huh"?
"Yep, and I for one, have learn a great deal from him. In those three days he was here. Enough for me to know, I've gotta step my game up. Cause God willing, I want to be on that level, the next time we meet".
"Jay, babe you can do anything, you want to do". Pam reasoned.

"Hey I'm about to go for a walk, I'll be back". Jay spat.
"You want some company"? Pam offered.
"No I just need to clear my head, you know"?
"Okay, I'll be here then". She kisses him. He gets dressed, he grabs his hoodie, and walks out the door.

As he continues down the street. He notice, it's getting real grimy now. He's in the hood, D.C.'s P.J's (projects) he comes up on a dice game, He touches his waist, to check his chrome. (gun) For assurance, as he ask, can he get down.
A fat kid, not much taller than Jay said.
"Hey, if you got cash! Get yours".
Jay sees the bet, and lays down. He wins the first

three passes then losses, but he waits for his turn again. The second time, he came up sweet.

Fat boy, wasn't feeling it. As he tried to pick up Jay's money. Big mistake, out came the chrome. As Jay back handed the boy across the side of his head, with his piece the boy fell to the ground. Balled over in pain, as the other boy tried to help out. Jay turn the hammer towards him, he quickly, changed his mind.

" I don't want to die, just take, your money!" The guy spat.

"You telling me what to do, when I'm holding the heat? You D.C. cats got some nerve!" Jay spoke, his eye's seeing red.

"Matter of fact, break bread son! Everything that blings on you. I want little bitch ass fucker. If you know what's really good, don't hold out or I'll put your brains, across the street in that sewer right there. Come on son, come up off that!" Jay ordered.

The fat kid, pulls off his chain. Followed by his rings, he hands it to Jay.

"Naw kid, put that shit in that fitted, you got on! And put it on the ground. Oh and don't forget your fronts, nigga.(platinum teeth) smiling ass. Now kick off one boot, and start running that way, and who ever else, don't start running wit this nigga! Is getting all this".

Jay said waving the heat (gun)

They all start running down the street. Jay picked up the hat with all the money and the jewelry. Jay turned and walked away, until he turn the corner. Then he jogged, until he got back to the hotel. He busted into the room, breathing hard. He spoke,

"Pam! Get everything packed we outta here now".

"Jay what"?-

He cut her, a sharp look

"Never mind, we'll be ready in ten minutes baby". She replied.

"That's, what I wanted to hear".

She scrambles to get everything ready. Jay's in the corner counting the little, stick up money.

Damn! that's almost five and a half G's here. And the jewels, that's a nice little come up. He thought to himself.

She takes the key back to the office. Jay Grabs the bags, they head the other way, towards the bus stop. They get the tickets and sit in the bus depot for only ten minutes. Before their bus arrives and just like that, their gone.

Chapter 3

Almost 72 hours later, they were in Boston. They would have probably been there earlier, but their bus broke down. Therefore they had to wait until another bus was sent to continue on. Jay and Pam did a lot of talking on the long trip. Things in this new town, were going to be different.

They walked around until they found a reasonable hotel. Once they got settled in, they went to get something to eat. They go into the local diner. They both got the looks like, who are these two?

The young girl came to them, and spoke in a strong Boston accent "Just two?"

"Yes! Non smoking please". Jay stated.

"Follow me". as they sat, they paid no attention, to the stares, as they got into, their conversation.

"Jay some how, we gotta get a used car, this bus thing is gonna cost us to much money. And be to slow, if we gotta get outta town that fast again".

"Yeah, your right! Well we'll figure out something. I got enough for that off that dice game, back in D.C"..

"Are you serious?" She asked.

"Hell yeah, I was fucking em up, until the fat boy tried to test me. And lost". As Jay said this a bum walked in, and sat at the counter. The manager went up to him, and asked him to leave. Jay got up, and went over to them.

The manager said: "Look, either you leave now or I'm calling the police".

"Hey Hakeem! What's up? We over here. Sorry, he's with us."

Jay grabs the man's arm, and leads him to their table.

As the man sits down. Not really knowing, what's going on.

"Thanks young man! But I need him to call the cops. So they can take me, to jail. That way at least, I'll have some food, and a place to sleep. for the next 90 days". He replied.

"Hey, if that's all you need. Look here, order anything you want off the menu, and we'll talk". Pam was looking at Jay, like what the hell is he thinking. The girl comes back over to them, and takes all of their orders. five minutes later, she comes back with their drinks.

"Okay, young man. Lay it on me, what am I into you for?"

"Relax! Look I figure, we can help each other out. As you noticed, were kinda young. So we need some one, to be there. when we need them, feel me? Where gonna be in town for a few days. And for those few days, trust me. Where gonna take care of you. As long as you help us out, got it? Tick for a tack". Jay stated.

"First order of business, we need to know your size, In clothes, that is". Pam sized him up, after they finished up with, their food. They where out.
" Listen! Go handle your business, I'm gonna take him across the street to get a hair cut. Cool! Meet me back, at the spot. Okay?"
"Gotcha!" Pam answered.
Just an hour and a half in this town. And with the help of people running their mouth in the barber shop. Jay knew who was doing what. As a smile went across his face.

Once they leave the barber shop. And walk down the side walk
"So, what is your name"? Jay asked the older man.
The bum looking shocked. "Damn! Nobody asked me that one, in some time. It's Nate, and yours?"
"I'm Jay, and my girl is Pam". He responded.

As they continued walking, they were passing house after house, an saw
a young boy sitting on the stoop, with a radio playing: " look at that fake smile he gave me, it's breaking my heart, should I school em', or pull the tools out, and just break em' a part"
Jay-Z's Coming of Age.

"Damn, that's my shit right there!" Jay spat

They continue down the street talking. Until they get to the Hotel. Pam's Waiting With the new clothes. Spread across the bed, as Jay and Nate, entered the room.

"Good! That's the style, I was thinking about". Nate, look's at the two of them.

" Nate, go head take that into the bathroom, and get washed up, and put on the new clothes. And put your old ones in this bag". As he goes into the bathroom, Pam and Jay talk over their plans.

"Well, I found out he has a license so we can get a car, but tomorrow your gonna go to the bank in town, I believe it's a Citizen's and open up and account feel me? We gotta start stacking. Here take this money down to the office, and get another room".

"Why he can sleep here on the floor? I mean, he's use to sleeping on park benches an shit". Pam responded.

"Naw, fuck that! I don't trust him, to just let him sleep in the same room with us. Stop trusting every one, at the drop of a dime." Jay said looking at Pam, like she bumped her damn head.

" Okay Jay! Just give me the money".

He hands her the money, she turns, as he smacks her on her ass she walks out.

The following day… Jay gets up, to find Pam already up, and dressed. "Damn! Are you going some where?" Jay asked.

"Yes! Come on we got a lot to do today. Go next door and get Nate up. While I get washed up. So we can get some breakfast, or something".

"Okay I'll go I'll be back. Jay! Stop watching T.V. and get dressed I'm hungry".

Jay, snapped out it.

"Okay! Okay. I'll be ready go, go get em". He orders.

Pam goes next door and knocks, no answer. She knocks again just as she was about to knock, the third time. Nate's, coming down the steps.

"There you go, I was just getting you up. So we could go and get some breakfast, is that okay?"

"Sure, I just went for my morning walk that's all". He replied.

Pam, gave him this weird smirk. Like she didn't believe him at all but went along with him anyway.

She walks back to their room with Nate in tow. Once they get to the door. Jay was coming out.

"Okay! Everybody ready?" Jay asks. Jay puts on his head phones, and leads the way.

"I just don't believe, all the things people say, controversy! am I black or white, am I straight, or gay?" controversy. Prince- played through the head phones.

"Who's that, you listening to?"

Jay seen Nate's lips moving, and pulled down one side of the head set.

"what?"

"I asked, who are you listening to?"

"Oh, the man. Prince! You like Prince?" Jay asked.

"Don't tell me, you don't like Prince?" Jay questioned.

"I wouldn't say I don't like him, I just don't care for him that much". Nate shot back

As their walking up to the diner, this young kid Darnel. Pulls up in a rust colored Honda civic. System banging " Erick Sermon's" just like music- Jay thought. Damn that's my shit, but gave no acknowledgement towards the seemly, cocky kid.

That jumped out the car, looking briefly at Jay and Nate. But stared, a little longer at Pam. Just disregarding, Jay's presence.

Jay grabbed Pam's hand. He held the door open with the other, they walked in. Darnel sat at the counter, waiting on his take out order he had placed, awhile ago. Jay, Pam and Nate are seated. Darnel makes eye contact with Pam, once again.

Once Darnel gets his order, he goes over to their table. He pulls out a huge roll of money, and peals off a hundred dollar bill. And places it on their table and says,

"Hey no disrespect! But I notice you two walking. And I would like too, treat ya'll breakfast is on me and I think you two, should stop hangin' around the neighborhood bum. I mean new clothes, and some food in his stomach. And he'll still cross you, trust me". He stated.

Pam said thanks, as he walked away. Jay felt embarrassed, but more enraged. As he looked at the expression on Darnel's face. He knew he got nothing but pleasure, doing that to Jay. But that wouldn't be, the last time they would meet.

———————————

Natasha

Chapter 4

The following day…

Pam gets up early in the morning to hit the local mall, while she's walking around she runs into. No other than Darnel. He steps to her then looks around.

"Hey! Hi you doin?" A smile goes across Pam's face. it's something about this guy, that does it for her.

"Hello". She replied.

"So where's your, little friend?" He spat, referring to Jay.

At this remark, she knows he's just trying to belittle Jay. And that's her boo, she quickly replies.

"He's where he needs to be! Taking care of business, thank you! And if you'll excuse me, I need to be going myself". She said as she stepped pass him.

"Hold up ma! We got off on the wrong foot. No disrespect, I came out my face wrong wit that. I apologize for that! we cool? I don't even know your name, mines Darnel, how you be ma?"

" Fine! Thank you, I'm Pam nice meeting you, but really, I've gotta go".

" No problem, maybe we can kick it some time?" He stated.

" I don't think so". She walks away, he stand there admiring her ass. As she walks, like a model, on a run way. He thinks to himself "damn I got to get me, some of that".

Back at the motel, Jay and Nate get ready to go to the car lot, to get a little something. Ten minutes later, their taxi pulls up in front of the car lot. Jay and Nate jump out. Jay pays the cabbie, as the guy asked him. "would you like me to wait?"

"No! That wont be necessary". Jay turns, and walk around the lot.

"Damn Nate!, You where right. They have some nice looking cars here".

A young man walks up to them.

"Hello, can I help you find something?"

"Yes! I believe you can. You have some nice looking cars here. But I'm only working with three thousand but I want to drive out of here today, now the question is can you still help me?" Jay spat, eye's squinted looking at the guy.

" You got it, follow me." the man walks over, to the other side of the lot. Where he has, a clean Honda accord. A little pick up with tinted windows, and a Saturn.

All of theses are in your price range, that's cash right!?

"Of course".

"With that tax and tags, you ride today". He said.

Jay tries not to show his excitement, as he goes from car to car. Sitting in them starting them up, and listening to them.

When it's all said and done, Jay takes the little pick up, cause it sound the best, looked great. And it had a system, with the cd player.

They go inside, and handle the paper work. Almost a hour and a half later, and he and Nate are driving out of there. As a smile goes across his face, he leans over in the seat, and goes into his back pocket. He hands Nate a hundred dollar bill.

"Thanks man! We needed this, it's on now". Jay stated.

Minutes later… their pulling into the motel parking lot. Jay jumps out and walks around the truck with the biggest smile on his face, Nate calls out.

"Hey Jay! You need me for anything else right now?"

"No, I'm cool right now Go do you, oh and thanks again".

Nate leaves Jay goes up to the room.

About half an hour later, Pam comes in with two full bags. Jay's, laying across the bed.

"Hey baby, it's a cute little truck in the parking lot, so how did you make out.?" She asked.

" Well for starters, here's your key to our "Cute little

truck in the parking lot". At this, she starts jumping up and down.

" Baby it's beautiful, you're the best". She jumps into his arms.

"Wow! We got our first car together". Then she walks over to the bags, on the floor.

"Wait until you see what I got you, I've only spend thirty dollars".

"What! Your the only person, I know who can go into a store spend thirty dollars and steel three hundred dollars worth of shit". He stated with a light chuckle.

" I know! I'm good ain't I? who's your bitch?"

"Your my bitch". He spat

"And don't you forget it, babe!" As she pulls out this baby blue "Sean John" dress shirt, with pearl like buttons and a pair of dress slacks.

"This is a formal set, for when we need business attire". She stated.

"Good thinking baby, damn you're on your game".

"Jay, trust me. I know with you, where on to bigger and better things, I can feel it".

At this, they hear a loud system bangin' in the parking lot. Jay peps out the window, it's Darnel in his civic.

"Damn! I'm starting to run out of patience, with this dude on the real".

He stated, to no one in particular.

He closes the blinds, as him and Pam engage into their conversation.

Jay finished looking through the clothes Pam got him. She models some of the clothes she got for herself. Within' minutes their getting into each other, as they began kissing deep and passionate Pam takes Jay's clothes off. She leads him to the shower, this is only the second time for Jay. But this time he's more nervous, than the first cause it's all he thought about since the last time.

Once in the shower Pam's soaping Jay up. He's standing there with an erection that couldn't get any harder. He's breathing hard as she spends more time soaping up his dick she then rinse him off as she get on her knees, and starts to suck him off. At this, Jay can hardly control himself, he grabs the back of her head, and starts pumpin' in and out of her mouth first he's going slow then he finds he's fucking her mouth. As he explodes he slowly lets go of her head. He's still shaking. Wow, that was great. He thought to himself.

They get out of the shower. Jay turns on the radio. He pops in Jada Kiss. "ain't none of ya'll better." As he bops his head, and sings along

" If I don't like you, I'm a kill you, Not fight you, bite a little piece of ya ear off, like Mike do!"

As he nods his head a little more, he continues to sing "I'm God, minus the twelve disciples, I pop up all you see is shells and riffles"-

"All this is my shit!" He screams out.

"Jay babe, everything's your shit let you tell it so what's up, lets go for a drive?" She inquired.

No doubt, let's bounce. Jay slides his razor in his mouth.

"Damn! Old habits die hard". As he finished getting dress, he reaches down to his waist, and feels the heat. He's ready. They walk down the stairs, and run into Nate.

"Hey where you guys off too? ' All it ain't nothin' old head. I'm just taken my girl for a little drive, we'll be right back you straight?"

Jay reaches into his pocket, and pulls out his roll and peels off a twenty and hands it to Nate.

"Hey thanks! Young buck."

"No problem Nate, I got you dogg." As he opens the door for Pam, she climbs in the passenger side, he closes the door. Then walks around, and hops in, and their off.

Twenty minutes later… their pulling up to the park, it's a nice day outside. The kids are running around, chasing each other. Jay looked on in amazement, at a childhood, he never had.

The smile ran away from his face. Pam looked over at him,

"Come on lets get out, what's wrong baby?" She asked.

"Nothin'! I'm cool. I was just thinking, about something".

" Like what"? she questioned.

"Nothing come on let's walk". She grabs his hand, as they stroll through the park their walking as a Frisbee flies over. Jay caught it and half threw it back.

Pam laughed. She picked it up and threw it and it flew through the air so smooth.

"Hey! How did you do that Hold up, let me try again" Jay waved for the kid to throw it back.

The kid flew it back to him perfect. As Jay got ready to throw it.

"No, no, not like that like this!"

She grabbed it and showed Jay, how to hold it. This time, he flies it good not far, but good.

"That's It just throw it harder next time Come on, let them play. Let's go baby".

She grabs his hand, and pulls him away. As they continue walking down the path Pam sees a nice tree and pulls Jay off the path. As she backs him against the tree and starts kissing him. He tries, not to lean against the tree. Pam asked

"What's wrong?"

"Nothing I just don't want to get my new shirt dirty".

"Jay baby I'll get you ten of them shirts".

No Pam! You don't understand, I never had any clothes like the clothes you got me. I use to see theses, in the magazines and thought damn, if I ever got the chance to dress like that I'm gonna take care of my clothes". He stated.

"Hey I can respect that, So if I wanted to give you some right now it's not happening huh?" She questioned.

"I wouldn't say that, there's exceptions to all rules". He said as they both shared a laugh.

"Yeah, I should hope so". She kisses him passionately, some kids ride by on bikes laughing.

"Come on, let's go". He reasoned as he sprang from the tree.

" Humm! I see someone don't like their business, out in the street?"

" No doubt, I am not afraid to admit to that. I'm a personal dude".

"Jay, I've gotta tell you something I don't really know how to say this, so I'll just say it. You really make me feel like I'm worth something. I mean it's like, I've always felt like a big loser. But you except me for who I am. No matter what my flaws are and I truly think I'm falling in love with you because of it. And the person you are".

Jay, doesn't know how to respond.

" Wow! I'm a bit taken back by what you just said, cause I thought it was me that was the loser?"

"Jay baby, there's nothing about you that could ever make anyone who get to know you, think that. I could tell the moment I met you that you read a lot, and your are pretty smart by the way you put your words together" that's why I like being around you, you make me stronger and you give me the confidents, I've never had".

"Okay, okay your getting a little deep on me here. I mean, I'm just a guy, not a God!"

"I know, let just say I'm a flower. And you're the water I needed to grow".

At this, they start walking down the path. They

come to a tree with a flier on it, about an up coming carnival.

"Look baby! Have you ever been to a carnival before?"

"No I haven't, why do you want to go?" Jay asks.

" Hell yeah! Look, it's here next week that's what's up count us in"

Chapter 5

The following day...

Nate had felt sick, and went for a check-up. The hospital ended up keeping him over a period of three days, running all kinds of test. After visiting with him. They left when the doctor told them he would be there for at least three days. They went back to the motel and got his stuff out of the other room, and put it in theirs. Pam had said it's a waste of money, to pay for a room for three days If he's getting one for free.

"Hey that's why we make a good couple cause your always thinking what I should be thinking. But when I'm slipping, your not. That's good, I hope my old head, alright thou!" Jay reasoned.

"I'm sure he'll be fine". Pam goes to move, Nate's bag Some pictures fall out she goes to pick them up. It's pictures of Nate with a little kid that kinda looks like, Darnel.

"Jay, look at theses pictures that fell out of Nate's

bag who does this kid look like to you?" Pam asked. waiting for a response .

"Humm Kinda looks like that kid, Darnel".

"That's what I thought! You think- naw".

"What! Tell me?"

"You think that Nate's his father?" Pam questioned.

"Okay, but how do we go about asking him without him thinking we were going through, his shit?" Jay reasoned.

"Humm Good question I don't know, maybe we can just like bring it up one day in conversation". Pam stated.

"Maybe but don't push the issue cause I want him to continue to trust us I don't want him to think, we went through his stuff cool?" Jay said, looking at her.

"I got you, hey let's get some ice cream?" Pam suggested.

"Humm, I'll have a shake".

They walk up, to the glass.

" Hi! May I help you?" The girl behind the counter asked.

"Sure! I would like two scoops of chocolate ice cream in a sugar cone, And a vanilla shake thick!".

" Is that it what size shake, Large?"

"Yes that's it". Pam turns to Jay.

"What the hell does she mean "is that it?" what do I look like a cow or something? I can't stand when people ask dumb questions". She stated raisin her voice as to not care if the girl heard her or not.

"Calm down please! Your turning red, you light skin chicks kill me". Jay spat

"Shut up Jay! Your just as yellow as I, So what the hell are you talking about". She spat.

They both laugh.

"Oh I forgot to tell you I got us two of them go phones from 7 eleven all we have to do is charge em' up, they came with 200 minutes". Pam stated.

"Are you serious? Damn I always wanted a cell phone". He hugs her, as they kiss again.

" I think I'm gonna call "Jason" tonight to see what's buzzing. I miss him, he was a cool dude No doubt!"

They finish eating, their ice cream. As they walk through the park back to the truck. When they get to the truck, this guy and his girl are leaned up against Jay's truck.

"Yo! excuse me, that's my truck your leaning on". The guy brushes Jay off, and continues to lip lock with his girl. Pam just looks on to see how Jay's gonna handle this.

"Dude! Don't take this there get the fuck off my truck!" Jay said with venom, dripping from his words.

He stops. "Yo kid! You and your girl need to go play some where cause I'm busy".

At this Jay's face is blood red. As he goes into a rage he spits his razor into his hand. The guy has his hands around his girl as Jay takes the razor across his hands the guy let's out a loud scream. As everyone close by turns to look.

Jay moves with cat like speed. The guy reaches towards Jay his girl sees the blood streaming down his arm. She starts to scream. Jay dips the guys arm as he slices him again from his wrist to the elbow.

When the kid grabs his new wound Jay goes across his face. As the guy falls over Jay steps over him to get into the truck. As Pam runs around the other side shocked. But impressed how her man handle himself.

Wow he's a beast. she thought to herself.

Jay put the truck in reverse. As he rolls down the window and spits on the guy and pulls off, before the park ranger arrives.

As they rode in the truck not a word was spoken. They just rode in silence. Once back at the motel. Jay picked up the bloody razor off the seat as they went up stairs. Pam thought to herself I know he's not gonna keep that? They get to the top of the stairs, as Pam puts the key in the door opens it and steps to the side as Jay walks in first.

Jay goes to the closet and pulls out a bottle of solution and a small box as he pours the solution into the box he puts in the razor. As it starts to fizz.

"Jay! What the heck is that?"

"It's a sterile solution it's get my razors clean like new".

"Are you gonna put that razor that you just slice the boy up with" back in your mouth?" She questioned.

"Not right now but hell yeah".

"This is the stuff doctors clean their tools with, and they cut people open every day. Not to mention these aren't just regular razors these are my razors".

"What's that suppose to mean?"

"Never mind." He stated.

"Hey I'm a bout to jump in the shower". Jay said.

"Well when you get out I'm gonna get a bath, you want to get a movie they got a few new ones, on the list".

"We can order to the room?".

"Yeah, yeah yo do they have "Scare face" on there?"

"Yeah! You want me to order that?"

"No doubt yo you feel like going to the store to get a bag of popcorn?"

"Yeah I'll do that". She answered.

"Cool".

Jay turns on the shower. Then he turns on the radio, and pops in his Jigga C.D. the blue print. And skips to song number 9 "Never change" as he listens to the course. " never stop fuckin' wit crime, cause crime pays, out hustlin' same clothes for days, I'll never change, I'm to stuck in my ways" "Damn that nigga J, keeps it real".

As he steps into the shower. It's piping hot, just the way he likes it.

"Awe! Damn this feels good". As he thought about the guy he just fucked up for life. He taps his head, stomach, shoulder, shoulder as he looks up. "God, I'm not sorry for what I've done I can't live my life with regrets it was either him or me, and I'm good, amen"-

Jay put his hands on the wall. As the hot water ran down his back he thought of his next hustle. He quickly snapped out of his thought as he heard Pam come back in. He soaped up once more rinsed and got out. He rinsed out the tub and started Pam's bath water. He walks out with the towel around his waist.

"Umm! what you got there?" Pam said licking her lips.

"I started running your bath". He began looking in the bag,

"Hey what else you got in here?"

"I got your slim jim, and peace tea Snapple".

"That's what I'm talking about well go in there take your bath so we can kick back and chill". Jay looks over at the cell phones charging. He goes over and unplugs the one. Goes to his bag and grabs his little black book with two numbers in it. And he calls "Jason" Jason answers on the second ring. " Hello?"

"Hey Jason, what's up? It's Jay".

"All it ain't nothin' young boy what's crackin'?"

"I was just about to get at you, on the "I need a favor tip" you got me?"

" No doubt! What's up? Talk to me". Jay stated.

"Well, I'm in Syracuse New York, and I don't really want to back track but I'm gonna need this money by the time I hit Kentucky, feel me? You know that dude, I was taking to in D.C.?"

"The old head "poppa rose"?" Jay asked.

"Yeah that's him well he got some loot he had owed me. If your not that far can you scoop it for me?"

"Yeah it's whatever that's it! Oh we got a car now".

"That's what's up youngster I'm feeling you on that tip. Theses buses are a mother fucker, I tell you. Well look it's $60,000 dollars. Listen use it to make some money off it until we meet up again. I trust you'll do the right thing. As you grow up in these street out here just remember, if you need anything or you run into something. Ya'll can't handle out there by yourselves, drop me a line cool?"

"Yeah Jason I got you thanks".

"No doubt stay up I'll call my man and let him know your coming to get it, alright?"

"One"- (they hang up) Pam comes out of the bath, wearing a yellow lace bra and panties set.

"Damn! Girl ya look good".

"Thank you! You don't look half bad yourself". She replied.

She goes over and takes off his towel- Jay roll her over and begins to slowly lick, from her neck down to her chest. He pulls her bra down, as gentle as he can, an caress her breast. Before he slips her now hard nipple into his warm waiting mouth he takes his other hand and clumsy find her ' freshly shaven' swollen lips. He slowly slides two fingers, into her love tunnel her back arches, he hears her pantin', as he thinks to himself damn, I'm getting better. He pulls his soaked fingers out of her, and puts them in his mouth. At this she grabs hungrily at his dick she rolls him over, and mounts him. He's pumpin' she's jumping up and down you can tell their each others first.

They last about ten minutes their done before the movie comes on.

Jay goes back into the bathroom and washes up then joins her in the bed to watch "Scare face" as It comes on Jay starts saying everything Tony Montana said word for word.

"Jay please! Can we both just watch it?" She ordered.

"Oh! I'm sorry babe it just that this is that movie you know?"

"Yeah I know". He opens his slim jim and cracks open his Snapple Pam watches as she eats her popcorn. " Oh by the way Jason wants us to go back to D.C. and pick up some money owed to him".

"Oh really! And just how much is he giving you to do this?" She asked.

"Well I didn't ask him that but listen to this he said I, I mean we can use it to make money off of until we meet him in Kentucky".

"Jay is it worth it?" She inquired.

"That's what I was thinking we can use it as bait to get big money feel me, It's $60,000 dollars we talking about and my mark is that kid Darnel". Jay reasoned.

"Oh really!"

"Yep and I know just the scheme". He stated with a sinister smile.

"Well, you gonna let me hear it or what?"

" Listen"- as he starts to explain to her, the whole set up.

"Sounds like a plan hey can I ask you for a favor?"

"Sure what?" Jay asked.

"Can you teach me how to hold a razor in my mouth?"

"Are you serious? Okay pull that chair over here". He sitting on the edge of the bed, she's sitting in the chair right in front of him. Jay gets up, and get his extra razors out.

"Okay now look, stick out your tongue like this." Jay spits out his razor into his hand and placed it on the tip of his tongue.

"First things first don't try to move it around that much at first just get use to it being in your mouth, then do this he shows her the razor in his mouth. Then he closes and flips the razor as he opens his mouth back up the razors backwards. She tries she flips it the first time and opens her mouth. Jay notice a little bit of blood.

"That's good, but not smooth enough you gotta keep practicing we'll start with keeping it in your mouth two hours a day at first cool?"

"Yeah that's good so when are we leaving, to go get this money?"

"First thing in the morning we will go get some donuts or something and be out.

" Babe if this works out the way you plan it we can pull this scheme in a few different towns".

"No doubt!" Jay spat.

Jay goes over to the radio. With a smile on his face and puts on Prince's. " Baby I'm a star" as he starts to sing the course "baby, nothing comes to easy, but when you got it baby, nothing comes to hard, see what I'm talking about, even it I have to scream and shout baby I'm a star".

" Baby, what is it about Prince that you like so much?" Pam asked.

"That's easy his talent and that fact that he don't give a shit about what people think about him. He wears heels pants with the butt cut out, that nigga just makes great music and he does him". Jay replied.

"I feel you on that he don't care about what people think. And that's the way to be, real".

" And that's why I like Red Man cause he's the same way, I mean his music is all that, he's one of the hottest rappers out there, cause he does him". Jay spat.

They talk a little more, then Jay falls asleep, while Pam's talking to him. She gets up, and cleans up. And packs all their things so in the morning, they can just bounce.

———————————

The next morning... Pam gets Jay up. After Jay brushes his teeth.

"Hey let's stop by the hospital and see my old head before we roll cool? Drop some loot off to him. And tell him we'll be back in two days. We'll fill up the tank, grab something to eat, and we out".

"Sound like a plan". Pam stated.

"Too D.C. baby!"- Jay screamed.

Chapter 6

Two hours later–

Pam lays her head in Jay's lap, first she's talking. Then she nods off she fast asleep, her head on his lap and her feet out the window. Jay looks out the window and thinks Damn! She has some pretty feet. About an hour later Pam wakes up.

" Hey baby where are we"?

"Rhode Island we should be hitting Connecticut soon". He shot back.

"You want me to drive for a while so you can kick back for a little bit?"

"Yeah that's cool we'll switch at the next rest stop, that coffee got me having to pee like a " Russian race horse." At this, Jay sees a sign for the next rest stop.

They pull into the rest area, Jay parks. He gets out, and goes to the bathroom. Pam waits, for him to return then she goes. Before she leaves she turns to Jay

"Hey you want anything to snack on for the road?"

"Yeah if they have it get me the usual".

"Gotcha! A Snapple and slim jim coming up". As she walks through the parking lot an older guy sees her go into the ladies room. He gets out of his car, and walks towards the ladies room as well. Jay sees him but thinks nothing of it until he notices the guy stop at the door look around, then slips in.

Jay reaches under the seat and grabs his gun sticks it in the small of his back, as he jogs over to the ladies room as well. Jay looks around same as the guy, and slips in.

Jay opens the stall door with his right hand as he sees the guy with his hands around Pam's neck. Jay swings the gun and hits the guy right on the side of his head as the guy turns to fall. It's then that Jay sees Pam got the best of him with her new razor skills. While he was holding her neck she was going back and forth across his face and chest and neck, with the razor.

"Baby are you okay? Baby"-

"Jay I'm fine! Let's just get out of here before someone comes in here, Hey! Go watch the door". Jay picks up the dude and sits him on the toilet, and closes the stall door.

"That should buy us some time, Pam just go to the car and change that shirt I'm gonna go into the store okay"?

"Alright hurry thou please!"

"Baby calm down, I'll be right back".

"You want something?" Just as he said this, a police car pulls up along side of their truck. Jay doen't wait for her reply as he turns and continue across the lot, to the store. Once he gets everything, he needs and get in line. The cops right behind him in line. Jay pays and walks outside of the store. Once he gets to the curb he sits the bag down and acts like he's tying his sneaker, as the cop walks pass him. He gets to the car and leaves. Jay exhales, just then a lady comes out of the ladies room screaming at the top of her lungs. At this the cop stops and puts his car in park. And Jay tries not to look like he's hurrying to the truck that's only 10 feet away. But seems like a foot ball field away.

Once in the truck they leave… Jay exhales again.

"Oh my God baby! I've never been that scared in my life".

" Pam baby calm down, where out of harms way". Jay stated.

Jay thought to himself damn I sound assuring. But I'm not really convinced myself. As he puts in Red Man's C.D. "Doc's Da Name 2000"

He forwards to track #4 "Get it live" he starts to sing along-" ya nigga's ain't ready for Reggie, I be steady to rob that bank in Philly, break cool C out and ask him what the dealie? Pass him the A.K. so we can get busy"

Pam just looks at him. Wondering, how he could be so calm.

"So how much farther do we have to go?" Pam asked.

"Are you serious? Babe just lay down and go to sleep. We still have to go through, New York and New Jersey, so just relax". Jay ordered.

———————————————

Mean while, two detectives pull up to the rest stop. Jay and Pam just left, as they look over the seen det. Jake looks to his partner ms. Roberts and says. " I believe we have a slasher, on our hands".

Jay continues to change C.D. after C.D. and 6 hours later, their riding through Jersey City. Pam wakes up, and ask where are they?

" Where in Jersey City babe where making good time. But I'm tired and I gotta pull over cause, I got to go to the bathroom. How about you"? Jay asked.

" Yeah I got to go, but this time I want you to stand outside while I go please"? She stated.

" No problem I got you". She goes to kiss him. " Whew!! You need a breath mint."

"Yeah you too I'm gonna get washed up at this stop and brush my teeth". Pam said, while turning her head.

" Me too."

Almost 11 hours later... Their pulling into D.C. the first thing Jay does is get his gun from under the seat. Pulls the clip out, looks it over. Puts it back into the gun as he steps out of the truck. He tucks it in the small of his back. He turns to Pam.

"You ready"?

"Sure thing!" She replies.

"Well lets go get this money here's the plan where gonna make the pick up, get something to eat and get a room the next town over. And where back on the road in the morning got it?" Jay explained.

"I'm with you babe".

" Cool lets go get Popa Rose!"

Once they get to Popa Rose house, he opens the door.

Heyy, the the therre youngster. I been waiting oon yoou two as he turns to Pam my ain't you a sight for sore eye's? yya'll coome on in here now. He stated with his strong stutter.

He steps back and let them pass. Old dude can't keep his eye's off Pam's ass. Pam takes notice of this and starts to flirt just a little stronger Jay just looks at her. And shakes his head.

"So how long are you two in town for?" Poppa Rose questioned.

"Humm.. who knows old man. We might just stay until Jason comes back through". He stated lying.

Popa Rose gets a smile on his face as he looks over at Pam thinking how much he wanted to sex her. He continued to look on with lust in his eye's. Until Jay snapped him out of it. Buy clearing his throat. "Okay old man enough with the small talk, let's get down to business where's the loot?" Jay asked as he turned around, with his hands crossed in front of his crouch, and his eye's squinted.

"Okkay, well lett me go get it out of the other rooom".

Popa Rose leaves the room. Jay turns to Pam

"What the hell! Are you doing?" He asked her.

"Jay this dude got money and I for one want to find out how much, are you feeling me now?" She snapped.

"Fuck it! Do your thing then". Jay shot back.

Popa Rose comes back into the room, with a large brown bag as he puts it down.

"Here it is Youngster count it." Jay opens the bag and his eye's get big. As he pulls out stack after stack. Once the bag is empty, Jay began to count minutes later he's done. "It's all there, $60.000 cold cash".

"Heyy, wwhy don't the twoo of you come by tonight, I'm having a little get together Bar-b-que out back all yoou can drink I know you two are a little young to be drinking, but hell ya'll to young to be doing a lot of shit, but ya'll do". He said, this looking at Pam. Jay answers him.

"That's a bet old man. We'll come through for a minute no doubt". He gets a smile across his face, still looking at Pam. As Jay packs the money up, they head out the door. Pam turns His head is slow coming up cause, he was looking at her ass.

"So what time?" Pam asked.

"Coome about, 10:00- 10:30 okkay? Now putt that monney up, youngster I'll see you two, later".

Their walking to the truck this little kid couldn't be more than 7rs old came up to them. And opens his back pack "Yo! I got C.D's and DvD's you want to look?"

"Naw shortie, we cool". Jay floats him a twenty anyway. As They continue to the truck. Pam gets in

"Ha! Little man was getting his grown man on, he look cute".

"So what's the deal you think we should call Jason before we hit his man off?" Jay asked.

"What! Jay, we do our own thing we don't need permission from no one we out here trying to eat, just like he is, this is the streets baby, survival of the fittest, baby it's either them or us." She spat.

"Your right your right." They pull off- once they get over to the next town, and get a room. Jay just lays across the bed Pam sitting on the edge going through the bag.

"Wow! This is a lot of money". She said as she ran her hand across a few of the stacks.

"So here's the deal were going to get as much money out of this town as we possible. So it's what ever tonight but keep your head about you, always know where I'm at at all times feel me?"

"I got your back baby! Trust me were here". (she does the Martin thing with her hands) Martin Lawrence, is her favorite show on t.v. as they lay together, on the bed they start kissing.

Hedi

Chapter 7

Later that night...

    Their getting dressed for the party. Jay's sitting on the edge of the bed, he has on some Roc-a-wear jeans a white tee, and a fresh pair of air force one's. As he stands up and tuck in the front of his shirt as to show off his Roc-a-wear belt buckle. He looks himself up and down in the mirror. Just then, Pam comes out of the bathroom looking hotter than hot sauce.

    "Damn baby it's like that!? You stepping kinda hard, ain't you?"

    "So you about ready?" Jay questioned.

    "Yeah let's bounce". She shot back.

    "Cool look don't get to far outta each others sight alright?"

    "I got you! Baby". Pam had on a little jean skirt a nice belly shirt exposing her wash board stomach. As her hair just laid on her shoulders. While going out the door Jay grabbed her ass. She jumped he smiled, as they continued to the truck.

Once in the truck. Jay starts it up, as Kanye West new song came through the speakers. "Diamonds are forever"

"Oh this that shit! I'm in the mood already, no doubt!" Jay screamed. "I feel you baby this thing is hot, I'm ready".

Ten minutes later their pulling into town. Ten minutes after that. Their at the party Jay parks a little down the street, as he steps out he checks his face in the mirror. Then walks around, and opens the door for Pam. Poppa Rose is out in the yard, cooking on the grill.

Once he sees Pam, all his attention is on her. Jay comes through the gate first. Followed by Pam, now more eye's are on her as some guys were looking at Poppa Rose to see what he was looking at. The one guy being real disrespectful.

"Damn shortie, all that? My bad son she's with you?"

"Yeah dogg! You seen her come in this mother fucker, with me right?" Jay spat. As his face got red he twirled the razor in his mouth.

"Hold up!" as the guy turns around looking at his boys.

" Who the fuck is this mother fucker? and who the hell does he thinks he's talking to, like that?" He spat as he stood and stuck his chest out.

"Yo Kid! I'm gonna need an apology". The guy gets

up Jay steps towards him. Poppa Rose steps between them. "Hold up, this my party ya'll little young mother fuckers, ain't starting that shit up in here pump them brakes". Poppa rose stated. Without stampering his words

"Jay fuck that nigga! It's cool come over here with your prettty little woomen and get something to eat". Poppa Rose reasoned.

"That's what's up! I'm with that".

He and Pam walked with Poppa Rose. Remmie walks over behind them an taps Jay on the shoulder

"Yo man my bad, I didn't mean to come at your neck like that it's all good". He extends his hand Jay shakes it.

"Done deal man I'm Jay".

Jay said as he paused, waiting for a response. " I'm Remmie".

Remmie was just a little taller than Jay dark skinned. His girl was a pretty white girl with red hair. "This my girl Shawna". Jay was feeling her, no doubt.

The night went on nice. As everyone got comfortable with one another a couple drinks later. Jay was in the back room talking to this tall skinny kid "Mel" " so Jay, where did you meet Pam if that's what she's calling herself right?" Mel stated.

"Excuse me? Yo what are you talking about? Yeah that's my girl Pam and that's her name dude, are you drunk or what?" Jay questioned.

"Jay look I don't mean you no harm, but that girl's from around here and she's running game on you dawg, She's a hoe, who like's it rough, you don't believe me? I bet she's around here some where getting fucked as we speak".

With this, being said. Jay was furious

"Okay big man, I'll tell you what let's go from room to room, If she's in one of theses rooms getting fucked, Then I won't blow your fucking head off how's that player?" Mel looks down at Jay who had the barrow of his gun. In Mel's stomach.

" Let's walk". Jay, not knowing. Games being ran on him. First two rooms, are empty as they come to the third. Jay hears noises coming from behind the door as he pushes it open. He can't believe his eye's Pam having sex with Poppa Rose. Chained to the bed with a scarf around her mouth. Jay closes the door before she sees him. He storms out into the back yard where he throws-up. The only other person out there is Shawna she asks.

"What's wrong are you okay or you just can't hold your liquor?"

Jay holds his hand up as to say 'not right now.'

Shawna comes closer and hands Jay a bottle of water.

"Here drink this". She ordered.

"Are you sure your okay?"
"Not really!"

"Well just remember this, Nothing last forever, not even your problems".

"Hey I like that! What are you a poet or something?"

"Not quite, just a good listener if you ever need one".?

"You know talk about the right place at the right time". Jay reasoned.

"Let me ask you something".

"Sure shoot".

"How do you know Poppa Rose"? Jay asked.

"I don't Remmie does, If it were up to me we wouldn't be here. I hate that nasty perverted motherfucker".

"Why is there bad blood between you?" Jay inquired.

"Well I can't really prove it but I think, he put some kinda "date rape" shit in my drink cause I started to feel real dizzy. And when I started coming to, I was looking at this bed, with chains on it"-

At this Jay's eye's got wide as saucers.

"Wait right here!" He stated. As he jumped to his feet and runs back into the house kicks open the door by the time Poppa Rose reacts. Jay had cut him about twenty times Poppa Rose falls to the floor. But before he could scream. Jay smacked em' across his head with his gun, he fell out cold.

Jay almost had tears in his eye's. Thinking how he left his girl there for this old dude to do this. He quickly unchained her and hugged her, she got up and started kicking Poppa Rose in the face.

"Baby hold-up, I think I got an idea I wonder, if he ever heard of "a Chinese death?"

"Baby what is that?" Pam asked. Jay has her go to the bathroom. She comes back with alcohol. Jay has Poppa Rose chained to the bed now. He's still out Jay starts making tiny razor slits, all down Poppa Rose chest when he's finished the one side. He starts the other side then he covers Poppa Rose mouth.

"So are you gonna wait until he comes too, or what?"

"Oh no, he's about to wake up watch this".

He takes the alcohol and drips it on Poppa Rose nuts. Poppa Rose tries to scream, But the gag wont let no sound escape. Tears form in his eye's while he's thinking If Jay's gonna do it again. Jay gets a clothe and soaks it with alcohol then rubs Poppa Rose chest with it. When Poppa Rose saw him doing this he thought nothing of it, as he nearly went into convulsions chained up to the bed. Jay turned to Pam.

"Are you ready to go"? Jay asked.

"Yeah baby". They get up Pam grabs the clothe and rubs his nuts all over, then his chest. As their leaving the room all the noise of the party comes to them. Jay locks the door, to the room. And they leave.

While walking towards their truck, Jay hears someone call him. He turns, it's Shawna and Remmie.

"What's up? Ya'll leaving already?"

"Yeah we out! Jay steps closer an extend his hand

Look it was nice meeting you two baby give me a pen please". Pam hands him a pen.

" Look if you two ever in D.C., come through and holla at ya boy! Feel me?"

"No doubt Jay hey man, ya'll take it easy". Jay notice Shawna put the number in her pocket book. As Pam turn towards the truck shawna winked at Jay.

Chapter 8

Once in the truck…

"So baby what's up, you want to spend another night here and leave, first thing in the morning? or you want to bounce tonight?"

" No Jay! I'm too tired to be on the road tonight, let's just go get washed up and go to bed. Thanks again, for saving me back there".

"Come on babe, you don't have to thank me for that You're my baby, I love you".

"Thanks I love you more".

" I doubt that."

"Oh yeah! I love you more than all the stars, and all the cars, in all the world".

"Yeah well I love you more than all the grass, and all the trees, and all the"- (they both start laughing).

Jay pulls down the visor in the truck, and puts his Donell Jones c.d. in the first song comes across the speakers. "U know what's up"

"Yeah this is my c.d. right here, I can just put this

thing on and let it ride. No skippin' nothin' this thing, is fire baby". Jay spat

"That old ass c.d"..
"What? Please! This thing is a classic". Jay stated.
" I'm just playing I love this song, Put on track 4 "have you seen her" That's my cut right there"
" Ho, ho, it'll come up just relax and listen". Jay touches her leg, and she jumps.
"Are you sure you're okay? Do you want me to take you to the hospital?"
"No thanks! I'll be fine, I just feel dirty that's all". She answered.

Mean while... the two Detectives. Ms Roberts and det. Jake found a few pieces of Jay's hair at the scene. They toke it back to head quarters, and ran it through forensics. They come up with a match of a run away from a boy's home, Jay's face comes up.

"Damn! If I didn't know any better I would say this kid. Kinda favors you, Ms.Roberts". Jake reasoned.

"Hey you feel like getting a cup of coffee?" ms. Roberts asks.
"Sure is there something wrong?"
" No why?"
"Just wondering".

They go outside and get into the car.
"So where too?" She asked.

" Let's go to the diner". Once they reach the diner they sit in a corner booth. Det. Jake speaks.

"So are you gonna tell me what's on your mind, or what?"

"Well listen I usually don't discuss my personal business like this, but the two of us have grown close in theses last few months. Look what's spoken between us stays between us got it?" She spat.

"Come on Marquia! You know me better than that, Of course what's your big secret?" He questioned.

"Well when I was 17yrs old living with my mother thinking about going to the academy I thought I was in love with my boy friend at the time Tyrone, and I became pregnant, Well I learned quickly, he wasn't in love after I told him about our baby".

" So what did you do?" He asked.

"I'm getting there well my mother, being the christen woman she is don't believe in abortion So, I had a little boy I held him for about 10 minutes, before they took him away, I gave him up for adoption".

She choked back tears as she continued on,

"And every may 21st I get depressed thinking, what kinda life did he turn out to have. And I can't help to hate a part of myself that can't help this boy. That will never know, his real parents, mother or father".

Det. Jake just sat there. With this look on his face then he spoke.

"So why are you telling me this now, I mean is there a reason? Wait! Is that why you asked that we be put on this case? Cause you think there might be a chance that you might find your long lost son?"

"Look I feel for you really I do, but you can't put your personal life with your career, let me just ask you something if the time came, and we caught up to this guy where looking for, and he has a gun to me, are you going to shoot him or think about what if he's your son?"

"Wait, wait"- She said trying to cut him off.

"No! I need to know the answer to this question". He spat

"If it comes down to that I have to do my job, I took an oath to up hold the law and that's what I'm gonna do!". She screamed.

" That's what I want to hear, Come on let's get out of here". They both left after just a half a cup of coffee.

The next day.

Jay's up early he's doin' some push-ups. Before Pam gets up he tries to be quite but the floorboards under the carpet are squeaking. Pam gets up.

"Hey baby you about ready to go get something to eat?" Jay questioned.

"Yeah! I'm gonna be ready in about half hour". She shot back.

"Cool, I'm gonna get into the shower". She grabs

her towel off the back of the chair. And heads towards the bathroom. Jay thought to himself.

Damn, she took like three showers last night. But he under stood but he would never forgive himself for being played like that. As he turned on the T.V. he found himself watching the yard of Poppa Rose's house filled with cops. They were calling it a crime seen. As the news reporter went on to explain: late last night a body was discovered at what appeared to be a friendly bar-b-que, that turn bad for the person who was having it. A local man Marshal Kelly was found murdered he's known in the neighborhood as "Poppa Rose." He was found chained to his bed an slashed with a razor, What looks to be torture friends that attended the party found him. It appears he choked from his own vomit, cause he had a gag on. more on this breaking story, today at noon.

Jay turned off the set, and ran to the bathroom.

"Baby! Come on we gotta roll like right now, come on let's go!" Pam turns the shower off and steps out

"Jay baby! What's wrong?" She questioned.

"He's dead!"

"Who?" Then her eye's get big.

"Poppa Rose"?

"Yeah come on we'll eat a few towns over let's go".

"Okay Jay okay". She finished drying off and puts on some sweat pants a tee-shirt and her Yankee fitted. With her hair still wet she throws her hair things from the bathroom into her bag.

"I'm ready, let's bounce".

Within' twenty minutes their headed out of Boston headed back to D.C. Jay talks out loud,

"Damn! I just turned 17 may 21ˢᵗ and I got a body already, what the fuck happened! back there?"

" Baby you didn't mean to kill him, you were only looking out for me, I'm sorry". She pleaded for him to forgive her.

"No fuck that!, I wanted to kill him at first but then I thought, we would just make him suffer a little but it got outta hand I guess, Baby you don't never have to apologize, for being a woman. If I had to I would kill 20 mother fuckers like him, For you, I would no doubt". She leans over, on to Jay's shoulder and within' minutes. She's fast asleep. Jay continues driving, as he slows down. When he sees a state trooper's car parked, in the medium on the highway.

Hours later... Jay pulls over for gas in "Norwalk" Connecticut. Pam awakes, once she feels the truck come to a stop.

"Where are we?" She asked.

" I don't know, I seen a sign a little while back that said now entering Norwalk". Jay answered.

" Norwalk? So are we staying here over night or what?"

"Yeah that sounds like a plan". After Pam gets up, Jay's pumping gas Pam goes inside to get Jay some hot chocolate and she gets herself some hot tea.

As she's about to get into the truck some young boys pull up. One's hangin' out the window.

" Yo! Shortie, what's crackin'?" Pam looks at Jay and gets in. Jay's still pumpin' gas when the guy runs into the store and comes back out.

Jay finished up, then gets in and pulls off. The car follows them their on the highway for about 5 minutes. As Jay pulls off the exit the car pulls off behind them, Jay let's them pass as he sees a hotel up ahead. He pulls off into the parking lot.

" Hey if theses punk mother fuckers come over here and talk to you when I go to the office you know what it is."

" I got you baby!" She replies.

Jay gets out, and go into the front office, to get a room. He comes back out fast. He turns the corner and just as he thought the car was pulled next to his truck. Pam's smiling all at the guy hangin' out the window like he's the shit.

It's always the guy in the passenger seat that think they got the most game, when the fuck will they realize a bitch don't want the mother fucker, that got less then them. Hold up, Not true. I'm giving theses bitches to much credit myself some hood rats love a broke ass nigga or a baby dad, that whoop that ass every now and then. He thought as he smiled to himself.

The driver sees Jay coming. He hands Pam a piece

of paper. They pull off Jay acts like he didn't see. He turned and saw the passenger smiling as they rode by.

He starts talking to his boys.
"Damn I'm gonna fuck the hell outta
that little pretty bitch right there! that's my word."
As they continue down the street. Jay reaches the truck
"It's a no go they told me my parent had to come get the room, let's take a ride down the street". Jay reasoned.

Jay gets into the truck, as they pull away,
" So what did they say"? He asked.
"Oh you were right! The guy hangin' out the passenger window, does think he's the shit his names Jamal, and he wants to meet with me tonight".
"That's good we need a hit cause we been spending money like crazy lately".
"True that"! She replied.
"We'll use the old bate and hook, get him to feeling good about himself then ask him why he don't have a car. See what they got or what they moving cool?"
"Baby trust me, I got this".

"Hey no skirt wear something sexy, but not to"-
"Jay baby! Calm down, I got this".
"Okay, okay, look I want to be close by cause the last thing I need is for you to get hurt, So I'm not gonna be that far cool?"

" Well here we are motel 6 they leave the lights on". (they both laugh)

"Jay let me go up and get the room".
"Okay hey if they have one with a whirlpool in it get that one".
Pam grabs the money from Jay's out stretched hand. Once she gets to the front office. There's an older man who helps her. She gets the keys goes back around Jay's just leaning against the truck.
"Hey baby were in room 724 on the other side second floor, and yes we have the whirlpool". She said.

"Are you serious? That's what's up!"
"Well I'll drive around back, and you can take the bags up then what do you say we find a diner and get something to eat?"
"That's cool baby".
"I could go for a tuna melt". Pam said as he got into the truck.
"Umm that sounds good Me, I can eat just about anything right now, I'm hungrier than them African kids for real! Shit, all I'm missing is the flies".
"Baby you know your wrong for that come on with your crazy self!"

Once up stairs and in the room. Jay drops the bags just inside the door as he goes and dive on the bed. He turns over Pam jumps on top of him they kiss passionately. They break.
"What was that for?" He questioned.
"Jay that's because, I love you babe I love you for

excepting me for me for staying with me, and for being my first love, and for being my partner, out here in these mean streets. Jay ain't to many people got what we got. I love you, for trusting me. When I met you, you said "you don't trust anyone". Thanks for letting me in".

They kiss passionately, again.

Out the corner of his eye's Jay sees and older woman walking by the room window next to the door. Their kissing again and he sees the woman again. They chill in the room a little longer. Then they leave as their walking out. Jay locks the door he sees the woman at the end of the walk way.

He and Pam go down the other set of steps to the truck. Five minutes down the road they pull over to the diner.

1 hour later,

Their back in the room. Pam calls Jamal he answers happy as hell. He agrees to meet her. She tells him to meet her in front of the state store she had seen about four blocks from their motel. He gets off the phone. And starts braggin' to his boys.

"Yo! That was shortie I told ya'll niggas I was about to fuck, She wants to meet me in front of the state store. Yo give me one of them pills Nas put in shortie's drink last week and fucked with".

Jay watched Pam get ready. As they went to the truck Jay dropped her off in front of the state store. As he pulled back into the motel parking spot he goes up stairs and puts the key in the door. But before he steps into the room he's greeted by the older woman. Jay seeing her up close for the first time noticed. How pretty she was.

"Excuse me! Young man are you and the young woman staying here without your parents, how old are you?"

Jay eye's lit up. "I'm 17yrs old why what business is it of yours, what were doing?" Jay said, with a little attitude.

"Cause the two of you look like some run-a-ways! And I should call the cops on your little smart ass". She snapped back.

Then Jay took it down with his tone.

"Hey look! I'm sorry I came off like that but please, don't call the cops on us were not run-a-ways thou but"-

"Say no more, come here". She grabs Jay by the hand and pulls him three doors down. To her room and opens the door. She goes in before him and lays down on the bed. "I wont call the cops if you give me some of that young dick? You think you can do that"?

"Do I have a choice!" Jay asked a little nervous, at the older woman coming on to him.

" Yeah you have a choice! Either fuck or leave before I call the cops?" Jay starts to pull her clothes off once she's naked his dick is hard as a rock. He thinks damn she's beautiful she takes his clothes off. She lays him on the bed, he's nervous.

His feet are on the floor she's on her knees between his legs. She takes his dick in her mouth. Jay's whole body starts to shake he never felt like this before she was much more experienced than Pam he grabs the back of her head as he starts pumping into her mouth. She pulls away an puts his balls in her mouth and starts jerking his dick.

Jay don't know how much more of this he can take. Before he explodes. She slips a condom into her mouth and starts to suck his dick again as she stops. The condoms on as she mounts him.

" Come on! Young boy fuck this pussy!, You like this shit huh?"

She smacks Jay across the face. It caught him totally off guard as he pushes her off of him. She's on her knees on the floor layin' on the bed Jay gets behind her He enters her he grabs a hand full of hair as he pounds her from behind.

" There you go! Ride this pussy oh that's my spot, fuck me, fuck me harder, harder!."

Jay pumps a few more times as he cums. She feels him stop. He gets up.

" Damn young man! What's your name?"

"You don't need to know, all that!"

" Your right my names Debra. But were gonna have to do this again cause you didn't get me off, got that?"

Jay puts his clothes back on and leaves. While he's walking back to his room all he could think about was how good the sex was. And him being with an older woman, a beautiful older woman.

Jay gets back in the room and jumps into the shower. Once he's done He puts on some Sean John jean shorts with a white Sean John tee shirt. He tucks his gun. But tries to sit down an pulls it back out lays it on the bed. puts on his white on white air force one's he looks in the mirror checking himself out. Then he grabs his gun and tucks it, an leaves out the door. Jay goes down the steps and gets in the truck and he's off to watch out for Pam, On her date with Jamal.

Jay sits in the truck just thinking about Debra. His first mature lesson in fuckin' a woman. He had thought he handle his business until she told him, she didn't get off. He snaps out of his thought as Pam and Jamal appears, their coming outta a little restaurant. Jay's enraged at the sight of his woman with this guy. Thinking he's pullin' a fast one on Jay.

I should pull out my gun an blaze this fake ass thug! He thinks to himself as he looks on he continues to flip his razor in his mouth he almost looses it, when Jamal grabs her ass. As she gets in his car. They pull out the lot. Jay stays, about three car lengths behind them.

Ten minutes down the road. They pull up to an arcade/ sports bar type spot.

"Look this is the spot, it's cool in here so just chill here I'll get you something to drink is that cool?"

"Sure! Why not". She replied.

When Jamal comes back with the drinks Pam

excuses herself. And goes to the ladies room. She gets on her cell and calls Jay.

"Hello?"

"Babe what's up? Look I'm gonna leave this car key in the ladies room. In the second stall under the back okay use it to get the bag out the trunk and put it back so I can put it back cool?"

"I got you! You cool with that clown?" Jay asked.

"I'm trying to handle it but I don't know how much more I can take".

(they hang-up) Pam goes back out and sits next to Jamal. To her surprise he ask her

" So what's up with us getting a room?"

"Excuse me? What do I look like to you a whore? Nigga! I'm not feeling you like that, A little appetizer and you think your gettin' the pussy? Naw son, it ain't, that type of party nigga!" She spat.

Jamal's mouth drops.

" Well look here shortie!, yeah I did think it was that type of party bein' the fact that you slipped out on your man, for what for a free meal and to talk my ear off? No I didn't meet you for that! I met you here to fuck. Bottom line, so we fuckin' or what?" He stated. With serious attitude.

" Hold up! Okay okay let's go to the motel down the street?" She says, thinking of his next move.

" Naw fuck that! I already got a spot, we can go to my man's crib".

"Alright let's go". Pam answers.

Jamal, gets a smile on his face.

"Hold-up! Let me run to the bathroom again."

"Damn what you nervous?" He asked, with a chuckle.

"Maybe a little" She dips into the bathroom she's met by Jay.

"Baby what was in the bag?"

"I got about a pound of weed, two ounces of coke, and like four g's you did good". He answered.

"Look! He wants me to go to his boys crib with him, what should I do?"

"Go! I'll follow you two there and your gonna have to go real slow get him ready, I'll go back to the room get our shit and we out I'll call you on the cell, act like you gotta go outside to get a signal, jump in the truck and we'll bounce cool"?

"Gotcha! That sounds like a plan, but hurry".

"No doubt". They kiss she goes outta the bathroom first, two minutes later Jay slips out unseen. Pam goes over to Jamal and hugs him an slips the keys back in his pocket. As she thinks about what Jay told her what he got outta the trunk.

Jay gets outside he sees them pulling out of the parking lot. He runs to the truck and follows them to the house. Jamal just stopped and got out of the car he told Pam to stay. He just had to drop something off he gets out the car and goes to the trunk. Jay's pulled over as his eye's lit up at the sight of Jamal going to the trunk. He just grab the bag without looking in it and goes to the door of the house.

Pam cell rings. She answered "hello"?

"Babe as soon as he goes in get out the car, were outta here.

A guy answered the door Jamal went inside with the bag. Pam gets out the car. But not before shutting off the engine and taking the keys. She gets in the truck and their out-

"Damn Jay! That was close".

"What did you put in the bag, for weight?" Jay asked.

"Just some bullshit! He had in the trunk".

(They both laugh.)

As they continue down the road. Her cell rings. She answers.

"Hello? You little bitch you could have at least left the keys to our car". He spat.

"Our car? Ya'll share everything huh?"

"Yep just like we was gonna share your ass, back at the crib you little whore!"

"Oh I'm a little whore now, huh? But you and your little bullshit crew are the only one's that got fucked! But I'm the whore? You little bitch ass nigga! you got some nerve, I'll be a whore, suckin' my man's dick while we spend ya'll money, how you like that?"

As she hands Jay, the phone. He still talking. "So was your name really tonya?"

Jay screams into the phone. "I'm Rick James bitch!!" Pam's laughing her ass off as Jay hangs up.

" Well that's the end of Norwalk C.T. what an experience, it was."

"Yeah that goes without say".

"Hey babe what do you say we treat our self's to some seafood?" Pam inquired.

"Humm that sounds cool to me, maybe we will run into a nice one as we ride".

"Yeah maybe baby you sure you don't want me to drive for a while?"

" Not now maybe a little later". Jay answered.

"Cool hey how about I put in some "Kel" (R-Kelly) on?"

"Okay put on track 8, "fiesta!" that's my shit!" As he starts, to sing along " Bout to be vip for the night, pull up to the bumper baby, beep twice, jump out the car like I was the police, didn't have a gun but my wrist said freeze"- 'Damn this nigga be hurtin' this shit, that's what's up.

They drove on, he kept singin.' Pam fell asleep.

———————————

Chapter 9

Few hours later, Jay pulls over to a little motel in "Yonkers" New York. Pam lifts her head.

"Damn I'm tired baby, I need a bed". She looks out the window.

"Damn! Where are we in the country, what suburbs are these? They look familiar".

"Where in Yonkers, New York". Jay answered.

A chill ran down Pam's spine. Jay looks at her.

"What's wrong with you? You look like you seen a ghost, are you cool?"

"Jay, are we stayin' here tonight?"

"Yeah I thought we would and leave early in the morning, why what's up?"

"Nothin', nothin' lets go in". They park and Jay goes up to get the room. An older woman comes up.

"Hello can I help you?"

"Yes I would like a room please."

He pays she hands him a card. He fills out some print out slip then he leaves.

Back out at the truck. Pam's inside cause it starting to rain. Jay reaches in grabs the bags and they go inside. They open the door. Jay looks around

" Damn what a dump! Hell yeah, we out of here a.s.a.p"

"Thank GOD!" she chimed in.

"What's with you and this place, have you been here before?"

She ignores the question.

She returned "Well I'm bout to get in the shower then to bed I go".

"Can I join you?"

No it's that time Sorry baby, but nothin' going on tonight". She replied.

Jay just shakes his head. As he gets the bag with the sixty Grand in it. And opens it and just looks at the money.

"Damn! That looks sweet". He lays back on the bed and tries to come up with their next money move.

I got it! Oh it's on now baby. He says to himself. Pam gets out of the shower, Jay runs it down to her.

"Yeah I'm feeling that". She states.

"It'll work just fine we'll run it on Darnell, when we get back cool?"

"Gotcha!" Jay goes to get into the shower. As he's in there he starts to day dream about the boys home. He's brought out of thought by Pam knocking on the door. "Damn! Did you fall asleep in there or what?" She screamed.

"I'm comin," he puts some shampoo in his hand.

And works it into his hair, then he rinses and he gets out.

"Okay here's the deal we gotta make as much money off of this sixty grand, as possible before we meet back up with Jason okay"?

" No doubt". Pam reasoned.

"Well when we get back to D.C., we'll stay there for a week we'll run as much game, as we can, And where out got it"?

"I'm with you baby we gotta be at the top of our game In order to make it happen". They both lay down, and soon, there fast asleep.

Brooks

Chapter 10

The following morning... Jay gets washed up, he's brushing his teeth as Pam packs the few things laying around. Jay finished in the bathroom. Pam goes in and gets ready. Once she's out they leave.

Night falls, their back in D.C. and the first person they see is Nate. Jay greets him.

"What's up old man?"

"All I can't call it so I see, the young "Bonnie and Clyde's" back!?"

"Yeah something like that, what you been up to?"

"Nothin' just hangin' in there you know how it is young blood".

"Yeah I hear you, you ready to get this money again?"

"Of course". Nate shot back

"Well where gonna set something up and all we need you to do is bring people in got it?"

"Just say the word! And I'll take care of the rest".

"Cool! So have you been takin' care of yourself sense you got out of the hospital?" Pam asks.

"Oh yeah, I've been going for long walks every morning trying not to eat all that fried stuff you know".

"Well that's good to hear".

The three of them are just chillin,' leaning against the truck when across the street, Pam sees Darnel pull up in his boy's car.

"Jay babe! There's our first mark". Pam adds, as she rolls her eye's in his direction.

She goes across the street to get his attention. Jay explains everything to Nate about the set up.

While Pam's across the street talking to Darnel. A guys walking around handing out fliers. Pam asks

"What's that he's handing out?"

Darnel answers, "Yo, that's for my man's party kicking off, tonight!" Darnel waves the guy over, and gets a flier and gives it to Pam.

"Look you need to be at this party tonight! It's my man Swizle's party and trust me, he goes all out he sells "E," you don't fuck wit that thou, do you?" He said while looking at her, waiting for her response.

"No! I don't but yeah I'll stop through, can I bring a friend?"

" No doubt as long as you don't ignore me?"

"Of course not baby" She said while lightly touching his face and kissing him on the cheek. Pam's cap up game was definitely up to par. Cause she had him eating out of her hands.

Darnel goes into the store Pam cross the street. Jay was coming out with the room keys.

"Hey we got rooms right next to each other, again". He hands the other set to Nate. Jay turns to Pam

"Baby you hungry?"

"Yeah a little somtin' somtin", .Jay then turns to Nate. "How about you old man?"

"Yeah".

"Say no more let's go". Jay ordered.

Once they get to the restaurant an order. Jay starts to tell Nate about the store front they needed to rent.

"Well we'll get in touch with the owner tomorrow morning, were looking to rent it out for a month even thou, will only use it about two or three weeks".

That night at the party... Pam and Jay show up together. But Jay steps off and starts to mingle. As he sits talking to a pretty girl sitting next to him. He sees Darnel walk up to Pam. And kisses her on the cheek. Jay didn't like how easy she took to him. But he knew, it was only business.

Pam and Darnel leaves the room. Jay gets into his own conversation with Heidi. Heidi's a nice size girl nice blonde hair, pretty blue eye's and when she got up to get a drink. Jay couldn't help but notice the most sexiest hips and ass, he's seen on a woman Dammmnn!!

Was all he could say. When she came back Jay made her aware he was looking,

"Hey I didn't want you to leave, but I love to see you go. Let me ask you something?"

"Sure what?"

"Do you know what you got there?"

"Jay your nasty, huh?"

" No it's not like that! It's just, you look sexy as hell".

Jay turned his attention across the room. Some guy was talking to two girls, being very loud. Jay asks

"Who's the asshole?"

"Oh! That'll be my man Mark". She stated.

"No I'm talking about the loud dude, with the two girls hangin' all over him".

"That's who I'm talking about". Heidi spat.

"Does he know you're here?" Jay questioned.

"Of course! We came together he don't give a fuck about me, I guess you can tell that huh?"

"Come on baby why would you put up with that shit! from him? Are you slow, or something?" Jay inquired. With a light chuckle.

"Jay your funny, I just like talking to you can we go for a ride?"

"Well I'm here with a friend also what the hell, I can't turn down them pretty eye's?"

"Hey do me a favor wait out front for me? I'm gonna tell him, I'll be right back".

"Sure" Jay makes his way outside. Five minutes later Heidi comes out. She grabs his hand as she kisses him on the neck.

"Come on let's go". They walk over to her car she turns towards him as she leans back against the car. She pulls him close and kisses him again this time on the lips. As Jay palms that ass he pulls away

"Look let's go some were else with this, I don't feel comfortable out front Knowing your man's right inside".

"Yeah I feel you well get in". She unlocks the doors Jay gets in she gets in. And starts up the car and pulls off. As their driving along she lights up a blunt takes a couple pulls and passes it to Jay.

Jay takes a few hits and passes it back. As they pull up to this big pretty house down a long drive way. She pulls up to a what looked to be a barn the garage door open up they drove in and parked. The door closed they got out.

"Who's house was that we passed?" Jay inquired.

"Oh! That's my parents house, yeah their rich but this is my apartment". As they go up stairs to a living room over looking where they just parked.

"Wow this is nice". Heidi goes to the bedroom as Jay continues to talk. She comes back out wearing nothing,' but her black thong and matching bra with a see threw blouse.

Jay's eye's lit up. "Woo damn! You look good". Jay goes towards her as he grabs her this time he kisses her. He's palming all ass as they fall to the couch. She grabs the remote and turns on the music. She puts on fat Joe's "get it poppin'" as they start to take each others clothes off.

"Hey! What if your man comes home?" Jay asked.

"Who cares he don't live here!, He don't even know where I live".

"That's all I needed to hear!" Jay shot back.

She gets on her knees with a cough drop in her mouth as she licks his dick all over, she pulls it out of her mouth and starts to blow on it. Jay feels a chill down his spine as his eye's roll in the back of his head. Then she puts ice in her mouth and continues. When Jay couldn't take it any more he put on a condom.

He had her doggie style on the side of the coffee table. Jay was smackin' that ass as he rode her for about twenty minutes. Then he turn her around laid her down and reentered her as he grab her legs he pushed her knees up to her chest. As he pounded away as they both looked on her big screen t.v. watching the whole thing as it unfolds.

They lay on her thick carpet both out of breath.

"Damn! I needed that I haven't had sex in two months".

"So why are you with that guy?" Jay inquired again.

"Well cause he's not up my ass I hate when a guys

are up my ass all the time, he's cool to chill with when he's not being an asshole".

"Hey if he wasn't being an asshole tonight we wouldn't be here".

"Well in that case I'm glad he was an asshole tonight". Jay spat.

"Jay I know your not from around here but I hope we can do this again soon?"

"Sure can I use your bathroom?"

"Yeah it's over there" she said pointing.

"So you ready to go back to the party?"

Jay comes outta the bathroom.

"Hey I'm ready when you are". He answered.

She goes to the bathroom. within' five minutes she's back. "Yeah I'm ready".

"Hey Jay you got a cell phone?"

"Yeah why what's up?"

"Can I see it?" Jay hands her his cell. As they get in the car she hands it back.

"That's my number when I call, I hope you make it your business to get out!"

"Well with the way you handle your business, I don't see that being a problem at all babe".

"Jay don't take this the wrong way but you haven't had that many sex partners, have you?"

"Why! Was I that bad?" He stated.

"Know, know, like I said don't take it the wrong way you where good, you just seemed a little distracted or inexperienced I can definitely help you get better, and trust me, Your girl will appreciate it no doubt".

"Look I want to get back together tomorrow night If that's possible?"

"Well I can't promise anything, but I'll try". At this she's unzipping his shorts she pulls his dick out, and starts stoking it, Jay just lays back as they listen to Kanye West's " Champion" she puts Jay's balls in her mouth as she jerks him off. He starts to pump harder in her mouth. He grabs the back of her head he holds her there as he cums she swallows. She smiles at him as he zips his shorts.

Within' fifteen minutes their back at the party. They get out of the car they stand outside and talk for a while. A girl comes up to them with jello shots. They each take one then she hands them some warm water Jay takes it and starts to drink it. He leans to the side and spits it out. Heidi asked " Did you just spit?"

"Yeah why?"

" I don't know how to spit".

" Are you serious?" He asked.

"I gotta swallow". As they laugh together, and walk back inside.

"What was the fuckin' warm water for?"

"The tubes! Were kinda sticky they were for your hands,.. sorry".

_____

The following day.. Jay gets up and get ready. He goes over to Nate's room and tell him to get ready cause their about to go eat. As he gets back into the room Pam's getting ready. Jay sits on the edge of the bed.

"So how did things go last night?"

"Jay baby this guy is sweeter than cotton candy, he started to show off he gave me $300.00 dollars, he showed me his safe, and told me just about everything about his whole team".

"Yeah he is sweet huh? Cool".

"So here's what where gonna do, your gonna need to hang with him again, but work this idea into his head and see if he bites feel me?"

"Oh and that chick you were talking to her nigga, is on their team too".

"Oh really?""

Yeah his name's Mark right?" She asked.

" Yeah, yeah I think that what she told me his name was".

Jay tried to sound like he wasn't talking to her like that.

"Babe! What's wrong? You look nervous, or something what's up?" She questioned.

"I'm cool I'm just ready to make this money grow feel me?"

"Hey you know I'm with that".

They leave the room after they finished getting dressed. Nate's waiting outside. Jay greets him

"Good morning old head, you ready to make it happen?"

"Good morning well if it ain't the young "Bonnie and Clyde."

Jay just started laughing.

At the diner... after they all finished eating and talking. The waitress comes back with the bill. Jay goes up to pay. Just when they get up to leave, Darnel comes in with his boy and two girls. The hostess shows them to their seat as Darnel gets back up and comes outside and grabs Pam's arm. Pam stops Jay just looks back and continues to the truck.

"Sorry I didn't mean to grab you like that, but I need to see you again tonight, is that cool?"

"Yeah that's cool I'll call you when I'm ready, okay?"

" Gotcha! I'll holla at you later shortie". Pam gets to the truck.

"That's it baby! He wants to get together tonight".

"Cool what time?" Jay inquired.

"I said I'd call him when I'm ready, I was thinking about 8:30pm cause I really wanted to spend some time with you tonight If you know what I mean".

"Baby trust me If we pull this thing off, like I know we can we gonna cop a spot, and jump on a plane to where ever feel me?"

"Are you serious baby? No more of this hotel shit?"

"You said it baby! We gotta do it". Jay explained.

Later that night... Jay went for a little drive. Pam

was back at the room getting ready. Jay cell phone rings. It's Pam.

"Hey babe what's up? Jay are you coming back before I leave?"

" Yeah I'm stopping at the store first, then I'm coming you want anything?"

"No I'm straight".

"Okay I'm on my way". (they hang-up)

Jay calls Heidi she answers.

"Hey I was just thinking about you, I was watching our video earlier so you ready for part two?" Heidi asked smiling over the phone.

"Are you serious? Hell yeah!"

"Jay let me ask you this, what's your favorite color?"

"Green why?"

"Cause I got a surprise for you so what time are we getting together?"

" Humm I was thinking in about an hour, how's that?"

"That's good for me but don't drive here, meet me at the diner down from your hotel".

" Cool, I'll see you then." (they hang-up).

Jay thinks to himself wait! I never told her what hotel I was staying in? As a puzzled look came across his face.

Jay mind starts scrambling. He thought about everything under the sun. Was she setting him up?, Was she a stalker type? Or was she crazy? One thing for sure, Jay would find out. When they get together in an hour while still in thought, Jay pulls over to the store. He gets out of the truck and he can't believe his eye's, sitting in the car next to his was Debra. The older woman Jay slept with a few states over.

Damn! what is she doing out here? Jay walks over as he leans his head in the car. "Hey stranger, what you doing out here?" Jay inquired.

"Oh shit! Hey young man I'm out here visiting family, and to think I was wondering, what to get into out here now I know, don't you owe me young man?" she asked looking him over.

Jay starts to blush, loving the feeling the older woman gave him the last time they had sex.

"Well here take my number down and give me a call tomorrow okay?"

"Oh yeah you can count on that". She takes the number folds it and puts it in her bra.

"You still never told me your name?" She stated.

"It's Jay". He replies.

Jay goes in the store he gets what he needed. Plus some more condoms thinking, It's gonna be a long weekend might as well suit up for it! As he laughs to himself and gets in his truck.

Meanwhile… Det. Jake and Miss. Roberts. Get a set of finger prints which they ran through the system and they matched? Jason Banks a 17yrs old run away. As they get the address to the foster home. They make their way there to find out more about this child their looking for.

Jake speaks to Miss Roberts. "

So what do you think, this kid could be thinking out here killing people at random?" He spat.

"Well don't be to quick to Judge, maybe it could have been out of self defense, I mean they where older guys that have been killed, they could have tried to rape him or something never know, it's a sick world out here, and it's gotta be scary for a 17yrs old, trying to make it on his own". She shot back.

"Can I ask you something? How old would your kid be now?"

"You know, I was just thinking the same thing 17yrs old".

When they get to the foster home. They go into the office where their talking to the social worker who was on Jay's case. When she pulled a picture of Jay out, a chill went up Det. Jake's spine, as he showed Miss Roberts the photo. Their eye's met as they tried to hand her the photo back.

" No! You can keep that picture, we have it on file so, may I ask you something?"

" Sure what's that?"

"I know he escaped from here, but other than that is he in any trouble?" The social worker inquired.

"We'll as of now, he's just a suspect we found his prints, at a murder scene but they could have been there before hand, where not sure but we gotta start on our only lead".

"Now can we ask you a few question? How well did you know him? What kinda kid is he? Is he violent, would he have reason to believe someone would want to hurt him?" Det. Jake asked with his pad out waiting to jot down her reply.

"Well Jason's a very smart kid he's a thinker and he's definitely a survivor he's short, and he can carry a razor In his mouth very well, I use to find him sleeping with it in his mouth". They both looked at each other again. She went on.

"Kids, he didn't trust any one you have to earn his respect and his trust just for myself, I wanted to know where he's at but as far as his well being? I know he's doing good he's a nice kid, that got a raw deal. He got dealt a bad hand, early in life". She answered as she talked, with sadness in her voice.

"Well thanks for all you've done but we must be going now they get up, and make their way towards the door.

" Excuse me, Det.? Would it be possible, for you to call me when you find out he's okay?" She asked.

"Sure! We'll give you a call as soon as we know something okay?"

"Thank you, and God bless you two".

Meanwhile… Jay sitting with Pam drinking a cream soda. Jay talks,

" So are you looking forward to making this happen or what?"

" No doubt! But I think, he's falling for me pretty fast". Pam stated.

"Baby, who wouldn't fall for you? Look at you".

Jay turns her towards the mirror over the dresser in the room. "You look beautiful, how you think I fell for you?" Jay reasoned.

"Jay stop, your making me blush so what are you going to do tonight, when I'm gone?"

" I'm getting worried Jay, me not being able to spend that much time with you theses "chicken heads" around here, might start thinking your single and I don't want to have to beat the shit outta one of theses bitches, But you know I will".

Jay starts laughing. "You crazy babe I couldn't picture your little ass fighting."

"I know, you ain't just call me little? Nigga you shorter than me!"

She spat.

Chapter 11

That night...

Pam, went out with Darnel on business Jay on the other hand went to meet Heidi. And had nothing but pleasure, on his mind.

Once they get to Heidi's apartment. They couldn't keep their hands off of each other. Jay stopped Heidi and had her get him a drink. That night, Jay got introduced to. "Hypnotic" and Hennessy together known to the world as "the incredible hulk." After a few of them in Jay's system. He's kissing on Heidi's leg she's on the couch. He's on the floor on the thick carpet. As he reaches up her thigh he feels her ass.

" Humm somebody don't have any panties on?"

"Reach a little, higher". She ordered.

Jay does as she gets off the couch. And gets up on the coffee table and starts dancing she pull up her skirt. She's wearing his surprise a green thong and bra set.

She also has her finger nails and toes. The same color. Jay stands up and picks her up off the table. And carries her to the bedroom. Where he's amazed the first night. Jay and Heidi never made it to the bedroom.

Jay laid her on the bed as she's getting his shorts off Jay's admiring the set up. She had a 42" plasma t.v on the wall at the foot of the high canopy style bed. Jay sunk in the satin sheets and thick down pillows she had. At this Jay felt fire as she took his dick into her mouth. Her mouth was hot Jay in an instant felt he was about to cum any second.

As he pushes her away she's pulling hungrily at his dick. Jay takes off his shirt he turns Heidi on her stomach. That's when he noticed the tattoo of a 'black panther' on her ass.

This, excited him even more. He licked her, from her calf to the bottom of her ass. Once there he slid two fingers in to her hot and waiting pussy for a second, his experience with Debra was coming to him. As he finger fucked her While putting a hickey on the cheek that didn't have the tattoo on it. She moaned loud, Jay pulled his soaked fingers out. Then grabbed a hand full of her blonde hair and pulled her to her knees. And mounted her from behind, as they went through.

" Like Prince would say, 23 position in a one night stand." After, they both just lay there completely sexed out. Then Jay did what no one cheating should do, he laid there and fell asleep.

Good thing Heidi, didn't want to get him in trouble.

So she only let him sleep, for a half an hour. Jay got up showered and dressed. Heidi took him to his truck.

Pam and Darnel was sitting in a hotel room. Sitting in the Jacuzzi sipping on moet, Pam never tasted anything so good in her life.

She was really starting to feel Darnel's charm. He wasn't quite the asshole she made him out to be. A few more glasses of moet and Pam found herself naked in the bed laying next to Darnel. He touched her with experienced hands, as he rubbed her down with lotion Pam didn't know if it was the way his hands felt on her body. Or how sexy he looked naked. Whatever it was Pam was feeling the effect of the moet and the ambience. She was in the mood, and went with the flow-

Jay got back to the hotel room and waited on Pam's arrival. His cell phone rang, as he answered expecting Pam's voice. He got Heidi's. "Hey Jay! I need to talk to you about something".

"Yeah what's that?"

"I got this thing well how can I tell you this?"

"Heidi? Whatever it is, give it to me straight please!" Jay reasoned.

"Okay are you interested in making some fast money?"

"Heidi babe are you still a little drunk?" Jay asked.

"No Jay look I'm serious are you interested, or what?" She snapped.

"Of course what's the catch?"

"I'll talk to you about that later I'm gonna need you, to meet me tomorrow about 2:00pm in the after noon cool?"

"No doubt! I'm there where are we meeting?"

"The diner on chamber street okay? Be there".

"Gotcha! Later" (they hang-up)

Jay takes his clothes off and walks towards the shower. Thinkin' what money? Where, and how much. He gets into the shower then he starts to think bout how the night went with Heidi. As he washes up Then while he's washing his hair he starts to think about tomorrow with Debra. He's quickly taken out of thought when he hears the door slam.

"Hey babe, I'm back!" Pam calls into Jay. She starts to get ready for bed. She's still floating on cloud 9 when Jay steps in the room.

" So, how did everything go?" He questioned.

" Wonderful, just wonderful!" Then she caught herself, by then It was to late.

"What's that suppose to mean? Are you still on your grind, or are you slipping? Cause your starting to like this nigga?" Jay stated with adidtude.

"Jay baby what are you talkin' about? You know I only do this for us! come on, don't act like that".

She was talking with a slight slur, so Jay knew it was the liquor talking. So he thought it best to just talk to her in the morning.

The following day…

Jay gets up he let's Pam sleep in. He and Nate go and see the landlord about the store front. Jay writes Pam a note and he and Nate leave. While their in the truck Jay goes over the plan with Nate again. About what to say how long he wants to rent it out for and so on and so forth. Before they get out of the truck, Jay hands Nate the money him and the guy talked about over the phone. The last months and first months rent.

As they step out of the truck their met by this skinny little Jewish guy. All three of them shake hands as they talk business.

When all was said and done. He handed the keys to Nate and they shook hands once more and sealed the deal. They didn't even have to deal with him any more, it was and address they sent their rent to and that's that. They waited for him to pull off. Jay spoke,
"Well now it's all in motion, let's go get my girl and lets go eat breakfast".

Jay couldn't have felt better his plans were coming together like clock work. Now if he didn't lose Pam in the transaction then everything would be great. He wondered on the drive back.
When they got back to the hotel. Pam was up when Jay came in.

"Hey baby you hungry? Come on let's go eat, I got great news". As they walked to the truck Jay turns to Pam. "Baby we got the store, it's on and poppin' now believe that".

Nate was outside talking to a friend Jay turns towards the window. When the waitress asked, how many?. Jay told her three he looked out the window again Nate was motioning for Jay to come outside.

"Baby go sit down I'll be right back cool?"
"Okay you want me to order the usual?"
"Yeah that's cool, do that".
"Okay hurry up". Jay goes outside.
"What's up old head?" Jay asked.
"Young buck! You didn't tell me, you was messin' around with the dude Mark's girl how you swing that youngster?"
Jay tried to sound dumb, "what are you talking about Nate, who?"
"Look Jay, I'm just trying to tell you that's the jackpot. You've been waiting for, Everything about that girl is money why you think he fucks around on her but he wont let her go?"
"Nate old head stop talking in riddles, put me up on the bitches game dogg!" Jay inquired.

"Jay I'll put it to you short and simple she's a rich girl, and I don't mean through her family, she lives on their property that's it they don't have shit to do with her any more, come on young blood let's go eat".
They went in and joined Pam. They all ordered as

Pam ask Jay about the store. Jay was in deep thought about what Nate had told him outside. Not to mention the phone call he got after being with her last night. He also thought about their meeting early that coming after noon.

"Okay well first we need to get over there, and clean up a bit".

" Look everybody remembers how it's all to go down right?"

Once their food comes. Just then Darnel walks into the diner. Jay locks eye's with him. Nate looks at Jay, then turns to see what he's looking at as Pam cracks a smile and gives a little wave while Jay's not looking at her.

"Young man don't get yourself all wilded up over that nigga, cause he's got one foot in the grave already". Pam eye's lit up at the statement being made about Darnel.

"Nate! What did you just say?" She asked.

"I was just saying, he's on his way out anyway he's got "the Monster.""

"What's that?" She questioned.

Jay and Nate both look at her- Jay answers.

"Baby that's Aids, that's what the streets, call it, " the Monster,'" his ticket etc".

Pam stomach flips. As she gets up to go over to him. Pam gets right up on Darnel. "You mother fucker! I can't believe you, you fucker you knew you had that shit and you laid down and gave it to me? I hope you burn in hell".

She leaves out of the diner Jay gets up, and follows her out.

"Baby what happened?" Jay asked.

"Jay don't worry, I'm sorry and I'll leave you alone, I'm sorry baby I never wanted to hurt you, Jay "I love you." And this is how I treated my one, and only love". She rambled.

"Pam baby slow down what are you talking about?" Jay questioned.

"Jay did you not hear me in the diner?"

"Baby you where whispering, I don't think anyone heard you".

"Jay baby, I slept with Darnel last night!!! Jay, baby I slept with Darnel last night!!! Jay I slept with Darnel last night!!!"

Jay just sat on the curb. As it echoed, on and on in his head. He couldn't think he didn't know what to say. What seemed like an hour went by, was only five minutes Jay snapped out of it.

"Hold on baby we watched videos about this in the boy's home about Hiv and Aids there's been cases, where people slept with people who had it, and didn't get it we'll go get you tested, okay? Baby I'm not gonna leave you to go through this, by yourself you're my ride or die chick! Believe that, Come on we got business to handle". Jay stated.

"Were going to stop by the planned parenthood on the way to clean the store, cool?"

"That sounds good, thanks baby"-

"Pam you don't have to thank me, you're my girl". At that statement Pam cracked a smile.

Twenty minutes later…

Their pulling up to planned parenthood. Nate stays outside to smoke a cigarette. Pam and Jay goes inside.

Lady at the counter "yes may I help you?"

Jay walks up to the counter. He asks her, about Hiv testing.

She answers, "we'll have our next one tomorrow between 9:00am-12:00 noon. Would you like to set up an appointment?"

"Yes". Jay answered.

As the lady took their information. She handed Jay a bag of condoms and they left. Nate was leaning against the truck. He asks " So what's up?"

Jay answers.

"We got an appointment for tomorrow".

"That's cool, it's gonna be alright Pam I just know it, try to relax".

"Thanks Nate but that's easier said, then done". She responded.

A little down the road and their at the store. Jay gets the brooms he brought from the dollar store out of the back of the truck and the bucket.

Nate opens the fence in front as he rolls it up. They open the door and go in. Jay being at the library sent off for all the permits they needed. They all started cleaning and talking and just having fun. And before long, they were done.

"Okay, baby where ready for business tomorrow we'll order some candy, chips, soda and a bunch of other stuff, set it up nice and neat, then where gonna get a fake title from the boy brooks then it's on, we look for a buyer as we make money until we pull off the big caper got it?"

"Sounds like a beautiful plan baby, I'm with you".

"That goes for me too". said Nate, "You a young smart motherfucker I wish I had someone like you to run with, when I was younger". Nate spat

They all get back into the truck.

" It's on baby, it's on and crackin' no doubt!" As Jay said this, a smile went across Pam's face.

A week went by...

And the results came back from Pam's test.

She was found to be, HiV positive. Jay couldn't believe it, a million and one thoughts went through his head.

As he tried everything to hold back his tears. But they came anyway. He left the store and went for a drive. All the while just thinking how all his plans where gone. Then he started to think about Heidi's offer he had told Pam about it she thought it was cool.

Heidi had asked Jay to let her help him get his

hands on some crazy money. Her girl friend who she " helped out" a while back was paying Heidi back by giving her different people's info to get credit cards. The first week she gave Heidi a list with people who had outstanding credit.

And Jay had her send them to the store. Both had $75.000 credit limit. Jay would wait till they arrive then he would hold on to them until they sent the pin number behind them.

Then Jay would go out and buy DvD players, digital cameras, big screen tv's etc. Then when he couldn't charge any more. He would get as much money out as possible. Then he would call and ask for an increase. Some times they would give it to him then he would sell the card for $200 dollars. If he got a $500 dollar increase. If he got a $1,000 dollar it would go for $400 Jay with Heidi was a money makin' fool.

Now Jay had Heidi, Pam, Nate, and the young girl, lulu on his team. And everyone was eating good. Lulu was the counter girl, she was from the town over she was looking for a place to stay. And found it with Jay he put her down with the team, and the rest is history.

Lulu was a young hustler, she helped move most of the camera's, dvd players, and she sold 4 big screens In one week. Lulu, Just turned 18 yrs old, and had no idea she was older than Jay.

"Wow, I can't believe he's only 17yrs old?

I know he looks young, but to see him handle business I guess just makes you think, he's older huh?"

" Yeah I guess to a point, but then you never seen him act a fool either I mean don't get me wrong, he's really fun to kick it with".

Little did she know later that night, she would find out more about Jay.

As the day turned to night. The store closed. Pam was tired, and just wanted to go back to the room and lay down.

Jay didn't tell Pam the good news yet. But Him and Nate found out about an old couple, who was renting out a split level duplex not far from the hotel, they stayed at now.

Even thou Jay was bring in the money he was always looking for ways to save. This way Nate and Lulu, would be on the bottom and he and Pam would be on top. And the fact that Heidi, was moving with them when they were about to leave town.

Pam hated the fact that Jay was hooking up with Heidi right in front of her eye's. Jay tried to hide it, but the fact of the matter was it was bound to happen.

It's two week later… The store doing great. Jay, Pam, Nate and Heidi are still setting people up, for next months deal. Jay push back there time, being the deli was really making money.

They all been moved into the duplex. For a week now and everybody loves it. Nate and Lulu were going to get her a car. About three o'clock today. They where just waiting for Jay to get back with Heidi.

They couldn't just leave Pam at the store alone. Cause the medication she was on made her weak at times. Pam was in the back store room signing an order in when Jay and Heidi walked in Nate was out front sweeping the side walk. Lulu was bopin' her head to the head phones she had on. As Jay got closer he heard the music.

"What! I know that ain't no Prince, I hear you listening to?"

She takes off the head phones.

"Yes it is why?" She asked.

"What do you know about Prince?" Jay asked with a slight smirk on his face.

"Are you serious? Naw! You didn't go there". Lulu spat

Jay turns to Heidi

"Did she just go there, with me?"

"Looks like that to me". Heidi replied.

As they all hear bottles breaking in the store room. They all run back. Pam's double over in pain. Jay runs over to her.

"Baby are you okay?" As he helps her sit down.

"Heidi baby can you take her home, for me please?"

"No problem come on Pam". As she reaches her hand out to Pam. They walk through the store. Jay tells her he'll see her later. And if there's anything she needs, to call him.

Then Jay tells Nate and Lulu to go. "I got this, ya'll go".

As their about to leave. Jay grabs Lulu's arm.

"We'll talk about this, Prince thing when you get back".

They both smile as Her and Nate leave in Jay's truck.

Heidi and Pam were talking on the way to the duplex.

"So, you're his baby now huh?"

"Pam what are you talking about?"

"Oh, I heard him call you baby when we were in the back and look Heidi, that's cool just know I love Jay, but I did this to myself, I can't do nothin' for Jay any more, at least not sexual. Your good for him, he's a great guy, and all I want is what's best for him God knows, if I could take back the mistake I made, I would. But it's one, I have to live with, just don't break his heart, he's been through a lot". Pam stated.

They pull up to the house.

Heidi turns to Pam.

" Hey thanks, it means a lot to me to hear you say the things you said about Jay and thanks for giving me the go to hook up with Jay he has mad love for you, and even more respect just know that, thanks again". They hug as Heidi gets out of the car and walks around to open the door for Pam.

She helps Pam inside, Then she leaves.

Once back at the store. Heidi and Jay, are out front talking she had told him what Pam said. And their kickin' it when Nate pulls up in Jay's truck and minutes later. Lulu pulls up in a red Honda civic. She gets out she starts jumping, up and down as she goes over and hugs and kisses Jay. At this Heidi by the look on her face. You can tell she was hot.

"Jay thank you, thank you, thank you, so much! I've never had any money or anything I could call my own until I met you, and right hear an now if there's ever anything you need! Let me, be the first person you ask please I love you man" she hugs him again. "Your like a real life angel, I mean, who your age can not only get me off the street but give me a nice place to live, and put money in my pocket and help me get my first car, God you're a saint!". She stated, excitedly.
"Hey, it's cool hey were all a team all for one, no doubt where like that crew, in that book "Flawless" the B.F.L. no doubt". Jay replied.
"Well, I need to read that book cause I never heard of a crew so loyal".

"So Nate are you and Lulu cool with closing yourselves tonight?" Jay inquired. As they both gave Jay the nod okay. Jay and Heidi was out. As they got outside.
"So where to baby?"

"Well if you don't mind, let's go get a room, I just want to be alone with you for a while". She stated.

"Hey you gets no argument from me babe, lets do this

I got this game, we can play".

"Oh really? And what might that game be?"

"Well we get naked"- Jay cuts her off.

"I like it already drive faster." They both laugh.

———————————————

Chapter 12

With in minutes… they where pulling up to a hotel. Heidi grabs her bag out the trunk and goes and slip into something a little more sexy, Jay knew that, as she disappeared into the bathroom. When she came back out, he couldn't believe his eye's. She had on an all black fish net body stocking.

"Wow!!" Was the only word that escaped his mouth. She came closer to Jay.

"You have got to be the sexiest, woman! I've ever laid eye's on dammnn!!" He thought she would put on the CD he made for her. But instead she put on some Tupac. Then she lit some candles. From there it was on.

She made Jay get on the floor doggie style as she sucked his dick from behind. Jay couldn't believe it. He had just over heard two guys talking about this position the other day. At the pool hall. Then she had him sit on the couch and lay back, as she sucked his dick a little longer and rubbed his chest. She grabbed his dick and started to smack herself in the face with it. Jay couldn't take any more as he got up laid her down on the floor as he lift up her legs and entered her. He had her knees pushed back to the side of her ears as he pounded away, at her pussy.

As Tupac played on in the back ground Jay and Heidi fucked the night a way. Once they were finished. Heidi went down the side walk and got Jay a Snapple and herself a coke. She walked back in handed him his drink. Then she turned the music off, and put a movie on. Dave Chappell's, second season.

"All this is my shit! This dude is funny, as hell".

"So let me ask you this? Why do you really want to leave this town?"

"I knew this was coming well Jay, the truth is remember I told you Mark kinda has a hold on me?"

"Yeah, and?"

"Well it's not just him, I feel this town has a hold on me. and I need to break free now, while I'm still young".

She took a breath an continued.

" And if later I want to come back? At least I know, I saw something different got me?"

"Oh yeah I feel you I spent years just thinking, and reading and honestly that was my only escape, through books you see when I'd read, I see myself as the people I'm reading about an I envision that's me! That's doing whatever it is, their doing but now, I'm no longer that caged bird I'm flying now, playing by my own set of rules I'm a slave to nothin', but a master of all my mind can conceive".

"Jay baby your are one deep brother! That's what I love about you, you know what you want and you know how to go about getting it, an that's real".

"Look Heidi where only here for a short period of time This life ain't guaranteed! To nobody, so it's a must, you do the damn thing while you're here all the time you spend bullshitting, and fucking up? Is time wasted, no doubt".

"It's like a bad relationship, it's pointless. One man's trash is the next man's treasure, don't believe that,

Ha you believe that?" Jay spat

"Yeah, kinda".

" Baby that's bull GOD don't make trash! If a man makes you feel that low, he was never a man in the first place, A man is strong responsible, caring sharing, and loving to his kids, his family, and most of all his woman. If he needs to break you down, to feel more like a man, then he was lacking one, If not more of them quality's feel me?" Jay stated.

"Hey you feel like going to the diner for some coffee or something?"

"Sure Jay, we can do that".

"Cool well let me jump in the shower first then we out".

"Okay baby, take your time".

While Jay's in the shower Heidi gets a call from Mark.

"Hey girl why haven't I seen you in a while?" He inquired.

"Mark baby I've been busy but we can get together tonight, Is that cool?"

"Yeah meet me over my crib in about 10 minutes, got it?

And yo! Don't keep me waiting, alright?"

"Come on baby you know I can't keep you waiting I'll be there". (they hang-up)

Jay gets out of the shower.

"So Heidi you ready?" Jay had the water running but had came back out to get a towel. He heard the whole conversation. So now he's just waiting to see how she's gonna blow him off.

"Jay something's come up can we just get together tomorrow or something?"

"No doubt! Baby that's, cool". Jay replies.

"You sure?" As Jay walks pass her. And goes to the car, she's a little pissed.

"Your not gonna even ask why?" She questioned.

"Heidi the set of rules I live by no, they wont allow me too."

"Yeah Jay, what set of rules is that?"

"Don't ask for the truth if your not ready for it, or if you don't want to hear a lie". He stated as he cut her a look.

"So now I'm a liar?"

"Okay just this once, I'll bite what came up Heidi?" He inquired, with his words dripping with sarcasm.

"My mom wants to hang out, and watch movies So, so I'm staying here that's all why, what did you think?" She asked looking down at the floor.

"Oh! Your gonna really play this thing out huh? Well I know for a fact, that's bullshit!! But it is, what it is baby you mean to tell me, your mom can't wait for you to go out, and have a cup of coffee?"

"Jay I don't spend that much time, with my mom as it is Damn! Can I do this, one thing?"

"Like I said, are you ready?"

"Yes Jay, let's go". She snapped back.

Minutes later.. she's dropping him off at his truck. Jay sits there for a while, until she gets jumpy.

"Damn! Must be some movie, I'll let you go see him I mean it, c-ya!" She tries to kiss him on the lips Jay turns, she kisses him on the cheek. As he gets out.

"I'll call you tomorrow, okay?" Jay holds up the peace sign as he gets in his truck.

Jay gets home and the only one up is Lulu.

"Hey Jay look Nate rented this old movie "Bonnie and Clyde," you want to watch it with me?" She asked.

" Yeah he keeps calling me and Pam that and I told him, I've never seen it before go head pop it in".

Lulu had on some shorts she sleeps in. And a wife beater that kept sliding down. As she laid there, with some fresh popped popcorn Jay kicked off his sneakers and sat down next to her.

"Okay let's see what this movie's about".

Half way through the movie, the two of them are really cuddled up together. Jay started to feed Lulu some popcorn she grabs one and tries to feed it to Jay as she tries to put it in his mouth. He begins sucking on her finger. She pulls away.

"Jay! We can't do this".

"Yeah your right there's just so many quality's you have that attracts me, to you".

"Well that's very flattering but you have a girl friend, and I don't want to be the one to come between that".

"Okay, I respect that hey how about after the movie you go get a cup of coffee, with me?" Jay suggested.

Pam had gotten up, and was standing in the door way listening. Thinking, "Damn that used to be me". At that she turned around hoping not to get noticed, as she went back to bed.

The following day… Jay went and opened the store. Lulu and Pam was working, while Jay and Nate went to an appointment to see some would be buyers for the Deli. Nate didn't have any idea, until it came up. As they left the meeting their outside in the truck. "Jay did I hear it right? You want to sell the Deli, your renting?"

"Nate it's like this I got this kid Brooks who can make any kinda fake id photos even titles, and deeds Feel me? It's like this, after we get all the money from the scheme where running, Just consider this as some extra "get lost money," huh? You with me, old man?"

"Young buck I'm with you". As a smile, goes across Nate's face.

Debra

Chapter 13

The next day... everything's ready for play. Lulu brings Swizle, he gives the person behind the slot in the wall. An envelope with $5 G's in it. The voice tells him to come back In three days. Half hour later Nate brings in Jamal. He leaves an envelope with $7 G's. The voice tells him the same.

That night the store closes. Heidi comes by.

"Jay you want to go somewhere we can be alone? I got a surprise for you".

Jay answers. "Well me and Lulu had made plans".- Lulu cuts him off.

"No Jay don't worry about me! We can hang out some other time".

Jay turns to Lulu,

" you sure?"

"Yeah go ahead!"

"Well looks like I'm free!" He spat

Heidi gets this look.

"Okay well let's roll". They get to the nearest hotel.

She goes into the bathroom she comes out with a silver bra and panties "boy shorts" on. Jay stops her.

"Hold on a sec, what's up with me not seeing you all day, you not answering your phone then you just happen, to pop up 10 minutes before the store closes, That's how you think you got me?"

"Jay baby I don't want to fight, with you I just want to make love to you". She gets down, an starts to rub his dick through his shorts. He stands up. She undo his shorts, as she let's them fall to the floor. Then she slides down, his boxers. He gets on the floor on his knees, as she gets under him she's sucking on his nuts. He slides up on down "tea bagging" he thinks about eating her out until the picture of her with Mark pops into his head. Then he declines the notion. They drink some more Henney and coke then they go back to the " incredible Hulk" as they drink cup, after cup before Jay realize he's fuckin' her without a condom.

When he finally noticed they had went a few rounds, already. As Jay got washed up and left. He got home and he and Lulu sat up and watched "Empire". Jay couldn't help but to keep thinking about having unprotected sex, all he thought about was them videos he seen in the boys home.

Two days later… Jay went to the bathroom, and his dick was hurting when he urinated his eye's got big. He went back out in the store and told Pam and Lulu he would be right back. Jay jumped in his truck and went down the block to the plan parenthood.

" Excuse me, excuse me!" He yelled, to the woman behind the counter, finally getting her attention. He spoke.

"Is there any way I could get checked out for a V.D. today?"

The lady took down his info, and told him to have a seat "someone will be with you shortly". She informed him.

Jay sat there as he began to look around. He then closed his eye's, an said a silent prayer. The doctor came out and got him. Jay followed him into the back the Doctor had jay urinated into a cup. The doctor then took it to the other room. Within' minutes the doctor had came back. "Jason, you have Chamita." The Doctor stated.

"What's that? Oh I know! That's one of the most common also, curable form of V.D., right?"

The doctor looked amazed, "That is correct but, that doesn't mean you should go around having unprotected sex."

" Doc, Trust me! I know, It was a big mistake that will never happen again." Jay reasoned.

"Well do you know who gave it to you? Cause they need to come get treated for this, before you two engage in sex again".

"Yeah I know I'll have her come". Jay stated.

"Here, take theses it's for a week they start working right away, but finish all of it okay?"

"I gotcha Doc, thanks!"

Jay left out with a smile. As he got into the truck and went back to the store. Nate was walking another buyer through when Jay pulled-up. Jay was about to go in Heidi pulled up also.

"Jay baby what's up?"

"Well if it isn't the woman of the hour?" Jay stated with a sinister stare.

"What's that suppose to mean?" She questioned.

"Come here we need to talk." As they got into Heidi's car Jay pulled out his bottle he just got from the doctor.

"You need to go get some of theses this where I just came from, and you're the only person I'm having sex with! But you can't say that, can you? Unless it was them movies you were watching with your mom?" Jay questioned, with venom dripping from his words.

"Baby your right! I'm sorry will you go with me?"

"You're right, I'm sorry! That's all you got to say to me? are you serious? Look bitch! I don't know how you get down, but I care about my life feel me? That could have been "the monster!" you gave me, but thank GOD! It wasn't Look, if you still wanta fuck with that nigga, who don't give two shits about you anyway then yeah, I'll go with you to the doctor then, that's it cool?" He spat.

" No baby! I didn't mean it like that Jay, the last thing I wanted to do was hurt you". She answered.

"Well you did two times". He stated as she got this puzzled look across her face. He continued.

"That night I came out to get a towel I heard your conversation with that nigga, and I was just waiting to see how you were going to get rid if me, then you lied, right to my face yeah, so if you want to get back into my good grace, you need to work at it".

"Jay, baby I'll do what ever it is you want!"

"Yeah well I'm gonna hold you to that so let me ask you this re you done, with that nigga? No don't hold your head down look at me, are you? Okay well, get that nigga to get in on this game that's being ran cool?"

"I got you babe". Jay turned around, and said.

"Don't got me, get me!"

Chapter 14

The following day…

Heidi got up early in the morning, and came and got Jay. And took him out to breakfast before the store opened. At breakfast is when she told him she had Mark coming to the store about two o' clock to drop off $10 G's "Jay he's an easy mark cause he's money hungry before we leave, we can probably get him for about $100 thousand clean".

"Oh really! He's holding like that huh?"
"Oh yeah, I made him at least quarter million four months ago." Jay just sat there listening to her.

Later that day at least six people came through and got their money all left with smiles on their face's. Like they really couldn't believe it. Jay and his crew had the whole hood shook on his long con.

Later that night… after they closed the store. Jay

was talking to Pam but she kept nodding off. So Jay took her home and put her to bed. Heidi was doing all she could to win Jay over. But Jay was still a little hard on her as he sent her home. He and Lulu went out and just walked and talked. Jay had no idea how much they really had in common. For starters they both shared the same sign Gemini. They both liked Prince and they both where pretty much on their own until now.

Jay promised her that night if she stayed with him. He would change the rest of her life forever.

"Jay if anyone else told me that I wouldn't believe them but you, I'm gonna hold you to that cause I truly believe If anyone can, it's you." At that, they kiss. Only this time she initiated it, and neither one pulled away Jay pulled her closer, as they continued to kiss. They finished their walk. Hand in hand as they walked along the trail. Lulu grabbed Jay and turned him around until they were face to face. Then she spoke,

"Jay if your gonna stay with Heidi, I'm okay with that being I'm not sure, what I want but can we keep us, between us? I mean if it happens, then it happens but let's do us at our own paste, is that cool?"

"No doubt I'm feeling you hey you're a real cool person, to hang out with I don't want to lose that".

"Good then we understand one another?"

"I gotcha!" Jay spat.

"Hey you want a milkshake my treat?"

"A little sexy thing like you want to treat a guy like me? Hell yeah! But I got to warn you when some one offers me something, I like to splurge". This being said. Lulu looks at Jay,

"I bet you do".

Mean while…

Back in New Jersey, Det. Jake and Det. Roberts are at a stand still in the Jason Banks case. Being that he hasn't slashed anyone they heard of anyway. And their only other informer hasn't been in touch in a while.

In two weeks Jay and his squad would be even farther away from the "dicks" as the Deli had sold for $121,000. But Jay had Nate make a deal, if they paid in cash he would let it go for $98,000. So they continued setting people up until moving day. Three days before the store was to be brought was the last day for everyone to drop off any money. Mark did just as Heidi had said he would. But a little better he left $125,000. He wanted his quarter million back. And Lulu got Swizle who really wanted to come up in the Game being that Mark was making it hard for him to make money. He dropped $75,000. Nate had the young boy Jamal who was also on the come up dropped off $60,000. And a few young boys got together $15,000. That plus the money from the Deli, and they step away with $373,000 dollars.

As their leaving the following day. They ride pass

the Deli one more time they see everyone, standing outside waiting for it to open.

Nate spoke, "Damn young buck, I'm gonna miss that place".

"Come on old head don't look at it as the end but the beginning of a new era baby, cause were gonna do big things with this money no doubt!" Jay screamed.

At their next stop their in Scranton P.A.

"Damn! If this ain't the boone docks I don't know, what is." Lulu gets out her car.

"Jay where are you taking us?"

"That my dear I don't know all of ya'll need to know one thing, I'm not a world traveler I just want to get us to a place that looks cool a place that we'll all like some place quite something like this, what'll you say we give this place a few weeks?" Jay looks at the whole group. And wait for a response.

Nate nodded in agreement. Heidi wasn't really feeling it. But she was still in make-up mode, so she agreed as well. Lulu just walked over to Jay.

" Hey it's whatever! I'm with you babe."

Heidi spoke, "that's just it your not with him I'am. Remember that!" Lulu walked away with a grin on her face.

"Jay I'm gonna have to whip that bitches ass! If she keeps this shit up".

"Heidi come on she's cool you have to calm down

look were one team I don't need any of you, getting crazy on me now."

"Look let's find a place to eat then we can find out where we can rent either a house or get rooms at a motel or something cool everybody with that?" Jay questioned.

They all got back into the cars. As Jay, and Nate got into the truck. Nate had this little smirk on his face.

"What's with the face old head?"

"Let me tell you something young man, you can pull the wool over them young girls eye's but not mine, you know why them girls are acting like that?" Nate snickered.

"Old head what are you talking about?"

"I'm talking about you you're a young man who just met two nice looking women, and gave them security and who knows, what else you gave them (he said with a smirk) whatever it is, they want more."

Jay sees an I hop and pulls into the parking lot. Followed by Lulu and Heidi, as they all get out the cars. Jay goes over to Heidi as he's talking to her. Nate and Lulu go inside Jay calls over to them.

"Hey get a booth for four cool?" Heidi turned to Jay.

" Don't think I'm sitting with that bitch! No Jay, look I'm here with you nobody said anything, about the two of us being friends I don't pretend, to like people I don't. That's not my style." She spat

"Oh! You got a style now, huh? Listen to me (Jay said, in a stern voice) All this, I'm putting together I don't need none of this kid shit! On the real, and truth of the matter is If you told me that's all you're here for, is me I would have told you, don't waste your time look, I spent to many years thinking and dreaming about living like this free and on my own, so cut the shit with her right now or I'll give you your cut of the money, and that's that!! On the real now you feeling me now bitch!" Jay stated. As he stared her closely.

"Don't think I came this far to lose everything We got! and everything we stand to gain. Over a fucking "cat fight," Let me ask you something anyway why don't, you like her?" Jay questioned.

"Because she,... I don't know I just don't like her". She answered.
"Your simple as shit! Get your simple ass in there and let's eat please!" Jay ordered.
"Fuck you! I ain't simple either". As she walked pass Jay he smacked her on the ass.

As they ate, Lulu being the better person ignored every sly and ignorant comment that Heidi had thrown her way. Once they all finished. They all got in their cars they agreed to get some rooms that night. And the first thing in the morning they would go looking for a house or maybe another duplex to rent.

They got two rooms. Lulu felt comfortable around Nate. So they got a room together, two beds of course. Jay and Heidi were in the other. That night Lulu and Nate talked the night away Nate was a good teacher for Lulu. He schooled her on Just about everything, she asked him about. Their conversation became deep, at times.

In the other room Heidi gave Jay a full body massage. As they made love twice on the bed, and once in the shower. They had on Jay's oldie C.D. (Al Green) "Tired of being alone." There was a short rap on the door. Jay put on his boxers then answered. It was Nate.

"What's up young buck? Lulu and I was about to go get some coffee we we're just wondering, if one of you want anything? Damn youngster! What you know about Al Green?" Nate inquired.

"Naw we alright thanks for asking".
" Old head I'll show you my collection one day and you tell me, what I know?

About Al Green- Marvin Gaye- Sam Cooke- Harold Melvin and the blue notes- etc. holla, at ya boy! I'll talk to you later". Jay closes the door. Jay goes back to the bed and Lays with Heidi but he's thinking about Lulu.

"So baby, what do you want to do with the rest of your life I mean, your too smart to just want to do this?"

Next thing you know Jay's in a deep conversation, of his own with Heidi.

"You know what? Don't take this the wrong way but that's, by far the most interesting conversation we had since we met." Jay stated.

"So Jay are you telling me you think I'm a dumb blonde?"

"No let's just say I didn't have you that far from the stereo type."

"All fuck you! Jason, you know what you are the biggest asshole I know but for some reason, I'm so very attracted to you."

"Well on that note I'm about to do some push-ups, then jump back in the shower and go to bed we all got a busy day a head of us tomorrow so I'm gonna try my hardest, to not let you sex me up all night." (they both laugh).

After Jay's done in the shower Heidi goes in. She starts to run the water she comes back out.

"Jay what do you think is gonna happen with us?" She asked.

"What are you talking about? And where did this, come from?"

"Look just go take your shower when your out, we'll talk cool?"

"Okay".

She turns back around and starts toward the

bathroom, as Jay lays on the bed staring at her ass. He says to himself "Damn!, now that's an ass" whew!!

He goes and puts his razor up. Then gets on his knees and says his prayers. Jay gets up and he hears a rap at the door.

"Who is it?" He inquired.

"Jay It's us, Lulu and Nate open up". Jay opens the door in his boxers. Lulu just looks at him.

"Youngster we need to talk to you about something get dressed, and come over to our room okay?" Nate ordered.

"Alright old head ya'll go ahead I'll be right there, cool?"

"Gotcha!" Nate backs out with Lulu still staring at Jay. Jay sees her, as he starts to gyrate his waist. Then she looks away embarrass that she was caught looking. Jay grabs his shorts off the chair he goes to the bathroom. And tells Heidi were he's gonna be then he leaves.

Once Jay gets next door Lulu's sitting in the chair. As Nate stands Jay sits on the edge of the bed.

"Okay so who's gonna tell me?" Nate looks at Lulu, she looks back at him.

"Well I guess I will youngster there's some young punks at the diner talking about getting a few dollars for stolen cars, but that's nothin' you say right? But listen, I also heard them talking about unloading some diamonds". At this, he now has Jay's undivided attention as Jay tells him to continue.

"What I got from the waitress they meet there every night about the same time".

"Good that's our in I'll make it my business to be there also Cool good looking old head, we starting to think alike huh?"

"Jay can I talk to you for a little bit before you go?" Lulu inquired.

"Sure Lu what's up?"

"I mean can we take a walk or something?"

" I don't see why not, let's go".

They leave and as soon as they get away from Nate, she's all over Jay.

"What's going on you okay?"

"No Jay I haven't been okay since our first kiss Jay, I know we said we'll take it slow but damn, are you feeling me, or what?" She questioned.

"Of course it's just we need to get focused on what we need to do to eat, in this strange town.

"I tell you what how about after we find a place tomorrow the two of us, meet up some where away from Nate and Heidi cool?"

"No doubt! Where?"

"We'll find a place tomorrow okay?"

"Bet Jay I'm there." They kiss again this time longer and deeper. "Wow that's something to look forward too". He reasoned.

"Yeah I didn't want you to go back to Heidi, and forget about me".

"You women are something else, boy I tell ya!"

They come back around the corner Jay goes inside Heidi's sitting on the bed.

"So what's up baby? They got something on for tomorrow or what?"

"Something like that we got a little something, brewing I'll put you up on it later, okay?" He told her.

"Jay I think you should go and check on Pam I walked pass her room and I thought I heard her moaning, I knocked but she didn't answer Jay, could she be dying this early in her stages of AIDS?" Heidi questioned.

" Sweetheart! That, I don't know all I know is that it takes different tolls on different people I mean look at Magic Johnson, he's been living with it for some time now but I know other cases, boom as soon as they get it, it's over shortly after all we can do is pray for her."

———————————————

The following day… they all went out looking for a spot to chill while in town for how ever long. Pam was to weak so when Jay asked her she declined. He kisses her on the four head and left.

They all split up and went out Lulu went in her car Heidi went in hers and Jay and Nate went in the truck. Forty minutes later Lulu calls Jay on his cell.

" Baby I think I found the perfect place! It's a nice little house let's meet up at the hotel and everyone can follow me back to it okay?"

" I got you."

"Cool I'll see you there."

Jay called Heidi. and she met back at the hotel as they all followed Lulu when they got in front of the house for rent, everybody loved it. Even Heidi couldn't lie it was beautiful. They had Nate call the number and ask about the house. He talked for about ten minutes, with an older woman Sheryl. Who said she would be there in about five minutes to show them around. As they waited for the woman to arrive, they all just leaned against the cars, talking. To Jay's surprise, Heidi and Lulu was talking. Without screaming at one another for a change.

Sheryl came. And walked them all through the house and when they got to the back yard Jay noticed the hammock tied to two trees. That was enough for Jay to tell Nate to get it.

"I'm asking $1,200 a month if your interested?"

Nate agreed.

"So it's $2,400 to move in?" Cheryl looked puzzled. With the question. "No, it's $1,200 a month When I get $1,200, you get the keys".

"Okay? No problem" So Jay hands Nate, the money. As she turns back around Nate hands her the money.

"We'll move in tonight is that okay?" Nate inquired.

"That's fine! I'm looking forward to seeing you all If you need anything, here's my number and I'm right around the corner Okay?" She writes down her number and hands it to Lulu. As she shakes each one's hand she leaves.

That night… They move into the house Jay met up with the boys at the diner. Jay learned quickly they had a little crew they called them self's "Cream squad" it was four of them. "Buttons, smash, face and first come" what a crew. But Jay noticed, they had a little order with them.

Jay paid for their dinner and left a nice tip. As they agreed to meet up the following night. Jay left.

The next day… Pam got up early in the morning, and left.

Jay got up. And Him, Heidi and Lulu went to eat breakfast. Nate had already been up, and went for his walk he stopped at the local "Dunkin' Donuts." And was drinking his coffee and eating a Donut when they got up.

"So old head I guess you not eating breakfast with us huh?"

"Man! Young buck you all got college kids hours ya'll get up to late for me, I would starve if I wait on you Young cats, stay up all night sleep all day." They all just walked out and left Nate talking, to himself.

Jay thought that is what they do, but who else as young as they are have almost a half a million, and nothing to do?

Chapter 15

Later that day....Jay was out back laying in the hammock and called "Jason" on his cell. Jason answered,

" Yo! What's up with my young boi? How you doing out there in them streets?"

"Oh it ain't nothing! I'm living an learning, that's all how's everything with you?"

"Where are you at Jay, I mean what state?"

" Oh were in Scranton P.A. bout to set up shop, how about you Jason?" Jay inquired.

"I'm not that far from you I'm in Akron Ohio yo! Whenever you bout to bounce up outta there I'm gonna leave you with some nice connection out here If you want to come through here, got me? There's money to be made out here youngster did I hear you say where? You still building a little crew, huh?"

"Yeah something like that."

"Just remember when running in theses streets always be the sharpest in your crew, If your gonna have one feel me?" Jason stated.

"Words to live by Jason no doubt, words to live by well look, I'll keep in touch cool I'll holla! Later"- (they hang-up.)

Just then Heidi comes over with something to drink for Jay.

"Here baby you thirsty?"

"Yes thank you so, no one still haven't heard from Pam yet?"

"No baby, you want to go for a ride and see if we can find her?"

" No, she probably doesn't want to be found right now she'll come back when she's ready." But little did Jay know, that morning would be the last time he would see Pam.

Four day's later…. That night on the news, Two hunters found a body of a young girl who had died from a self inflicted gun shot to the head. Jay went into his bedroom and went to his guns. One was missing-Jay broke down crying. His first love was gone, he then went to their money box, where he found a letter from Pam- it read.

my dearest Jason, I know I've betrayed you, and hurt you dearly. But please believe me when I tell you this. You showed me more love an loyalty, then I ever knew existed. Your kind and caring ways are beautiful, my only regret was, not meeting you sooner in life. Please don't be mad at me, for taking this way out. But

I couldn't live like this any more. AIDS was killing me, but seeing Heidi and Lulu with you, and me not being able to give you what they could was killing me more, and I was only slowing the team down, anyway. I really wish you all the best in whatever you do. Just remember to keep me, in your heart cause I'll forever love you Jay. I was your first, but you were my first real, and only love. Good bye- one love. Xoxo P.s put your Sam Cooke on, and listen to "Sad Mood" one time for me. Jay went back in the room with everyone and told them the news.

Nate took it the hardest. Jay grabbed his C.D. player and listen to Sad mood by Sam Cooke. As he let his tears flow freely. Lulu sat next to him as she grabbed and hugged him tight. She began to cry also.

The following day...

Jay had Nate go and identify the body. As they planned for her burial.

Jay wrote a poem: IF I DIE

IF I DIE TODAY, JUST WISH ME WELL. I'M PROBABLY IN HEAVEN, FOR I WAS LIVING IN HELL.

IF I DIED A VIOLENT DEATH, IT MIGHT OF HURT A LITTLE.

BUT NOW I'M WITH GOD, PLAYING THAT GOLDEN FIDDLE
IF I'M TAKEN, REMEMBER THE GOOD TIMES FRIEND.

TAKE THE BAD, AND JUST GIVE A GRIN.

YOUR STILL HERE, LIVE ON FOR US
JUST KNOW I'M IN HEAVEN, CAUSE IN GOD WE TRUST!!

YES I'LL MISS MY FAMILY DEAR, JUST HOLD ME IN YOUR HEART and I'LL ALWAYS BE NEAR.

AND ONE DAY WHEN IT'S BEAUTIFUL OUTSIDE, LOOK UP IN THE SKY
SAY MY NAME OR JUST WAVE HI.
KNOW ONE THING, I ENJOYED LIFE I CHALLENGED EVERYDAY.

Jay finished and put on his headphones and listened to Sam Cooke's "wonderful world" Lulu came and just sat with Jay for awhile before she spoke.

"Jay baby I'm so sorry but I don't really know how to express myself cause I never went through anything like this before."

Jay put his arms around her, and held her tight.
" Baby I know how you feel it took me awhile to trust anyone, but it came natural with her she showed

me how to open up, and I love her for that but I hate her, for leaving me at the same time." Jay reasoned.

"Jay don't say that! She didn't want to suffer anymore she didn't want to leave you Jay, you were her heart, she told me this on more than a few occasions you meant the world to her she felt she owed you her life, and she was so sad that she would not be around to try and pay you back." Lulu stated.

"She told you all of this?" Jay inquired.

"Yes Jay all she would talk about was you." As Heidi walked up to them. "Yes she did Jay she was truly, your biggest fan It broke her heart, that she broke your heart I think that killed her more, than a bullet could have ever killed her." Heidi reasoned.

"Hey are you guys hungry cause Nate told me you two were out here and we were both about to get something to eat, so are you guys going or what?" Jay took off his headphones.

"Yeah my ribs are touching, let's skip." Jay spat.

They all jumped into one car.(that's a first) as Jay spoke to no one in particular,

"Tomorrows a new day for me, I'm getting a new truck and I'm buying a motorcycle." Heidi replied first.

"What's gotten into you?"

"Well babe it's like this, I need to turn over a new leaf so why not, now right?"

Nate just shook his head in agreement. As they rode on.

Later that night…

They all sat around talking about a little of everything. Jay was telling Lulu how he was going to the library the next day and get some books out on how to invest his money.

The following day…

Jay went to breakfast a little later than everyone else. Well they all went and he didn't. But Lulu had gotten some breakfast things, from the store and made Jay breakfast. She made him French toast with sausage and even got him a fresh cup of coffee, from his favorite "coffee spot" Krispy creame.

"I don't know why he likes this strong ass coffee but hey, it's for him not me."

Heidi sat in the other room with Nate.

"Nate, you can't sit there and tell me something's not going on between them! Look, the bitch is in there cooking for my man! I should go in there and force feed that little skinny bitch see how she like that shit?" She spat.

After Jay got up and ate. He had a nice agenda for the day. First he wanted to go to the library and get some books. Then he thought about it he and Nate was about to go find him a truck.

Then he could just drive to Barns and Noble, and chill then he thought about the "Cream Squad" as he gave Face a call.

He answers, "Yo! What's up? Who dis?" he barked into the phone.

"Face? It's Jay we need to talk business, at your earliest convenience." Jay shot back.

"Sounds like a plan, just tell me when and where we'll be there son."

"How about the diner where I met you at In about half hour, cool?"

" You got it dogg! We'll be there."

Lulu

Chapter 16

Jay gets to the diner. He sees Face and his crew. Jay walks over to them, Face and Jay go and sit over at the counter.

"So here's the deal you and your boys can really come up on the money tip, fuckin' wit me on the real I got mad connects son." Jay stated.

"Oh really! And why should we believe you?" Face spat as his eye's met Jay's stare.

"Cause you told me, that your in the car business well me too, kinda."

" I tell you what, there's a rumor in the streets that there's a Lexis key floating around the "Master key." If your serious, give us $50,000 cash and I'll make sure you get your hands on it let's say right here same time, tomorrow?" Face ordered.

"You happen to have a truck a little newer than that."

Jay said while pointing out of the window?

"I'll check on that for you."

"Bet". Jay spat.

"I'll give you $40 G's'?" Jay reasoned.

"$40? I'll call you." As he gets up and gives Jay a pound "I'll call you!" He repeated.

As him and his crew parted ways.

Later Jay gets up and leaves.

Once Jay gets back to the house. Everyone's gone he starts to think about Pam. Then he calls "Jason" he answers, "yo! What's up youngin'?"

"Awe, it ain't nothing! I got some bad news, Pam's dead." Jay just spat out.

The other end of the phone went silent.

"Damn! Baby boy, I'm sorry to hear that what happened?"

Jay went on to explain the whole thing to Jason. They talked for about an hour. At the end of the conversation. Jason had him feeling better, and he had the chop shop numbers it's on. "Yo! Stay true to what your doing, and stay 2 steps a head of the rest of em' cool? One"-(they hang-up)

Jay put on his oldie C.D. "Cruisin'" by (Smokey Robinson) Jay just sat back and thought about the cash that was about to roll in.

The following day... Jay got in touch with the chop shop connection Jason put him on too. Jay went to meet with the guy "Paul." The guy came out this guy was huge. He looked like Ruben from "American Idol" but smooth, like the rapper (E-40) As he spoke, his voice boomed.

"WHAT'S UP YOUNGSTER, WHAT CAN I DO YOU FOR?" He questioned.

"What's up? and the question is,

How many cars can you move in a week?" Jay shot back.

"And I know you from were?" Big Paul questioned.

"Jason Sauve?" Jay answered.

"Oh that's big money right there, How's Jay smooth doin'?"

"Well It just so happens I'm moving more up scale cars at a faster rate right now, people want the big names but don't have the big bucks to pay for it, feel me?" Big Paul answered.

"He's doin' good you know, Jason. You mean Lexus?" Jay responded.

"Especially Lexus, why can you serve up an order for me?" Big Paul ordered.

Jay trying not to look to excited.

"How many in a week can you handle he asked again?"

"Let's start off with five is that cool youngster?" Big Paul reasoned.

"I think I can handle that what's it going for?" Jay inquired.

"Step into my office I'll give you a list of different models and what their hitting for."

Jay follows close behind once they get into his office. It's laid out plush carpet big pictures framed of signed Jerseys from different sports stars Jay knew he wasn't hurting for loot, no doubt."

"Here you go" he hands Jay a list.
"Can I expect the first one in two days?" He stated.

"That shouldn't be a problem at all cash right?" Jay spat.

"I wouldn't have it any other way." As he extends his hand out towards Jay, they shake. As the man's huge mitt, seemed to swallow Jay's.
"That right there, seals our deal youngster I'll see you in two days."

"Is there any set time?" Jay questioned.
"No, there's always some one here mostly me because good help is so, hard to find." He shot back as the two shared a laugh.

"Ain't that the truth! Done deal in two days I'll see you then."
Jay walked out with a huge smile on his face.
He jumped into his truck and like clock work he gets a call from "Face"
" Hello Jay?

"Yeah what's up?"

"Okay here's the deal We got a nice new "09 Dodge 1500 pick-up truck" the key and the truck $50,000 how's that?" Face reasoned.

"How can I turn down a deal like that done I need to meet up with you a.s.a.p. what are you doing right now?" Jay asked.

"Come to the diner I'll be there in like two minutes cool?"

"Gotcha!" Jay answered.

Within' ten minutes their both at the diner.

"So here we are look for every car your team gets it's two grand, and I need five cars a week So where talking ten grand a week how's that sound?" Jay questioned as he laid the deal out for Face.

"You got it! We'll take that only if you guarantee, five cars a week?" Face reasoned.

"That's no problem but do you have a place to take them to until my connect can get em'?" Jay asked.

"No doubt Buttons baby ma works every night at the storage, but you'll be responsible for giving her the hundred bucks she wants.

"No problem I got it covered like a blanket." Jay spat.

They give each other daps as they walk out.

"So meet me back here in two hours with the money and I'll have your new truck, and the key cool?" Face replied.

"I'll be here".

Jay jumps in his old truck as he thinks to himself. Damn if I would have left the foster home last year, I would have been father along. He smiles as he heads back towards the house.

Once he gets there. Heidi and Nate are gone. And Lulu's out back in the hammock. Listening to (musik's soul child)
Jay taps her she jumps up.
Sorry I didn't mean to scare you but were's everybody at? I got great news."

"Oh I have no idea where they got off too." She answered.

"Well I guess you'll hear it first I got a connect and were about to make $35,000 to $40,000 a week how's that sound?"
Lulu started jumping for joy. "Jay are you serious?"

"Is our president black? Of course I'm serious."
Lulu got up and grabbed Jay. As they were face

to face they began to kiss Jay held her close he found himself palming her ass as they kissed deeper.

"You know what? If I'm Clyde then I want you, to be my Bonnie". Jay said as they kissed again.
"Hey let's get lost for a while how's that sound?" Lulu questioned.

"Jay I've wanted to be with you the first time I laid eye's on you."
"Well are you ready?" Lulu looked at Jay and said,
"Let's go let's gooo!"

They go as they walk to Jay's truck.
Jay says,
"Let's take your car, cool?"
"Sure that's fine with me, I was beginning to think you was scared to drive with me for a minute there". (they both laugh)

"Naw it's not like that, see Lu it's like this I feel like I've been caged for so long I need all the freedom, I can come by feel me? And right now, I'm about to take full advantage of life no doubt."

"Just know one thing Jay count me in for the whole nine yards, I'm with you till the very end baby believe that!!

As they drive along Jay tells her to pull up to this nice hotel. They go inside Jay and Lulu goes up to the counter Jay ask for a room with a Jacuzzi.

171

The young man behind the counter "Excuse me! I think your to young to be getting a room, can I see some I.D. please."

Lulu was about to say some thing but Jay cut her off. As he gave the guy One fresh hundred dollar bill. The guy got him signed in and gave em' a card to their room. A smile went across Lulu's face when see seen how Jay handle the guy.

"Pretty smooth "Big Daddy" pretty smooth."

"Well don't thank me just yet, the day is still young".

They get to their room Lulu gets completely naked and heads towards the shower. Jay takes off his shirt he walks over to the Jacuzzi, and starts to fill it. Then he walks over to the curtains an opens them.

There he sees what looks like Heidi and Nate. Talking to two Det. As Jay's eye's lit up he close the curtains a million and one thoughts went through his mind. Who was behind this set up, was all the money gone? Or are they still looking to get them on more things do they know about the murders? What the fuck is going on? He thought as he pasted back and forth.

As Lulu step out of the shower Jay couldn't help but to stare. She was beautiful but so was Heidi, Is Lulu in on it too? How could he tell?

Jay pulled out his gun.

"Yeah baby you won't be needing that gun but I want this one" She said grabbing his dick through his boxers.

"Okay Lulu! Or whatever your name is what the fuck! Is going on? What do ya'll want me for? Jay inquired, holding the gun towards her.

"Jay baby, your starting to scare me what are you talking about?"

"Oh you don't know what the fuck! I'm talking about? How about this." He goes to the curtains and pulls them open. She tries to cover up as fast as possible. But can't help but to notice Heidi holding a baby.

"Jay babe what did you do that for? And who kid is that, Heidi's holding?" As Jay peeks out of the curtains again.

"So your not a part of this?"

"Baby are you telling me were being set up?"

Lulu starts hyperventilating.

"Jay baby, Jay I I I can't go to Jail Baby Jay Babe! What, are we go go going to to do huh?" She managed to get out.

"Lulu baby try and calm down, Calm down trust me, I'm the last person in the world that's trying to get locked up believe that we gotta think, but first you need to calm down baby I need you, right now." Jay spat.

As Jay hugs her. He kisses her on her salty tear soaked cheek. As they fall back on the bed Jay slowly rolls on top of her and kisses her deep and passionate. Lulu closes her eye's and reaches for Jay's dick. And stokes it slow at first but as his dick gets harder. She pulls harder at it as she gets up and puts it in her mouth all that can be heard is his dick going in and out of her mouth. She's slurping loud her mouth is dripping spit out as she hungrily keeps sucking. Jay's about to pass out as he nuts in her mouth. But Lulu kept sucking like she never got it.

In less then ten minutes later Jay's back hard again. Then she stops "I want to ride this next one" she said as she got on top of Jay she bounced up and down with her hair in pig tails Jay just looked up at her about ready to nut again but she got off of him. Then Jay got up he position her "doggie style" on the bed he mounts her from behind. As he reaches for her pig tails now he's riding her like a sled. He pulls out and cums on her back. Then he lays on the bed.

"Come on big boy your not finished are you?" As she walks over and gets into the Jacuzzi. She motions for him to come join her.

"Damn baby! Give me a sec, I'll be there." He goes to the bathroom then comes out and steps into the Jacuzzi with Lulu.

"So we finally did it huh? Well what did you think?" Lulu inquired.

Jay looked puzzled. "What are you talking about? Oh! You were great! Were you not looking, at my face in the mirror? Did you not see, back there?" They both laugh out loud.

"Yeah I saw you, I was always wondering what your sex face looked like". Lulu questioned still laughing.
"Oh really? Well I was always wondering something myself." Jay replied.

"Oh yeah! And what's that might I ask?"
"Well with a body like yours, I was wondering if you knew how to fuck!" Jay spat.
"So! What do you think now?"
"Let's just say we can teach each other a thing or two but I can also tell you this, it's gonna be a lot of fun baby."

As they sit in the Jacuzzi facing one another. Jay's rubbing her feet under the water as she just lays her head back. Jay's in deep thought.

"You know what, I got it! Either Heidi nor Nate knows about this truck I'm getting or about the deal with the cars therefore you and I can go back like nothing happened stay cool get all the money together, and we'll just break camp on em' feel me?" Jay reasoned.

"This is what we'll do you know how we don't all

eat breakfast at the same time any more right? Well that's our out we'll go back, rap with them for a minute I'll get the money, we'll put it in two duffle bags take it down the street and put it into my truck as of tomorrow morning were history, got it?" Jay stated.

"Jay why don't we just leave at night?"
"Humm that's not a bad idea."

" Were gonna leave your car and my old truck and in the next town I'll get you that new beetle you want cool?"
"Baby it's whatever you say! I'm with you, all the way."

"That's what I'm talking about."

Chapter 17

Later that night…

Jay's listening to tupac's "hit em' up" (what he listens to too, get hyped.)

Heidi comes over to him as she tells him she wants to talk to him in the room. Jay thinks 'Damn I might as well hit it one more time as a going away gift. I mean she is, fine as hell'.

Turns out the truck Jay got was a ford "Lighting" a high performance pick up truck. Jay got Heidi completely naked. He told her he would be right back he grabs a towel and goes out back and tells Lulu to get the bags. And take them to the truck. "Make sure no one sees you baby." He kisses her she leaves.

Jay goes back into the room with a candle and a glass of ice cubes. As he looks over at her laying across the bed looking as sexy as ever.

Jay lit the candle.

As Jay thought "damn I'm gonna miss this ass" this bitch know how to treat a nigga, no doubt! That's when Jay went to put a hickey on her inter thigh thinking "well at least, she'll remember me for a week".

They went through about five different positions, before Heidi and Jay passed out. Jay was waken by Lulu pulling on his foot, as Jay sat up she motioned, for him to come on. Jay grabbed his shorts and picked-up his sneakers an walked outside the room.

"Baby Nate's asleep too let's go, the money's in the truck".

They were out!

The next morning. Heidi awoke trying to grab hold of Jay but he wasn't there. She put on her tee shirt and went out into the living room only to find Nate with a dumb look on his face.

"So were are they?"

"Well Heidi I can only assume they went out to breakfast together, but then why would they take the money?"

" I should have known this kid was smarter then we thought he was."

"Not to mention quicker to the punch!"

As they reported back to their captain.

"SO, WHAT HAPPENED? YOU TWO REALLY UPSET ME! YOU KNOW TWO SEASONED "DICK'S" AND YOU WERE TAKEN BY TWO TEENAGERS CAN I EXPECT YOU TWO TO STAY ON THIS CASE OR DO YOU WANT SOME ROOKIES TO UP STAGE YOU?" The Captains voice boomed. As he continued, to scream at the two.

Heidi answered. "No sir! We'll get them back I promise you sir just give us the chance." She reasoned.

"OKAY YOU GOT IT! WITHIN' TWO MONTHS I WANT THAT KID BACK IN THE FOSTER HOME WITHOUT A PEEP GOT IT?"

They both reply "YES SIR!"

As they walk out of head quarters without a clue to were to start looking for Jay or Lulu.

Meanwhile...

After driving most of the night Jay and Lulu pulled up into "Lancaster"

"Jay baby were still in P.A. don't you want to go farther?" She questioned.

"Lulu honey I made a promise to get that money and baby we can out smart a couple "dicks," to get it you with me?"

"So we gonna get in touch with Paul and tell him it's still on."
"But here's the deal were gonna get motorcycles so we can get in and out of there with the quickness feel me?
I'll teach you, how to ride okay?"
"Baby no offence but I'll teach you how to ride!" Lulu replied.
"What! You know how to ride?" Jay spat.

"Do I? Like a pro! I use to run with this biker gang until"...
"Until what?" Jay inquired.
"We'll talk about that on a later note." She replied.

"Well we don't have Nate to get us a nice duplex or rent a house so what'll we do?" Lulu questioned.

They pull up to a Dunking Donut. They get out and go inside they order get their food and sit down and eat. As their talking among each other, the guy sitting next to them came over.
"Excuse me hello my name is Percy and I couldn't help, but to over hear your conversation are you looking for a place to stay temperately?" Percy inquired.

Jay responded. "Yes we are, are you a renter?"

"Well not usually but my daughter just went away to college and we had our pool house fixed up nice for her to have her own apartment but yet still live at home It's got a kitchen, bathroom, everything an apartment has and I'll even grant you, access to the pool are you interested in taking a look? It's right up the road?"

Lulu answered. "Sure Percy we'll have a look"

Jay looked at her.
"Hold on not so fast how much are you asking for it a month?" Jay inquired.
"Humm! How's $350.00 sounds?" Percy shot back.
"We'll follow you there." Jay reasoned.

Once Jay and Lulu. Pulled into the driveway behind Percy. They knew they would love the place.
"Wow! Would you look at this house baby."

"Yeah it is nice isn't it?" Jay couldn't help but to get an uneasy feeling in his stomach. Trying to figure out Percy's angle.
Percy stepped out of his powder blue Porsche. He walked over to Jay and Lulu getting out of the truck.
"The two of you just follow me". He then opened the gate. And walked along side the path leading to the pool area. As they passed a few bushes along side the house. When they came to the clearing what a beautiful sight it was. The so called pool house looked like a small cottage. It was something, out of a "Norman Rockwell" picture.

Lulu was getting more and more excited. The closer they got to the pool house. Once they came around the pool. which was as clean as a fresh ran bath. They went inside. It was like the pool house from. (The fresh prince, of Bellaire) only it had an up stairs as well. Last they looked at was the bathroom. which was also perfect.

They went out to the pool area. As he laid down the rules and guaranteed them, privacy. He and Jay shook on it as Jay told him they would move in the following day.

"No problem I'll have the maid clean it up by then oh that's another thing me and my wife are newly separated It's just me and (the help) so once again, you'll have more than enough privacy I promise and also I'll let Megan know to give you two the keys tomorrow when you come with the first month's rent she's nice, you'll love her."

Percy said with a slight smirk. Jay and Lulu walked back to the truck once inside. Lulu slid over and hugged and kissed Jay as she put on Prince's (sweet baby) they pulled away.

Lulu couldn't stop thinking or talking about the place.

"Jay baby remember the duplex we had I really liked that place but you were with Heidi so that took a little away from it's appeal but this place is all ours and I love it."

"Well that's good baby cause if it all go well we'll be here for awhile no doubt so I'll give you some cash tomorrow to put your touch into this place feel me?"

"For sure babe for sure." She answered.

The following day...

They moved in. Once Jay pulled up to the gate he noticed a most shapely woman coming out of the house. Jay could not help but to stare in admiration. He thought it would be a much older woman but Megan was at the oldest Jay guessing about twenty two.

She came over to them getting out of the truck and greeted them with her warm 'perfect teeth' smile.

"Hello Jason and Lucile right? I'm Megan wow! You have to excuse me I thought you two would be older." She reasoned.

Jay toke her by the hand. "Please call me Jay it's a pleasure."

"And you can call me Lulu damn Jay! You forgot I was here?" Lulu spat.

"I'm sorry this is my girl Lulu." He stated late in introducing the two.

"Hey! It's great meeting the two of you but I'm just

to give you the keys, and get out of your way plus I have a lot of work to do I'll see you guys around but if you need anything don't hesitate to call me, I'll be around here some where." They all laughed looking around, the huge estate.

Jay handed her the envelope with the money in it. As she gave Jay the keys. Jay made it his business as Lulu had her back to them to hold her hand a little longer than necessary.

Megan started blushing. Jay knew she had to feel the attraction. He was feeling towards her as she blushed. He got the answer he was looking for.

"I'll see you later Megan." Jay said as he winked at her.

Lulu turned around and forcefully threw Jay's duffle bag. into his chest Jay looked at her in shock. Being she never displayed any Jealousy towards him before. He turned around she had a devilish smirk on her face.

Once they get into the pool house it comes out.

She drops the bags at the door. Jay does the same. She pushes him back onto the bed before Jay could ask what was going on- she started kissing him all over.

"humm baby seeing you flirt with that bitch! Made me so horny for you come on baby get my dick out and let's get to the " christen" of our new place.

she quickly undid his shorts as she grabbed his now hard dick. And rubbed it across her face. Jay was getting harder he hurried to get her undress. Once she undress, he turns her over and starts to eat her wet' bikini trimmed' pussy every time he hears her moan. He tries to push his dick deeper down her throat as their half on the bed in the 69 position. Out of the corner of his eye Jay not only noticed the door still open. But Megan was standing there taking it all in. With towels in her hand.

Jay kept sucking her pussy like he didn't see her standing there.

She must of like the show, because she just sat the towels down without making a sound and back away just so they couldn't see her or so she thought.

Jay pulls his dick out of her mouth like pulling a bone away from a hungry dog he turned her over and put her legs over his shoulder as he fucked Lulu long and hard for another twenty minutes, they were both dripping in sweat when they finished, for now. Cause with Jay and Lulu it was never over for long. Sense they met, they been fucking like two sex addicts.

The next morning, Jay got up early; as he walked to the front of the house and peeked in the driveway. He did not see Percy's Porsche and decided to take a morning swim. He went back into the pool house and put on his trunks an jumped in.

The cool water felt good an also helped to finished waking him up. After he took a few laps he just leaned against the side of the pool while in thought, Jay leaned his head back as Megan was out on the balcony over looking the pool reading a book. Laying in a lounge chair wearing a "peek-a-boo" cami set. Jay could not take his eyes off her.

He thought to himself, (damn this woman's got body) as he went on to play out in his mind her calling him up. As he made passionate love to her-

He then snaps out of it. And does some more laps Megan hears the splashing and goes down near the pool. And starts a conversation with Jay.

"Hey there! Going for a morning swim are we?" She questioned.

"Good morning pretty lady yes I am would you care to join me?" Jay responded flirting with her.

"No not now honey, maybe I'll take you up tomorrow morning how's that?" She replied.

"It's a date I'll be here until then." They both laughed out loud.

Lulu came out wearing a fish net mini dress that fit like a second skin, with a two piece bathing suit under it. That was to die for and she had the body to fill it out perfect. walking with ' a ha-ha gotcha, bitch!' look on her face. As she stood in front of Jay still on the edge of the pool. Staring at her and only her. She took off the fish net mini dress an jumped in. She was under the water for a minute but it felt like five. As she had swam over to Jay underwater. And pulled down his shorts she put his dick into her mouth.

Jay was blushing like crazy. As he continued to look at Megan like nothing was wrong until his eyes rolled into the back of his head.

Damn Lulu sure knew how to get her mans attention back. With the quickness no doubt. She then started jerking him off as she came up took a deep breath and went back under to finish up.

Your probably wondering can you cum underwater? Well young Jay was about to experience it, in a few seconds. As he could hold back no longer. Jay got turned out that very minute, by his "Bonnie" getting head in a rich man's pool. By a "10" while looking, at a "10" Damn! Life is great!

Megan standing there looking at the expression on his face.

"Jay I'll see you later It looks like you two, need to be alone". She slammed her book closed and dropped it on the lounge. And walked away as Lulu came up for air.

"So what happened to my muse? I knew she would get a kick out of that!"
"Your nasty!" Jay replied.
"But you liked that right?" She shot back.
Megan got up to her room. As she puts on her C.D.

player. "Donell Jones" comes through the speakers. 'it's a quarter pass three girl what's it gonna be, shortie got her eye's, on me. She undress in front of the window, as she looks out at the pool, at Jay and Lulu. Thinking to herself what she wouldn't give to be in Lulu's place with Jay.

Chapter 18

Back in Scranton...

"Heidi you really think for one second that they have a need to come back through here? I mean seriously two young kids with a little over a quarter of a million dollars?"

"Nate, I just have a hunch what's the worst that can happen? We already don't have a clue where they were headed or what they know about us, I mean did they make us? Or did they just fall for each other and got greedy and didn't want to share the money, four ways? That's what I'm hoping I pray to God, we didn't get made by two kids on our first under cover job we'll be the laughing stock of the force".

Meanwhile... Det. Jake and Ms Roberts are on their way to Scranton P.A. cause they just found out about the suicide of a young teen who's body was found fitting the description of their girl.

Back in Connecticut. Mark got back on and was determined to get even with this guy they call Jay-Razor. But not after he got that bitch he left with Heidi. He knew Jay got him for a lot of cash but he also knew that bitch Heidi. Set him up for the taken.

Back in Lancaster...

"Well Lulu baby are you ready for our little trip back to Scranton tomorrow? I figured well leave in the morning get there handle business, we can do either of the two you can drive back or we can get a room, and I'll drive back the following morning so what's it gonna be?"

"You mean your gonna let me drive your new truck?"

"Come on babe stop the bullshit! It's our truck and after the thing you did in the pool hell you can drive anything you want hey I knew you had skills, but damn!!! How old where you when you learned how to swim"

"I never really learned I just use to watch my friends swim and saw it on T.V. and I was always scared of water and every one used to say sink or swim so I started going in the pool at night, when no one was around and I just started trying to hold my breath as long as I could at first, then I started kicking off, from the side and swimming from one side of the pool to the other, until I got better and better, at it."

"Get the fuck outta here! Are you telling me you taught yourself, how to swim? Damn! I'm starting to love you more and more baby I mean I heard people say they taught themselves how to ride a bike and a bunch of other things, but swimming? Hell naw I gotta give you, mad props for that shit." Jay stated.

"Jay what are we gonna do here?"
" Damn! Baby don't you just want to chill we got money coming in from Scranton. Are you getting bored, on me?

"Never that! I'm not talking about that, are we gonna get some where and settle down and not do this, jumping from state to state shit?"

"Sure just not any time soon babe I'm on a mission now can we finish that conversation you know, the thing you said you would tell me later? What's your story?" Jay inquired.

"Let's go get some ice cream and I'll spill the beans to you babe you deserve that much no doubt".

They jump into the truck and Jay spins out of the driveway in a hurry. Making the "lighten" chirp, as it went into second, Jay looked over at Lulu, and for a second he saw Pam. As he shook his head, and tried to focus.

"Jay! You okay baby?"

"Yeah I'm straight! So you think you can handle all this power?" Jay questioned.

"Baby I can handle all you think I can't."

"I believe you can."

(they both laugh) As they pull up to the ice cream spot. Jay gets hard ice cream three scoops of vanilla bean in a waffle cone. Lulu get a extra thick large strawberry shake. Jay pays, as they get into the truck they drive to the near by lake as Jay parks. They get out and climb into the bed of the truck.

"Well Jay I hope you don't think any different about me after I tell you what got me to this point in my life but I'm about to lay it out here for you either way you ready?"

"Lu I would never want to be judged by my pass as I would never judge you for yours with that being said, let's have it."

"Jay my parents were rich my dad worked as a stock broker in New York city he was the best father a family could ask for, my mom on the other hand was a cokehead who spend up all my dad's hard earned money, on her habit and on her " behind the back" affairs with at least three, different man friends."

"Who used… to… rape me" She managed to spat

192

out after stiffening back her tears, she continued on, "after she would pass out after getting high the one guy would look for me when he came over and would tell me to go in my room, he and my mom would snort coke and drink and he would act like he was going to the bathroom but he was only checking to see if I was still there so when she passed out he could do whatever he wanted to me."

With that being said, a tear fell from Lulu's eye. Jay held her close she went on.

"Then it was this time I whew he was coming so I left and he beat my mom so bad when my dad came home she said that we got robbed and two guy's beat her an she told me to run and all my friends started saying, I was acting different at one time I thought about killing myself."

"Then I met this girl who was going through the same thing and she taught me the "Sweet revenge" that was worth looking forward too and I got that mother fucking rapist back so good Jay baby." She stated, as she let her head drop, She took a sip from her shake, and continued.

" What did, you do?"

"We had this magazine with theses in mate's addresses so we were writing them and they were these two big ass dudes I wont tell you their names but let's just say when they got out we gave them some and they gave old rapist ass "Warren" his and we video taped it every thing them beating the confession out of him,

193

and him begging for them to stop tearing his asshole up."

"Damn baby! I though I was cold?"

"And after that I packed up and me and Vanessa went on the road together but Vanessa started stripping and fucking nigga's and I wasn't with that shit so here I'am".

"I went back home but when my dad was told what was going on behind his back and he wasn't there for me he killed himself and I been on my own ever since, that's my story Jay bottom line I was never into that drug shit I ran with a biker gang until, they wanted me doing that shit, so I left I can't control everything but I can control that." She stated As she sipped on her milk shake.

The following day...

They pull into Scranton. Jay drives straight to the shop "Big Paul" greets him, and Lulu.

"HEY THERE! THERE'S MY FAVORORITE TWO MONEY MAKING YOUNGSTERS LULU CAN YOU EXCUSE ME, WHILE I HOLLA AT YOUR MAN IN THE BACK FOR A MINUTE?" Big Paul inquired.

" No problem! You two go handle your business I'll be here looking at this beautiful aquarium."

"COME ON JAY I GOT A BONE TO PICK WITH YOU!"

Once they get in the back room.

"Okay big fella what's the deal What's going on?" Jay responded.

"DAMN JAY! WHY DIDN'T YOU TELL ME YOU LEFT TOWN LIKE THAT? I MEAN THE WAY YOU DID IT WAS SMART, AND SMOOTH AS SHIT. NO DOUBT! BUT YOU GOT TOO MANY PEOPLE, FOR A LOT OF CASH. TO BE JUST ROLLING THROUGH HERE LIKE IT'S ALL SWEET LIKE THAT, YOU FEEL ME?" Paul's voice boomed!

"Yeah Paul I was thinking about that on the way here I shouldn't be taking chances like this no matter how much cash is involved so here's what I got planned.?"

Paul tried to cut him off-

"Paul just hear me out first okay? I think it'll be better if we make all contacts by phone and all cash exchanges, once a month I'll give you an extra grand per car on that, cool?" Jay spat.

"THAT SOUNDS LIKE A PLAN BUT CAN YOU GET THE "CREAM SQUAD" OVER HERE, A.S.A.P.?" Paul reasoned.

" No doubt." As Jay flipped open his "razor phone" and dialed Face's number. After the first ring he picks up.

"What's up baby I was waiting on your call Jay Your not gonna believe what the "Team" got for you baby."

"Oh really? Well look can you come through in five minutes?"

"No problem where you at?"

"I'm at the shop "Big Paul's" just you come on baby."

"Let me hang up Jay and I'm there kid." (they hang-up)

Not even two minutes passed. Face was at, the door.

As he came into the shop, he gave Big Paul some dap. As he kissed Lulu on the cheek he headed over to Jay showing much more love. As he grabbed Jay shook his hand as he patted him on the back in the hood hug, kinda way.

"So what's really good baby?"

Norma

Chapter 19

"Look Face we gotta make some changes not with the business just the way things are being ran feel me?" Jay stated.

"What are you talking about Jay you talking in riddles holla at ya boy!"

As "Big Paul" sits, next to Face.
"What I'm saying is were gonna handle all business over the phone and I'll call all orders into you you'll call me when you get em' and once there taken to "The shop," then the transaction is final I get the okay, from "Big Paul." then your team gets paid but instead of me coming through every three days, it'll only be once a month." Jay reasoned.

"JAY BABY! YOU'RE ONE SMART MOTHERFUCKING YOUNG BOY I TELL YOU."

"Ain't he thou I was just thinking the same thing big boy Jay that sounds better and you know you got me and my team in your corner all day with the cash you making us whew!!" Face replied.

"Jay step out back with me for a minute and I'll tell you what we got for you."

They go out back and talked they make their way around to the side of the shop. Jay sees a pick up truck next to his with two motorcycle's on the back.

" Damn who bikes are they?" Jay spat.

"That's the thing or should I say things the team got for you and your girl you like?" Face replied.

"Stop playing Face what sizes are they?" Jay asked.

"I'm not playing there 600's ones a Honda f4 an the others a Ninja 600rr."

"Damn baby! How much I owe you for em'?" Jay inquired.

"Come on Jay don't insult the team like that like I said, we wasn't getting half the money we getting now we down with you that's a present, matter of fact let me get a couple of Paul's people to put them on your truck and maybe he'll get this truck off my hands feel me?"

As they switched the bikes to Jay's truck Jay went back in and told Paul they would be in touch.

"HOLD ON BABY BOY ARE YOU TWO DRIVING BACK TODAY? WHY DON'T THE TWO OF YOU STAY AT THIS LITTLE HOUSE I JUST FIXED UP FOR ME and THE MISSES, IT'S ON THE OUT SKIRTS OF TOWN NO ONE WILL KNOW THAT YOUR THERE PLUS I NEED A WOMAN'S OPINION ON THE PLACE." While saying that, he was looking at Lulu.

"COULD YOU DO THAT FOR ME, PLEASE?"

Jay turned to Lulu "Well what do you think, baby?"

"Sure Big Paul sounds like a plan okay baby cause I'm a little tired of the road right now." Jay stated.

Paul hands Lulu the set of keys as Jay gives Big Paul a pound he and Lulu leave. As they walk towards the truck Lulu's eye's lit-up.

"Baby! Say you got theses for us?" Lulu spat.
"Nope the "Cream Squad" got them for us."

As she jumps into Jay's arms he spins her around.

They jump into the truck and head out to Big Paul's spot.

As they take off.

"Jay-Z's" change clothes, come through the speakers.

Lulu, turns it up

Ya dude is back, May bauch coupe is back, tell the whole world the truth is back. You don't got to argue about who can rap, cause the proof is back, just go through my rap, New York, New York, yeah where my troopers at? Where my hustlers, where my booster at?

Jay-Z (black album)

Jay and Lulu sing it together perfect.

"Yo! What's your favorite Jay-Z song?"

"This one, "Encore" and "never change" Jay answered.

"Yeah I love that shit too but I'm gonna say "nigga what? Nigga who"

"He just come on the track flowin' like that other jaun on Memphis Bleek album "Is that your chick"

"When he come on there like " I don't love em' I fuck em', I don't chase em' I duck em' then I replace em' with another one, hard to see she kept calling me big, when my name is Jay-Z".

"Damn! That shit is fire right there baby."

They pull up to the house on the outside it's cute the colors light the grounds are very well kept. They step out the truck Jay and Lulu walk up the walkway to the front door. Jay puts the key in and opens the door.

Lulu's stepped pass Jay as he held the door open. Her mouth dropped at what she saw. It was beautiful.

The Foyer was well lit with closest on both sides. As you went father in you stepped down into the sunken' living room right pass the foyer was a full bath next to the bathroom was a set of steps, they both went up. There was a wooden fence it was another living room. Over looking the first one with the huge window they seen when they pulled into the driveway looking out over the driveway.

"Jay baby this is beautiful I know Big Paul's women is gonna love this place no doubt." She reasoned.

"Come on let's look at the rest of the place." Jay inquired as she followed close behind.

They run down the steps like a couple kids. Next to the living room down stairs they notice the fire place. In the first living room the cathedral ceilings with sky lights there's another wooden fence. As you step up from the living room you step up again and your in the kitchen.

"Wow an island kitchen look he has a subzero refrigerator."

Damn! Lulu sighed.

"How you know about all of this stuff?" Jay questioned.

"Jay babe "Better home and gardens" all this shit is in there that magazine let you know What's, what."

"Well look I'm about to jump in the shower you want to join me?" Jay stated.

"Of course babe stop asking stupid questions." She shot back.

"Yeah I like how you kick it." He spat.

They go into the back bedroom. Lulu flicks on the light she's in awe once again. As she looks at the four post bed sitting in the middle of the room.

"Damn baby! We gonna have a ball on that!!" She inquired.

"You know it". He shot back.

Jay walks into the bathroom the lights turn on automatic. Jay looks around in the middle of the floor Big Paul had a tub like "Tony Montana".

"Damn! I see big pimpin' got his little "Scare Face" thing going on here I'm feeling it, I'm definitely feeling it."

Jay walks across the heated marble floor as he opens the double glass doors to a dual headed shower there were two benches in there as well. Jay turned on the shower an stepped in as he let the water just run over his head he soaped up and washed off. Then just closed his eye's and stood under the nice cool water.

He was in deep thought when he felt his dick getting hot and hard.

He opened his eye's and looked down only to see Lulu with half his dick in her mouth.

"Damn! I almost wasn't paying attention and fell in his tub out there". Lulu stated.

As Lulu stood right in front of Jay. He's looking at

her realizing how naturally beautiful she really is here she is no make-up hair wet looking hotter than ever. As he kisses her deep and very passionate.

"What did I do to get a kiss like that?" She questioned.

"Your were looking beautiful like you always do baby I want to get you something like this one day."

Jay then soaped up her wash clothe and began washing her up. Lulu just went with the flow as she soon found he was no longer holding the wash clothe but was between her legs with two finger in her pussy. Jay had worked her towards the bench. As he laid her across he got between her legs. He had one leg on his shoulder he was leaned over her sucking her hard nipples as he held her tits together. and went back and forth from nipple to nipple she looked like she was about to explode he stops he licks down her wet stomach, he slips his tongue into her hot waiting pussy.

Once they were finished Jay got some shampoo in his hand and began washing Lulu's hair she couldn't believe it. This was one of her fantasy it don't sound like much. But she always dreamed once she was married her husband would take showers with her and wash her hair.

She really felt loved and wanted for the first time in her life.

She knew Jay had her sexually even thou their both beginners but now he completely had her heart.

"Baby I'm gonna make you the happiest man in the world." She stated.

"Were did that come from?" He asked.

"Baby you showed me what life's about I use to see people smiling thinking to myself what the fuck are they smiling at? But then I was just breathing, day in and day out I wasn't moving forwards nor backwards I was just breathing no purpose, until I met you, you picked me up dusted me off and blew life into me".

"Come on lets get out of this shower before we get wrinkled." He ordered.

They wrap themselves in towels and make their way to the bedroom once in the bedroom Jay walks over to the C.D, player and push play, as he waits to hear what Big Paul got in there. As "the Black Eyed peas" come through the speakers "Don't phunk with my heart"

"Awe I like this song" Lulu says. Jay goes over to the dresser and gets the lotion and comes back over to the bed.

"Lay down and let me put some lotion on you baby." Jay ordered.

"Damn Jay! What are you trying to do to me your gonna have me asking you to marry me by the end of the night".

"Hold on a sec can I change the c.d. now sense that song is off?"

"Go ahead I don't care." She answered.

Jay goes to his bag and pulls out his c.d. holder and puts in "Marvin Gaye's" Distant Lover.

He goes back over to the bed and starts to rub lotion all over her back, shoulders, then her ass and the back of her legs, as he goes back over everything he just did. He whispers in her ear for her to turn over.

She does he puts more lotion in his hand. And works it in as he lotions her stomach. He can see her nipples getting hard, but he continues down, as he does her thighs. He has her leg up her foot is resting on his shoulder. As he rubs it in then he does her calves he starts sucking on her toes. He see's she ready but he's not he's just enjoying this relaxing time with her as things are really falling into prospective for Jay as he realizes. He's found true love.

He spends the next hour just massaging Lulu as she falls asleep.

Chapter 20

The following morning…

Lulu awakes with her head laying on Jay's chest. She just looks at him sleeping she thought to herself how peaceful he looked she kissed him, on his full lips.

Jay woke up.
"Hey good morning sweetheart did you sleep good?"

"Of course! And thanks for that very nice massage I needed that I owe you big time."

"Naw I owe you, for letting me". They both laughed.
"So are you ready to hit the road in about two hours?"

"Hey I'm ready when you are". She got up and put on her yellow thong and her little black half shirt. That had (I love me) written in white with a red heart. She looked so sexy as Jay just watched her cross the floor.

She picked up the phone and dialed Big Paul's number at the shop.
He answers on the second ring.

"BIG PAUL: WHAT'S REALLY GOOD?"

"Hey big Paul! What's up with you this morning?"

"HEY BABY GIRL SO HOW DID YOU LIKE THE SPOT,.. AND BE HONEST?"

"Paul I love it and I'm 100% sure your misses will feel the same you done it up, big time and that subzero frig? Perfect trust me, she's gotta love it."

"WELL THANKS I'M GLAD YOU TWO LIKE IT, THAT MEANS A LOT TO ME ARE YA ROLLING OUT SOON OR STAYING FOR AWHILE? IF I KNOW YOUR MAN HE READY TO BAIL, AM I RIGHT?"

"Yeah we'll be outta here within' the next hour or so thanks again, for letting us crash". She repeated.

"NO DOUBT! YA HAVE A NICE TRIP BACK."

She hangs-up. And gets off the couch and walks

back into the bedroom. As Jay's, still wet from just getting out of the shower.

"That's just what I was thinking as they make love on the bed one last time."

And forty- five minutes later their walking out to the truck. Jay throws the two bags next to the motorcycles in the back bed of the truck. He pops the hood and checks the oil before they hit the road.

As their on the turnpike headed back to Lancaster they pull over to a rest stop and have breakfast at Denny's.

At the restaurant, the waiter is flirting with Lulu like crazy. Jay act like he doesn't notice until he goes to the bathroom to wash his hands before he eats. Once he comes back out and starts walking towards the table. He can't believe his eye's as they waiter was sitting in the seat talking to Lulu like Jay was a sucker or something he'll soon see differently.

Jay came to the table and slid down next to the guy pushing him farther in the booth.

" Hold on young dude let me get out first". He spat

After he said that he noticed Jay had his gun in his stomach.

As the guy started to stutter. "Come on, loo look, I was just, come on man! Please, just let me" -

Jay spoke. "Look dude! Do you know me? Have you ever seen me before? Then why the fuck! Would you think it's sweet like that? Huh!,

now what I should do is have you on the news tonight for this shit right here, you feel me?" Jay questioned with venom dripping from his words.

"Hey I'm sorry! Your, your right, I I don't know what I was thinking but please! Don't kill me?" He stated, pleading for his life.

"See it's just like I told you baby Guns, make dumb mother fuckers smart again." Jay said, to Lulu.

Lulu just laughed. "Baby let that little bitch go it's like fishing, he ain't big enough to keep." As she continued.

"That sucker ass nigga! work at Denny's part time he don't even have enough money for gas let alone me". She reasoned.

As Jay handed Lulu the gun under the table. He got up and let the guy out.

They finished eating as they left. Lulu dropped a ten dollar tip for the waiter as they went to the truck. They could both see him eyeing them up as they rode away.

The following day…

Jay and Lulu was walking through the park. When they met this interesting couple the guy's name was Tyrone the girl name was Tamela.

Tyrone had asked Jay were the local "Pep-Boys" was at.

Jay replied. "You know what dog me and my girl like just moved here where still trying to get the feel of this place too." Jay reasoned.

"Oh really we just moved here too maybe we can hang out together sense we don't know anyone If that's okay with you guys". Tamela inquired.

"Your gonna have to excuse my girl she has away of just inviting people to just chill and shit." Tyrone spat.

Lulu looked at her and spoke. "That would be great I need a girl friend around here no offence Jay! But I do need some girl time".

"No problem babe well how about we all get together later for dinner that way we can get to know one another cool?" Jay reasoned as he invited the couple.

"That sounds good.. Jay is it?" Tyrone asked.

"Damn! My bad dogg yeah my names Jay, and this is my girl Lulu".

They shake hands as Tyrone introduces him and his girl.

"You guys like seafood?" Jay questioned.

"Yeah but we can't afford that right now how about, the diner or something?" Tyrone offered.

"Guys don't worry we invited you two that means! It's our treat." Lulu stated.

Tyrone looks at Jay as to get his final word of approval.

Jay shook his head in agreement. " How's 6:00 sound?"

"We'll be there with bells on." Tyrone answered.

Over the next couple weeks they got to know Tyrone and Tamela real good Lulu and Tamela, were always hanging out together.

Jay on the other hand. Was not that fast to trust Tyrone, not because of who he was. But because how Jay himself were with trusting people.

The next morning. Jay got up early, as he saw Megan out by the pool with the smallest bikini he ever saw he couldn't take his eye's off her, she was beautiful. She had noticed Jay looking at her but down played it as she got up and walked away.

As her hips swayed back and forth Jay stepped out of the pool house just so he could continue to keep her insight.

She was just about to enter the house as she turned and looked Jay right in the eye and motioned with her finger for him to come.

Without hesitation Jay was right on her heals. He got to the door he looked into the house he didn't see her. Then he looked up the stairs she was at the top he quickly ran up the stairs taking them two & three at a time then went into the room he seen her go in. And much to his liking Megan was laying across her bed naked waiting for Jay.

Jay looked at her in admiration are you sure, you want to do this?" He asked.

"Come on Jay I'm a big girl! I been wanting some of that dick, sense I saw you and Lulu fucking in the pool house and I know you want this pussy?" She stated, reading his thoughts.

Within' two seconds Jay was naked he went over to the bed he put his hands behind her legs, he lifted them up with his hands behind her knees he pushed her knees up to her ears he stuck his tongue in her waiting pussy.

Jay then let go with one hand as he circled her clit as he fingered her he felt her about to climax, he backed off her. He went over to the door were he saw the condoms on the chest. She was on her hands and knees horny waiting to see what he was going to do next. Jay walked back over to the bed she grabbed him. And put his dick in her mouth she took the condom out of his hand.

Jay was getting pleased so good he didn't realize she put the condom in her mouth and put it on as she came off his dick.

He entered her and for the next half hour they fucked with the passion of two people in love Jay took his time as she did exploring one another's body both not realizing the door was still open.

Jay heard Lulu's voice calling him. He got up, and went to the window. He quickly put on his shorts and kissed Megan. He went out the front door he came out next to his truck. As Lulu turned the corner she saw Megan in her robe standing in the doorway.

"Good morning Megan! Have you seen Jay?" She inquired.

"I think he's out front". She answered.
"Thank you". Lulu replied.

"Jay baby let's take the bikes and go get some breakfast."
"That sounds good babe let me go jump in the shower real quick first cool? I was just wiping down the Truck". He stated.

"Okay! Can I get in with you? Not to sex you just to kill two birds with one stone?"

"No problem."

"We'll do the sex thing later". She said as she grabbed, at his ass.

"No doubt!" He spat.

They start to walk back to the pool house as they both strip down and got in the shower. After they soaped up they are face to face as they just hug each other. Jay stares into Lulu's eyes.

"Jay baby what are you thinking?

"How much I love that your apart of my life baby you know I would never do anything to purposely hurt you right?" Jay stated.

"Well Jay I would hope not I'm here for you Jay you are the first guy to treat me like a person but when you make love to me, you made me feel like a woman and I feel love when you touch me baby I would die for you."

As they kiss, Jay pushes her under the shower head as the water falls on her little perfect body. Jay pulls away from her as he began to suck on her left titty.

"No baby! Not now I'm hungry lets get out of the shower and go get something to eat please I'll make it up to you later". She stated.

fifteen minutes later their starting up the motorcycles.

Jay has his Roc-a-wear sweat pants and a light blue wife beater (muscle shirt) Lulu has on her pink sweat pants and a black sports bra. As they put on their helmets and speed off. Lulu goes pass Jay on a wheelie! Jay just looks on as he speeds up to catch her.

They pull into the gas station and to their surprise. Tyrone was working inside.

"Hey Jay what's up baby?"

"Oh! What's up man you working here? That's what's up hey give me $20 dollars on pump 4, hey baby girls outside come out and holla at her thanks "T" I'll see you."

"I'll walk out with you."

"Baby look who it is."

"What's up T! I see you got the job, huh? So what's really good?" Lulu inquired.
"Hey I'm just trying to hold my girl down like this guys holding it down for you."

"Is that right? Well, we'll get up with the two of you later maybe alright?"

"Oh! Most definitely."

Jay puts ten dollars in his bike and then puts the rest in Lulu's bike.

As they shot down the street and pull into the diner parking lot.

They get off the bikes Jay could have sworn out of the corner of his eye he saw Heidi. As he turned his head he confirmed it.

"Hey Lu go inside and get our table cool?"

She shook her head in agreement and went up the steps.

Jay walks over to the car.

"So what's up? I knew it was just a matter of time before you found me."

"Oh really! So you where expecting me to come looking for you huh?"

"That's what your kind do isn't it?" Jay reasoned.

She got real nervous at the remark that was made. Now she just tried to figure out did Jay know she was a cop or was he talking about the money?

Then jay thought. Damn I better down play this I don't want her to know that I know this bitch is after me.

"So Jason what are you implying?" She questioned.

"I'm just trying to see where your going with this that's all just friendly conversation, it's all good right?"

"Well if you say it is look, enough with the small talk Is there a time and a place that we can get together, soon?"

"Humm it depends!!! What's it about?"
"Don't act like this now Jay, what's it always about with you and I?"

"That's what I'm talking about! Well tomorrow down the block from here there's a Hilton, meet me in the lobby at 2:00pm sharp and you know how I like it bitch! So don't front." Jay spat.

Heidi just looks at Jay and gets into her car.
Before she pulls off she says. "I'll see you then."

Jay thinks to himself, he goes and have breakfast with his baby. Damn, I'm gonna bust that ass as he thought of the angle he was going to come at her with being he was caught off guard by her.

He finds Lulu, and slides into the booth.
"Damn! Jay how did that bitch find us baby and what are we gonna do?" Lulu questioned.

"Oh! So you saw her huh? I know, I know this bitch is playing both sides of the fence but remember this, "Every dog has his day" I don't know what's next but I'm thinking it'll come to me, trust me".

They ate talked some more and went and got Lulu a new 2009 Beetle turbo convertible. Pink her favorite color. Jay loved seeing the look on her face when he did what he could to keep her happy as he could so she would never have to think about her bad days in the pass.

Chapter 21

The next day at 2:00pm. Jay was pulling up to the Hilton hotel in the parking lot he saw Heidi's car. Which means she was early, loosely translated she was horny as hell.

Jay walks into the lobby he sees Heidi. She dangles the keys to a room Jay walks towards her as they head to the room.

Once into the room she couldn't keep her hands or mouth off of Jay. She had it bad, for the young man.

Jay took full advantage he stripped her down to her thongs he quickly got out of his clothes. She went to the bag she brought in the room and got out an 10" vibrator.

"So! You got props huh? Well get on the bed on your back and hang your head off the edge you know how, I like it."

Jay got the vibrator as he walked over and put his dick in her mouth. She was spread-eagle as he started eating her out she was getting hot as hell. He turned on the vibrator and slowly started fucking her with it he continued licking her clit she was going wild.

"Oh bay! Baby hold on, hold on, I'm cumming, I'm cum ooh ooh don't stop" She cooed!

After Jay got her once. He had her get on all fours, as he had the vibrator in his one hand, and his dick in the other. He had her suck his dick, and the vibrator back-and-forth. Jay then took her and laid her down as he put on a condom he entered her as he took her legs and put them over his shoulders Jay pounded her for at least 20 minutes until he came. Heidi was in a light sweat hair all messed up Jay went and jumped in the shower once out.

"Well look, it was fun but I must be leaving." Jay stated coldly.

"Jay baby there's something I need to tell you and I know your not going to like it." She reasoned.

Jay turned towards her.
"Yeah! And what's that?" He spat.

"Jay! I'm a cop I was sent to get you I've been on you for almost a year but I began playing both sides and started sleeping with you at first for my job, but I fell in love with you Jay I'm quitting the force! Cause I want to be with you… I can't believe a 17yr old has me doing this."

Jay just sat there and took it all in.
He pulled his gun and aimed it at her.

"And why should I believe that this is not a part of your set up?"
"Jay baby what are you doing Jay! I love you and I don't want anything bad to happen to you I'm trying to help you, please!" She pleaded.

Jay lowers, the gun.
"I would like to be with you too but I knew you and Nate where the feds that's why we left when we did but you gotta let me think this thing through okay?" Jay inquired.

"No problem Jay". She kisses him deep and passionate, as she gets dressed, and walks him out.

Once they step out of the lobby. They hear a loud. "boc- boc" the glass behind them breaks everybody's screaming, Jay takes a bullet in the shoulder that spins him as he falls and pulls his gun he's laying behind a body as he shoots his whole clip off killing the two guys in the old Caddy as he noticed the body he was shooting over was Heidi's she blinks, as Jay leans over her.

"Baby I'm sorry I betrayed you! But I do love you

ooh it hurts! So bad baby" She pauses, tries to take a deep breath. "At least we made love one last timmm."

As she breathed her last breath.

Jay kissed her on her forehead as he tucked his gun.

He quickly ran too the car that had shot at them as he peeked in he couldn't believe who he saw. It was Mark her boy friend. Or was he an agent too? Jay fled the seen as he heard sirens in the back ground.

Once Jay made it back to the house safely he pulled Lulu away from Megan as they were talking out back.

"Baby listen up cause you might not believe what just happened to me I went to go meet with Heidi"-

"Oh so that's it! You crept off on me to meet with that whore!" Lulu screamed.

"Oh my God Jay baby! You've been shot". She barked.

At the mention of his wound Jay starts to feel light headed. Lulu's first reaction was to go and get Megan. Megan came into the pool house with a first aid kit. First she had Jay lay down flat, then she got a towel and tied it as tight as she could to stop the bleeding she ran back to the house and got one of Percy's pain killers, she came back she had Jay take it, she began working on his shoulder. Jay finished telling Lulu the story.

"Look let me finish she's a federal agent she told me that she's been onto me for almost a year" Jay thinks to himself. Damn she must have known about the killing of "Poppa-Rose" and the others.

And the one thing Jay didn't ask her was where was Nate?

"Anyway Lu like I was saying I think we should relocate, the heat could be right around the corner." Jay reasoned.

As he explains more of what she said to him. Lulu just listened, then she spoke:

"So Jay why would we relocate now? That should be the last thing on our mind first it sounds like she got info on your where-a-bouts from the streets so what we need to do is use our connects to put their ears on the streets and see what's out there why run when we don't know what were running from, or who?" She stated.

"Damn! Your right, your absolutely right." Jay replied.

Later that night…
Jay's resting up he gets up and steps outside of the pool house he sees Lulu talking with Megan. Megan gets up, and leaves.
Lulu walks over to Jay
"Hey babe how you feel?"
"I'm alright for a nigga who just took one". Jay spat.

"So what were you and Megan talking about?" Huh.

"Men she was telling me about her relationship with Percy."

"You mean business relationship right?" Jay asked.

" No I mean he can't get it up so he just eats her out relationship!"

Jay eye's lit up-

"Get the heck outta here! Your not serious are you?"

"Jay I'm dead serious! She said he has her lay at the edge of the bed he sits in a chair in his socks and boxers with his dick through the hole and he jerks off trying to get it up as he eats her out but she never seen his dick, until one day he had his door open when she was walking by he was naked sleep on his bed watching porn with his dick in his hand she said it couldn't have been longer than her middle finger."

"Stop playing! He don't look that old you telling me this guy got a house like this an a Porsche, and he still can't get no ass?" Jay stated while laughing out loud.

They go into the pool house an Lulu turns on the c.d. player. As John Legend's – ordinary people. Comes through, the speakers

"All this cat is smooth I'm feeling this." Jay stated.

Jay's laying down on his stomach as Lulu is rubbing his back.

Jay feels something wet on his back.

"What's that?" Jay painfully turns around. Lulu's crying.

"Baby! What's wrong?" Jay inquired.

"Jay baby what if I would have lost you today baby, you're all I have in this fucked up world."

"You scared me when Megan was working on you."

"Hey Lulu baby I'm not leaving you no time soon, you're my ride or die bitch! You know that, right?" He lift's her chin and looks her right in the eye's "right?" He repeated.

"Of course Jay I'm with you till there's no more of us."

"That's what I want to hear oh by the way we gotta make that run again in two day's you ready?"

"No doubt!".

Chapter 22

The following day…

Jay calls Jason.

They talk for awhile, as Jay tells him about Heidi. Later that afternoon. Jay and Lulu goes for a motorcycle ride they go way out as their riding down this long country road. They notice an old what looked to be abandon barn set way back off the road.

So they ride out towards it their off the bikes walking around not seeing any signs of any one. Lulu jumps on Jay's back, Jay shouts.

"HO, HO WATCH, MY SHOULDER!!" Jay screamed out.

"Oh I'm sorry baby! Are you okay?"

She lays him down she starts to pull off his pants.

"What are you doing! You want to fuck, here? We don't know if someone's here or not".

No sooner then he said that, a smile went across his face.

"Oh! Your nasty well come on with your freaky ass then".

As they stripped down and made love behind an old abandoned barn.

———————————————

Later that night…

Jay couldn't sleep one he couldn't get Heidi out of his head and all she said to him. Jay gets up as he looks back at the bed he see's Lulu sleeping like a baby.

He walks to the doorway as he tries to stretch his shoulder, it's still killing him. He looks up he see's Megan's light on as he grabs his nike shorts off the chair he dips out.

As he goes into the door she told him that's always open.

Jay turns the corner and surprises her just as she was taking off her bra.

"You need a little help there?" Jay questioned.

"I was about to ask you the same thing, how's your shoulder feeling?"

"Maybe if you give one part of my body attention the pain will lessen in the other part, you feel me?" He reasoned.

"Sure! Close the door and come over here."

Jay goes over to the bed she motions for him to lay down.

"So Jay why are you still up this time of the night?"

"Humm let's just say I got some shit on my mind."

"Well maybe a massage from me will help, huh?"

She grabs some lotion off the nightstand as she begins to massage it in.

Five minutes later...

"Damn! This feels good your right you are good at this."

"Oh I'm not even half way finished with you yet turn over, and I'll finish okay?" She ordered.

"No doubt! You don't have to ask me twice". He spat.

Jay turns over slowly and to his surprise she still had her thong panties on and that's it. Jay just couldn't look away from her beautiful breast.

"You like them Jay? Don't be shy touch em." She ordered.

She grabs both of Jay's hands and place them on

her beautiful firm breast. Then she takes the lotion and puts some on his chest as she begins massaging his chest he's massaging hers. He feels his manhood growing as she grinds on his dick.

"Do you have any condoms?"

"Of course I do but your just getting a massage remember?" She answered with a devilish smirk.

"Stop playing girl and get me a condom."

Jay gets the condom and puts it on she gets back on top of him he pulls her thong to the side as she slides down on top of him. She lets out a moan.

"Damn!"

As she rolled her head back and made all kinds of noises. This excited Jay.

At first Jay was a little taken back from the way she was talking. But as he fucked her longer and harder he got used to it and soon they where both talking dirty to one another.

They had sex well into the night.

"Jay not to kick you out or anything but it's 4:00am in the morning, what if your girl wakes up and your not there?" Megan questioned.

"Yeah your right! Well I'm at a lost for words do I thank you or bow to you, that was great well until next time, I guess." He stated as he dipped off.

He kissed her on the cheek put on his shorts and left just as quickly as he had come. "Boof"

Jay walked passed the pool and slipped into the pool house. Unnoticed by Lulu who was still asleep. So he jumped in the shower.

Once he washed off twice he washed his hair and stepped out.

To his surprise Lulu was standing in front of him.

"Jay baby you mind telling me, where you were?" Lu questioned.

"Hey babe! Yeah I was in the house talking to Percy". Jay quickly responded. Then continued.

"Yeah he wanted to know if I could move a few thing for him with the truck". Jay stated as he continued to dry off.

"Okay but why would you think of taking a shower this time of the morning?" Lulu asked.

"Damn girl! What's this 50's " 21 questions"? You cool? No, don't tell me you got your period?" Jay spat.

" Fuck you! You're an ass hole just come to bed will you.?"

"I'll be right there with your fine ass damn! Even wit sleep in your eye's, my baby fine!" Jay stated jokingly.

As she turns to walk away, Jay smacks her on the ass.

"Stop Jay! Don't think I'm not still mad at you either, cause I'm."

"Yeah whatever you don't even know why your mad at me, do you?"

"Jay no, I'm being serious you need to stop playing me for a fool."

"I'll tell you what, tomorrow we'll make that run to pick up that "cheese" (money) up in Scranton, p.a. Then how about just us two take a much needed vacation just to get back to some us time how's that sound?"

"Jay baby are you for real?" Lulu answered.

"No bitch! I'm the truth but are you down for that?" Jay spat.

"Hell yeah! I'll go any where with you any time just say the word." She replied.

"Okay well, we'll go get this money and then we out." He answered.

Jay goes across the room and put on a C.D. as he pushes play (Donell Jones) comes threw, the speakers "It's a quarter pass three girl what's it gonna be, shorty got her eye's on me, we been talking sense two girl what ja' gonna do?" His voice cooed.

"Awe, this that shit right here! You don't know nothin' about this baby, this "grown folk music" right here! Holla at a nigga, what!" Jay screamed.

"Yeah okay let you tell it, your grown huh?"

"Damn right! All I need now is a glass of Henney,

and a smoking jacket girl. And I'll put on some steppin' music and keep it moving."

"Yeah is that right? And guess what, nigga! You'll still be seventeen with a smoking jacket, and a glass of Henney." As she laughed out loud.

"Well if it makes you feel good, go a head and keep cracking them lame ass jokes". Jay stated as he slowly looked her up and down.

"All come on baby don't go getting sensitive on me now." Lulu replies.
As Jay throws his hands up in the air.
"Awe, this my shit"

He goes over to the remote, and turns up the radio.
He starts to sing along with the C.D.
"Are you down to swing and "f" with me,
or could it be your blinded, by all this ice you see, I'm willing to give you all this love I got, no relationships involved- all this luv'-

"This grown folk music Bitouch!! Ha-ha!" Jay screamed, as he laughed on.

The following day...

"Whew!! What a night damn you put it on me, girl."

"Yeah there's more in store, when we get to our vacation spot "believe that". Lulu replies.

"Well I'm really looking forward to that." Jay reasoned.

They both get in the shower together as they both wash up Jay's thinking to himself. How many car orders he took and how their money's gonna look. He and "Big Paul" had spoken about getting bigger but Jay was continent with the way things were, at this point at least. But now he knew they had to take it to the next level. But with more power, comes more jealousy, that just goes without say.

They get dressed as Jay grabs some old school music for their road trip.

They jump in the truck, and go to get something to eat. Before they hit the road.

"Jay, when you were in that foster home did you ever go on a trip where you went, horse back riding?" She asked.

"No but I always wanted to do that, why have you?" Jay shot back.

"No but I plan on doing that with you, no doubt".

"Hey! You want to stop at that Bob Evan's, breakfast spot?"

"Oh yeah that was hitting last time, cool I'm up for that."

As they pull up in the parking lot, there's a young man out front.

They park and get out of the truck. Jay never took his eye's off the kid until they went into the restaurant.

They were seated right away a booth next to the window.

Jay peaked out of the blind and saw the kid looking in the trucks window. Jay sprang, from his seat and ran towards the door.

He got outside Lulu was right behind him. He yelled over to the kid.

"Yo! What the fuck are you doing looking in my shit? I don't know you kid, give me a couple feet alright!" Jay spat sizing the kid up, as he flipped the razor in his mouth.

"Baby! What's wrong?" Lulu chimed in.

"This little peeping Tom was to close to my shit that's what's wrong." Jay answered.

"Excuse me sir my names not Tom, it's Noah and you are?"

"Somebody who's about to dive right off into your ass! Look I don't care what your name is just stay away from my stuff friend, cool?" Jay said, sounding annoyed.

"Fare enough, I apologize" as he goes to shake Jay's hand he pulls him close and pats him on the shoulder.

Lulu can't believe what she just seen.
She goes over to Noah and does the same, only she kissed him on both cheeks and stepped away.

Jay was a bit taken back Noah was blushing.

Jay and Lulu went back into the restaurant and sat back down.
"So what was that all about?"
"He got you Jay so I just returned the favor, you can thank me later okay?" Lulu replied.
"What do you mean he got me?"
As Jay begins to feel for his money.
"What the fuck!" He stated. With a look of shock on his face.

Lulu hands him, his money.
"Is this, what your looking for? By the way here's his too he'll relies he's been got, and he'll either come in or he'll be waiting outside for us". Lulu reasoned.

"Damn! He was smooth huh?" Jay spat.

" Actually your just sweet like that baby no he's good to a regular person, but to a street person he's an amateur come on Jay, your slacking on your pimping baby". Lulu stated. As she giggled.

"Never let some one you don't know touch you like that".

"Style dropped, lesson taught I got you" He returned.

The server comes over to them, they order their drinks, she goes away. They become engaged in conversation, about their vacation.

Lulu was talking about getting a full body massage, when the server came back with their drinks.

"I'M SORRY, ARE YOU READY TO ORDER OR DO YOU NEED MORE TIME?" The waitress questioned.

They both answer together in unison, " No, were ready!"

"I would like to have pancakes with your Canadian bacon".

"Umm, that sounds good but I'll have the French toast, with bacon and a side of sausage please." Jay closes the menu, and takes Lulu's and hands them, to their server.

"THANK YOU I'LL GET YOUR ORDERS IN RIGHT AWAY."

"Now where was I ? Oh a full body massage oh baby I just can't wait." Lulu answered sounding excited.

"Yeah I could use a massage on my head too." Jay reasoned.

"Just your head?"

"Oh not that kinda massage some neck work on my other head, feel me?" Jay answered. As he laughed out loud.

"Jay your nasty but if your good, I might be able to grant your wish soon". She replies.

"Naw baby! It's to many people in here."

"No, no, not that soon damn, is that all you think about is me sucking on your dick.?" She questioned.

"Come on baby I think about us fucking, and money too so don't even play me, like that".

As the two of them, start laughing.

"You're an ass hole, but I love you."

As their server, came back with their food.

"DO YOU NEED ANY THING ELSE, RIGHT NOW?"

"No were good for now, thank you".

"Damn I don't know if this just looks this good, or I'm just hungry as hell."

"Probably a combination of both, cause it does look good but I'm starving myself." Lulu chimed in.

They sit eat and talk a little more, and their server comes and ask if they wanted, anything else.

"No, were good can we have the bill please!" Jay replied.

"SURE HERE YOU ARE I HOPE YOU ENJOYED EVERYTHING HERE YOU GO, HAVE A NICE DAY." She stated. As she pushed their bill on the table.

"Thank you! You do the same."

They get up to leave once outside. Jay and Lulu sees Noah leaning against the truck.

"I told you he was gonna come in or be waiting." Lulu reasoned.

"What's up dude! You played me, and my girl played you we even now right?" Jay spat.

"And now theses three remain faith, Hope, and Love but the greatest of theses, is Love... Come on brother! Show me some Love, baby I owe you please?" Noah pleaded with Jay.

"I like that when did you write that?" Lulu questioned.

"That's the Bible, he's quoting babe". Jay chimed in.

"Yes sweet heart, he's right! That's a blessed man to know theses words." Noah reasoned.

"That's 1ˢᵗ Corinthians 13 verse 13, you must be into the church am I right?" Noah questioned.

"No I'm not I've read some of the Bible, here and there you know." Jay shot back..

"No brother your knowledge runs deep, I wish to talk to you some time if that's possible?" Noah inquired.

"Look what's your name again?" Jay asked.
"Noah and yours?"
"Jay that would be cool but not now where on a mission, maybe at a later date cool?" Jay answered as he hurried to end the conversation.
"No doubt where can I reach you?"
Jay reaches into the truck and writes down his cell number and gives it to Noah.
"Call me tomorrow, cool." Jay stated, as he handed him the paper.

"Of course I will have a safe and peaceful trip you two." He spat.
Noah clear's his throat.

"Oh my bad! You would like your money back, huh?"
"Your kindness would be appreciated".
"I bet it would." Lulu said, looking him up and down.

"You know what Noah you seem like a cool dude today's your lucky day." Jay replies.
Jay gets his wallet from Lulu and hands it to Noah.
"When we meet again I'm gonna show you what it's all about and if your serious, about getting money we'll see."

He grabs Jay's hand and holds it as he looks at Lulu.

"He will have no fear of bad news his heart is steady fast trusting in the Lord, his heart is secure he will have no fear and in the end he will look in triumph, on his foes". Noah stated.

"That's PSALM 112 verses 7 and 8." Jay answered.

"You Love the bible huh?" Lulu reasoned.

"Sweet heart because he turned his ear to me, I will call on him as long as I live." Noah replies.

"That's PSALM 116 VERSE 2." Jay answered.

Jay shakes his hand good bye Lulu does the same as they jump into the truck, and head out.

As their riding.

"So Jay baby why didn't you tell me you were into the Bible like that?" Lulu asked.

"I'm not! I'm just a person who would rather know a little bit about everything, than a whole lot of nothing feel me?"

"The more I learn about you the more you turn me on baby." Lulu stated.

"You think you can handle this?" Lulu questioned.

She said as she started to unzip his pants as she

pulled his manhood out while he was driving. She went down, on Jay.

He was nervous at first, but he slowly began to relax as she went on.

Chapter 23

Then minutes had gone by as Jay felt he could hold back no longer.

"Ho hold baby! Your gonna make me crash." Jay screamed.

She came up and kissed him on the neck and just laid up against him as they drove on.

"Baby where do you think we'll be, in a year from now?" She questioned.

"Were did that come from? Look sweet heart, I just left behind the worst part of my life and I met you, and started wit the best part and trust me this is all new to me to, and sometimes I can't believe it the trips, this truck our motorcycles, etc."

"But as far as tomorrow goes, your guess is as good as mine let's just do us, until we figure it out how's that?" He answered.

"You got it baby! You got it." She replies.

They continue driving, within' an hour and a half, their pulling into Scranton P.A. about ten minutes after that they pull in the back of "Big Paul's".

Big Paul comes out, and greets them.

"WHAT'S REALLY GOOD? YOUNGSTER, WHAT I NEED TO CALL YOU TWO ARE THE BAKER'S CAUSE YA'LL GETTING' ALL THE DOUGH, NO DOUBT."

"What's up big daddy! Where the "Cream Squad" at?"

No sooner than Jay said that. Face pulls up with the rest of the crew in a black "hummer h2" with 24" rims on it.

Face was driving, and Smash was riding shot gun they parked Face jumped out with a fresh cut, looking like he just came out the barber chair lined up perfect wearing a white and butter, button down Jil Sander's shirt, with some Sean John Jeans with a pair of silver framed shades. Face was a dresser. He knew how to but an outfit together without a doubt.

Smash got out looking total opposite. But clean as a whistle he had on a gray Michael Jordan sweat suit, with a fresh pair of gray and blue Jordan's on. Smash was a hustler, and he dressed the part.

First come and Buttons where in the back. They didn't look like a crew the four of them together but you had to have muscle, to go with the brains. And that's what First come and Button's where, to Smash and Face.

Jay and Big Paul greeted the men with hand shakes and hugs as they all went inside. First come Button's, and Lulu stayed in front. As the rest of them go into the back and handle business.

Jay hands Smash, the new list. Big Paul goes over to the table and gets a silver brief case, and opens it.

"JAY HERE YOU GO BABY! THAT'S ALL YOU. THAT'S $360,000 CASH IT'S BEEN A GOOD MONTH, BABY BOY".

Jay looks over it, and takes out $40 grand, and gives it to Big Paul.

Then gives, $20 grand to Face.

"What's this for Jay, naw baby I don't want that no me and my team's cool Jay trust me, we eating great baby keep that and buy that pretty thing you got out there some thing good, or put it away for ya'll kid, cause I know you got one on the way?" Face said smiling at his own comment.

" Take the money, dogg!" Jay reasoned.
"Jay I'm serious! I don't want it I'm good".

"WELL YOUNGSTERS IT'S BEEN REAL, BUT UNTIL NEXT MONTH MEETING OVER STAY UP AND STAY UNDETECTED, FEEL ME?" Big Paul stated.

" No doubt big man! We'll see you". Face replied.

Face and Smash leave as they go out front, Button's and first come follow behind.

Jay talks with Big Paul some more. Then He goes, and him and Lulu leave with the silver brief case with $320,000 in tow.

They jump into the truck and drive until they reach "Wilkes Barre" and they get a hotel room.

As they pull into the parking lot, of an okay looking hotel.

Jay pull into a spot. Jay pulled out some money and told Lulu to get a room.

She opens the door and slides out of the truck. Jay watches her as she walks up to the entrance.

She has on a pair of capri's, khaki color with a short little tee on and her low top blue and white Jordan's. Jay looked at her ass as it bounced up and down showing Jay if she had on panties, they were thongs no doubt he would find out shortly.

She gets up to the counter.

"YES YOUNG LADY AND HOW MAY I HELP YOU TODAY?"

"I would like to get a room please, one of your nicer rooms." Lulu inquired.

"WELL, I WOULD LIKE TO THINK ALL OF OUR ROOMS, ARE NICE."

"I'm sorry, I didn't mean for it to sound like that"-.

"I'M JUST KIDDING, YOU LOOK A LITTLE YOUNG TO BE GETTING A ROOM." The woman implied.

"I know, I get that all the time but me and my brother are coming from college, and we want to surprise our mom and dad so if you could please, let us get the room without calling them I would appreciate it?" Lulu pleaded, selling the lady with her lie.

"NO PROBLEM, GOD KNOWS I HAVE A SOFT SPOT FOR A CLOSE FAMILY"

"Thank you."

She pays, he hands her the key's.

She goes outside, only to see Jay leaning against the truck talking to a girl.

Lulu walked over to Jay. And grabbed his hand,

"Hey baby our room is ready I'm sorry, who's your little friend?" Lulu spat, with a tone of sarcasm.

"Oh! I didn't get her name." Jay reasoned.

"It's wendy and your name is?"

"Oh I'm Lucy, but my honey calls me Lulu and this is Jay my baby".

"Oh! Yeah.. you made that quite clear".

"Well maybe i'll see you around huh?" Wendy questioned.

"Yeah it was nice meeting you, Lisa was it?" Lulu replied.

"No, it's Wendy."

She answered in an annoyed tone.

Wendy's walking away- Jay calls out,

"Hey maybe we'll see you again soon".

Lulu loves, how Jay shows no interest in even the prettiest of girls.

Wendy was indeed a pretty girl, I'm kinda shocked at how Jay just blew her off. Lulu thought to herself.

Jay thought to himself - Damn that Wendy, she was built like that, damn honey was wearing the hell, out of them shorts too. Whew!!-

"What are you thinking about baby?" Lulu inquired.

"Oh what? Oh I, was thinking about you, and I testing out the springs on this bed in this room". Jay answered, lying.

"Good answer!, That's what you better be thinking about." She stated, With a smirk.

They walk into the room, it's decent. A little less then, what their use to but their just there for the night it'll do.

Jay puts down the case on the bed.
"Baby you ready to see some of our come up money?"
"Go a head Jay, show me they money!" She screamed.

Jay pops open the case, Lulu's eye's lit up.
"Oh my GOD! Jay baby that's all your's?"
"No baby that's all ours!"

Lulu just looks on in total awe.
"Get the fuck outta here! Jay babe that's a lotta loot you know what were gonna have to do, where gonna have to learn how to hide this money, make it look legit you feel me?"

"And how do you plan on doing that?" Jay asked, with a puzzled look on his face.
"Well I know a little about computers we'll have to get a lap top for starters get some one we can trust to put this in the bank then we can move it around from here to there, you got me?" Lulu reasoned.

"I'm feeling you babe No doubt! But were talking about a little over a quarter million dollars here girl plus with the other money DAMN!!"

"Jay babe just think if we get caught with all that

money on our person what cop or whatever part of the law is gonna do with us or the money? Better safe than sorry and who knows what doors this can open up for the both of us?" Lulu continued.

You know who could probably really help us out with this? Brooks, the dude Jason had make us, the fake I.D.'s huh, how's that sound?

Good thinking! Well, let's get the ball rolling. First thing in the morning, but as for tonight, it's me and you.

Jay gives Lulu a few dollars, as she goes out to the store for God knows what. Jay just strips down to his boxers, and lays across the bed, but gets up and goes to his bag and pulls out. "Bonnie and Clyde" and puts it on, as he goes back and lays, across the bed.

He's watching the movie, as he slowly begin to drift off. Twenty-minutes later Lulu comes back in. And sees Jay asleep on the bed. She begins lighting the small candles, she got from the store. And placing them all around the room,.

"Umm, fresh lining. I love this smell."
She goes over to the bed where Jay's laying on his back, she goes into the front of his boxers, and pulls out his dick and slowly starts sucking, Jay lets out a low moan.
As she begins to pick up the past, Jay's getting

hotter, his eye's open to what he thought was a dream, he sees the candles, he reaches down and grabs the back of her head, and starts to pump slow. He pulls out of her mouth, and reaches down into his bag and gets a condom. he puts it on and turns her around, and mounts her from behind, Jay can see her face in the mirror as he grabs a hand full of her hair and gives it a pull, as he smacks her ass, she rocking back meeting him as they fuck in sync, with the crackle of the candles burning.

They go through as many positions they could think of Jay sucked her toes, put hickeys on her ass, etc. When they were finally done they sparked up a Blunt that was on the night stand, Lulu had rolled earlier.

Jay took a few pulls,
"Damn! That's some good shit where you get that from?"
"That's that shit I got from out of the trunk remember? Good shit right?"
"Shit, you can say that again!" Jay replies.

Lulu goes to the bathroom while she's using the bathroom, she noticed how big the tub was.

Once she was done she started to run the water as she hollers out to Jay-
"Jay this tub is big enough for the both of us to get in, you care to take a bath with me?"
Jay comes to the door, and peaks in with the blunt hangin' at a 45 degree angle.

"No doubt! What nigga, you know that's gonna turn down a women asking him, to take a bath with her?"

"Just let me know when you want to see my swan dive?" He spat.

Jay step into the bathroom and drops his boxers now he's standing there "butt naked" with a blunt, in his mouth. As he hands the blunt to Lulu she takes it, he then starts to take off her thong.
Now their both just standing in the bathroom naked, smoking a blunt. Lulu turns around and bends over to turn off the water, Jay steps closer so once she turns, he's right up on her.

" Damn baby! Can you give me a little room?" Lulu stated.
Jay puts his arms around her and pulls her close.
"Damn baby, you got all the space you need."

Jay kisses her long, deep, and passionate. His hands now on her ass.
"What you need space for, where you going? I love you come on lets get in."

They both get into the tub.
"Owe! This feels great". Lulu stated as she slipped in

Jay eases in, real slow.

"Damn girl! It's hotter than fish grease, up in this bitch! Whew!!"

Lulu's already laid back, Jay's still easing in.

Jay finished sliding in.

"Aahh! Damn babe your right ooh, this feels good!" Jay reasoned.

"You like it, baby?"

" Like it, I can get real use to this no doubt." He answered.

"What do you say, after this we go get a bite to eat?" Lulu suggested.

"Hey little momma, it's whatever I'm with that! My ribs, are touching."

Chapter 24

The following day...

Jay and Lulu went to " Circuit City" as they walked around for a while, a older man came up to them.

"HOW CAN I BE OF SERVICE, TO YOU TODAY?" He questioned.

Jay answered,
"Well sir, I would like to see your top of the line lap tops." Jay responded.

"FOLLOW ME THEN."
He takes them over, they look at a few.
"Humm, there's some nice looking ones big ones, small ones etc it's not going to be as easy, as I thought". Jay said, out loud.

"WELL YOUNG MAN, IT'S REALLY DEPENDS ON YOUR USAGE".

Jay tried not to look puzzled.
"I'm sorry, what do you mean?"
"WELL, DO YOU PLAN ON USING IT ALL THE TIME SAY, OVER TEN HOURS A DAY? THEN YOU WOULD GET THE ONE WITH THE LONGER BATTEY LIFE."

" No, we just need one that's light weight fast, with a nice size screen with a burner on it, how's that?" Lulu answered.

"THIS WOULD SUIT YOU FINE THEN THIS ONES GOING FOR $1,430.00
IS THAT IN YOUR, PRICE RANGE?"
The older man said with an attitude, and a sly smirk.

Jay stepped, back and looked at the older man an excused himself.
Jay told Lulu to say there, while he went up to the service counter where he asked, to speak to a manager.

"Hello I'm Terri, the store manager is there a problem?"
"Terri, do your people get a commission for sales?"
"No but, they get recognized for fine performance and they get a bonus for a lot of sales." She replied.

"That's nice but I would like to get another sales person to help me and my girl friend with a sale, cause this old guy is giving us to much attitude I mean, I don't want to start any trouble, I just"-

" No it's no trouble at all, I know who your talking about, we've been having problems with this guy all day and today's, his first day".

Terri gets Jay another sales person, to help him. Then she calls the "older guy" off the floor as they step into her office.

Jay goes back over to where Lulu was.
"Hey, were did you get off to? You looked pissed that "old head" was getting on your nerves, huh?" Lulu questioned.

"Oh! You saw that huh? Whew let me tell you, that'll never be us." Jay spat.

"What do you mean, that'll never be us what! "Old and bitter?"
"No! Old and working still." Jay inquired.

They both laugh, as the sales girl comes up to them.
"HELLO, ARE YOU THE COUPLE LOOKING FOR A LAP TOP?"

"Yes we are! We would like to get this one right here, please." Lulu stated. Pointing to a nice one.

"THAT'S A GOOD ONE, WILL THE TWO OF YOU BE NEEDING ANYTHING ELSE?"

She said this looking right at Jay, giving him a little sexy smirk.

Lulu stepped between the two.

"No, that'll be all for now I'm sure thank you for asking." Lulu answered looking her up and down.

The sales girl rolled her eye's, and turned and walked away.

Two weeks later....

"Okay, here's the deal that kid Noah has proven to be able to handle his business but you know that, trusting just any one isn't one of my strong points, so?" Jay paused.

"Come on Jay, you let him take your truck you even let him ride your bike and that's your baby! Come on babe, stop lying to yourself". Lulu ordered.

Jay listens, as he walks over to the curb. He has a hand towel in his right hand it's humid out, as he grabs the center of his shirt. And gives it a pull a few times.

"Damn it's hotter than a " fire cracker" out this bitch!!" He spat.

Jay takes the towel and wipes his brow, then folds it and sits on the curb.

"So what are you waiting for me to say Jay, if we put him down, I'm responsible for him, Huh?" Lulu chimed in.

As Jay's sitting, Lulu's standing in front of him.
"Oh shit! Here he goes."
Jay said, as the local "crack head" came up behind Lulu.

As his smell greeted Lulu's nose, she makes a face. She sees Jay's eyes widening, Lulu turns around and looks, at Tay-Tay.

"DAMN GIRL, WHEN I GET STRAIGHT YOU MY DATE!!"
He said with stain yellow teeth, wit hot breath to match.

"HI YOU DOING MISS SEXY?"
He said as he stood, next to Lulu.
Then he moved the conversation towards, Jay.

"JAY BABY, HELP ME OUT LET ME WASH THIS TRUCK UP FOR YOU".
Jay's truck is parked a little down the street, where there's a few young girls, jumping rope.

One of the young girl's started pointing towards the three of them, and Jay heard one of the girls say.
"Hey Tasha, isn't that your "crack head daddy?" She inquired as her and the other girl laughed together.

Jay turned back to Tay-Tay, As he seen him drop his head even lower

"You know what, jump in the back". As Jay opens the door and gets in Lulu goes around and gets in.

"Where we going?" Tay-tay questioned.

Jay reaches into his back pocket and hands Tay-Tay a $20 bill as they ride down the street towards his daughter.

"Hand that to her." Jay instructed to Tay-Tay.

As Jay pulled the truck to a stop Tay-Tay handed his daughter the money she took it. And beamed at the girls she was playing with.

"Thank you!" She yelled.

Jay pulled away.

"Damn! Young man, no one's ever looked out for me like that I appreciate that". He stated.

Once they got to the spot Jay pulled the truck up and told Tay-Tay he would pay him when he got out the shower.

"Oh, and look wipe my girl's car down too don't forget the rims son."

"Baby boy, I'll have em' sparkling when you get back! "Believe that".

The aged "crack head" said smiling, showing his yellow teeth.

Jay turned to Lulu

"Come on woman let's jump in the shower".

As they left Tay-Tay, to finish the cars they walked through the gate and was greeted by Megan.

"Hey where have you two been?

"Me and my baby had to take care of some business." Jay answered.

They continue walking past her as they open the door to the pool house. They where greeted by the cool air from the air condition.

Jay and Lulu both let out a sigh of relief.

Lulu showed no hesitation, as she began to strip while making a bee line towards the bathroom Jay followed as they left a trail of clothes from the door of the pool house, to the bathroom.

Twenty minutes later, they were finished. Jay put on some khaki colored short, his Sean John light colored button down shirt white with sky blue, and khaki stripes. His white (S dots) low cut. He put on his watch, as he grabbed his money out of his pocket from the clothes he had dropped on the floor. He picked up the rest of their clothes, as well.

Lulu has on her Lace pink, French cut thongs with matching bra looking as good as ever Jay thought, as he looked her up and down.

"You like what you see? So I got your attention right, that's what I want all the time if you gotta think of me naked nigga! Then that just what you need to do." She spat.

"Yeah I see your sexy ass over there but feel me on this, if I wanted some one or something else do you think I would be out here getting this money, for us? Now ask yourself that!, And if the answers no then you answered, your own question." Jay reasoned.

As Jay steps outside he sees Megan laying out tanning. Looking sweet enough to eat but Jay says nothing, and just tries to walk by.

As she clears her throat.
"Damn! Just gonna walk right by huh? Just cause you feeling guilty about giving me her dick, don't mean you can't give me some conversation, does it?" Megan stated.

Jay plays it off.
"Naw it aight even like that! With them shades on, I thought you were sleep so what's been up?" He asked.

"Oh it aight nothing Jay, but what's really good? Can I get some play, or what? I mean damn your young it aight like you two are getting married any time soon, right? Be young, have fun and fuck me tonight about 8:00, I'll be waiting." She spat

Jay just looked at her like she was crazy as he got up and walked around and saw Tay-Tay. Leaning against his truck that was shinning like it just came from the dealership and Lulu's had the same shine.

"Oohh hoo damn old head! You put your thing down, what this hitting for huh, holla at me!?" Jay barked. Showing his appreciation

"Hell man, you gave me a dove for my daughter just give me a little, so I can get me a taste."

"Look, I'm aight no preacher but if you left that shit alone, and opened up a little detail shop here in the hood! You could kill em' baby no doubt but here you got my shit, glassy."
Jay handed him, a fifty.

Tay-Tay's eye's lit up like spot lights he had just met Jay about a month ago. He heard that the young man had cash, but being a crack-head he was use to the other dealers throwing him ten or fifteen dollars for double the work on their cars, and bikes. But Jay treated people with respect, and never when against his better judgment, and that's why people took to him, like a moth to a fire.

Chapter 25

Jay and Lulu decided to take the motorcycles for a spin.

Megan ran around the side of the house when she heard the sound of the bikes start up. Being that Jay said he would take her for a ride next time, he had it out.

Jay was kneeling down on one knee, checking his bike as he revved it up. Lulu was sitting on hers doing the same, as she put on her helmet, she turned to Jay.

"Catch me, if you can babe!"

She turned back the throttle, and popped the clutch as the bike screamed smoking the tires and all. Jay quickly put on his helmet, and took off after her. Not seeing Megan calling for him, to wait.

It took him awhile, but he finally caught up with her, as they continued to ride. They pulled into a gas station that had to have been people coming from a motorcycle meeting or something. Cause there were about 20 bikes, in the gas station. This one girl came up to Lulu.

"Wow, nice bike my name's Petra that's my bike over there."

She said pointing to an older 600 hurricane.
"So, how long have you been riding?" She questioned.

"Bout 5yrs give or take, why how long have you been riding?" Lulu replies.
The girl turned and walked away, while Lulu was talking, she goes over and starts up her bike and pulls over to Lulu.

"You should get something smaller if your just beginning, that's how people get hurt out here thinking theses are toy trying to look all cute, and shit!"

The girl said with a strong island accent, looking Lulu up and down.

Jay had paid for the gas and was on his way back to the pump when he saw the two, both off their bikes up in each others face arguing.

Jay came in between them.
"Ho, hold on what going on out here?"
As another guy from what Jay thought was from their club, came over.

He spoke

"Well it looks to me like your little girl friend just argued herself in to a race, that will cost her that nice little bike of hers."

Jay turned to the guy

"Is that right? Says who?" Jay barked.

Then Jay turned to Lulu.

"Baby, what's going on?"

"This chick thinks, cause she got a motorcycle jacket on

and I don't, that she can ride better than me, or something".

"So, are you gonna sit there and talk about it, are ya'll gonna find out?"

"I'm sorry, but who are you? I didn't get your name". Jay asked the guy with an annoyed look, on his face.

"All you need to know boss! Is that theses are my grounds, your on so theses are my terms, the race is on and the bike is up, pink slips you got that?"

"Yeah, well it's like this being that for the time being it's just me and my girl, what's the guarantee if we win, you won't stiff us and not give us your bike?"

"Tell you what, I'll call my man mike right now he has a pick-up truck he'll meet us at the race sight if she wins, where a club of our word her bike will be loaded on that truck, and my man will follow you to where you need him to go cool?" Mike answered.

Jay and the kid shake hands.
"I'm feeling that, damn I always wanted one of them, bike too."
Jay said with a chuckle, as they walked away from one another.

As all the members of his club started up their bikes. He yells "follow us" Lulu finished filling up, as she looked at Jay.

Jay seen Lulu ride at high speeds, but could she race? That, he would soon, find out.

As they come from behind this old warehouse. They come to a long straight rode. All the bikers park lined up on one side. Jay park across facing them, Lulu did the same.

"This is and old air port strip, it's about a mile long small planes used to use it it's smooth straight up and down If you care to ride down and see for yourself now there's a white line here".
He said pointing towards the ground.
"And there's a red line a mile and a quarter down that's the finish line but here's the deal each side has a sensor If she rolls over that side this radio will go off and if our girl wins, this side goes off so we will both know from here who won, got it?"

Jay looks at Lulu as he waves her over to the line. The girl Petra is already behind the line.

Lulu pulls up to the line, as she holds her front brake and spins her wheel, she slides from side to side. She sees the girl Petra give her a nasty look.

"Okay, on the count of three it's a go 1, 2, 3."

They both take off in a hurry. Only Petra, spun her tire a little too much because Lulu got a nice jump on her, and from there It was no catching her, Lulu Leaned down on the tank, as she peeked in her mirror, she saw Petra trying to catch up she just gave her bike a little more throttle a smile went across her face, as she blew pass the guy with the truck. Tickled cause she burned the girl.

Happy, she won Jay his bike.

Jay rode his bike down the run way to greet her.
"Damn! Baby girl, were did you get the race track, reflexes? You were great".

Jay picked her up, and spun her around they kissed as they both turned to Petra.

Who gave them, a look of death.
If looks could kill, Jay and Lulu would have both dropped dead.
"Well a bet is a bet, key please."
Jay said as he held out, his hand.

She threw it at Lulu, but Jay caught it.
Lulu said to Jay under her breath
"Humm so ones, a soar loser".

"Excuse me! My man please hand back the key, please."
Jay tossed the key back at the guy, as a blank look went across Lulu's face like they, were about to be robbed.
"Now bitch! I need you to walk over to them, and hand them the key and this title, you think you can do that?"

He said in a hostel tone towards Petra, her eye's lit up as she took the key and the title from him and slowly walked it over to Jay and put it into his hand.

As two other guys where putting the bike into the back of the truck.
Jay turned towards the guy.
"Thanks your right, you're a man of his word, I like that it shows great character."
Jay went to shake the guys hand.
After he shook Jay's hand, he turned to see Petra crying.
The guy goes over to comfort her, as he lifts her chin he violently smacks her.

"You stupid bitch! First you embarrassed me, by telling me you could beat her now that you lost, you want to cry I tell you what go with Mike in the truck, so you can see them load your bike off, like they loaded on then just then, maybe it'll sink in, that you can't race for shit". He spat

His words crushed her, more than losing the race.

She stands there trembling, with her mouth open.

He puts his hand over her face (mugs her) as he pushes, her away.

"Go, and take off that jacket your no longer with this club until you prove yourself by winning a race or something, oh I almost forgot, and until you get your own bike." He stated as he laughed out loud.

Jay looked at the guy like he wanted to do something, but quickly decided against it, seeing he was really out numbered. Lulu told the guy Mike, sitting in the truck to follow her and Jay.

Jay started up his bike, as Lulu did the same Petra climbed into the truck as they took off.

Chapter 26

Meanwhile...

Noah meets a girl he's been talking to at his new Job. She's short pretty "Rican" jaun he's feeling her, plus she's throwing the pussy at him like a quarter back, no doubt. Well one day their talking about sex and Noah's kicking it to her.

" Okay! It's like this if you aight all talk, ride with me to lunch my cars out front." She ordered.

At lunch, they roll down to K.F.C. they go in order their food, get it and go out to the car.

She tells him to get in the back seat, she gets in the front drives around the building and parks on the side. Before he can ask what was she doing, she had got in the back seat with him, as she put his food up front she had him pressed up against the door kissing him on his neck, his ear as she fought to get his pants down.

"Stop being nervous, the windows are tinted." She spat.

At this Noah got a little more aggressive, he pulled out her hair clip her hair fell in her face. He could see the lust in her eye's as they almost rip each others clothes off. They were both naked in the backseat as Noah struggled to get in a position as he caught a glimpse of that pussy, she pulled at his stiff dick she got in position to suck it.

As her hot sexy lips slid over his dick head Noah thought he would explode he looked down, she was looking up with her deep brown eye's he then grabbed the back of her head and almost cause her to choke, as he pushed his dick down her throat as he watched the spit form out the corner of her mouth.

He then got her up, he slipped on a condom. As she got on top of him she was nice and wet, as he got into her with ease, she was bouncing up and down on him while facing forward, holding the back of the front seat Noah grabbed a hand full of her hair, and pulled her back she then had her feet on his knees as he sucked on her neck, she moaned

"Damn! We gotta get back, to work." She reasoned.

Noah pound harder, into her pussy from behind as her face turned red, and she started talking dirty

"Awe poppy, fuck me poppy, fuck me oohh!" She screamed.

They where both out of breath, as they scrambled to get their clothes back on. Noah ate on the drive back to the job, Serenna just talked.

But when they showed back up at work, by the next break. It was all over. People whispering. " look at the hickey on her neck her hair all out, she didn't leave like that."

Serenna didn't care, however Noah didn't like everyone, in his business.

Noah pulled her over to the side.
"So what's up, with that?" He questioned.

"What's up with what! Noah chill jealously is and ugly trait let the haters hate." She spat.

"Okay maybe your right! But if anyone ask you, it's our business cool?"
"Of course Noah baby I'm feeling you and trust me I'm not gonna let a few assholes get in between what we got here".

———————————————

Meanwhile…

Once Mike reached where Jay and Lulu were

staying, when he pulled up behind Jay he noticed the Porsche in the drive way.

"DAMN! THESES KIDS ARE LIVING LARGE, LOOK AT THEIR SHIT."

That's what Petra did as her tears flowed freely down her face all she could think about was her bike was about to be gone.

It wasn't even her's, it was her brother's who was away at college.

She thought of what could she tell him about his bike, after all, he was always telling her she couldn't ride, she didn't have the reflexes it took to race. How could she tell him he was right, at his expense?

Mike called her name, she snapped out of her stupper.

"I KNOW YOU DON'T WANT TO DO THIS BABY GIRL, BUT RULES ARE RULES."

"I know, I know but you think there's a way I could make a deal with them?"

Mike looked at her wondering, could she really be this naive?

"BABY GIRL, YOU NEED TO TAKE THIS ONE ON THE CHIN, AND LEARN FROM THIS EXPERINCE, NO DOUBT. THAT'S WHAT YOU NEED TO DO." He repeated.

Mike hopped out the truck, and began taking two

boards off that he put together, and then slowly rolled down the bike.

Mike shook Jay's hand, and jumped into the truck and took off.

A smile went across Lulu's face, as she looked in the truck at Petra crying her eye's out. Not knowing, that Petra had plans of meeting her again.

Chapter 27

Meanwhile…

The two dicks (detectives)where getting close to Jay and Lulu.

They had actually rode pass Lulu while she was outside washing her V.W. bug but they had no clue, to who she was.

Jay was out by the pool on the lap top he had become accustom to, looking for a nice house for him and Lulu.

She was not aware, but he had put in a bid for a nice little house he had even hired a guy, to act as his father. For him to go look at the house.

A week had pass sense the race, Jay had put a lot of thought into what he was going to do with the bike Lulu had won, and gave to him.

That night…

Jay was creping with just his shorts and his sandals to go hit Megan off a little dick. When he saw Mike and two other guy's from that "motorcycle club" getting ready to steal Percy's, Porsche. They hadn't seen him so he quickly went back to the pool house where he got his gun and shook Lulu.

"Baby get up! These's nigga's trying to play us, sweet".

"What are you talking about, what's going on?" She said still half sleep.

He repeated himself, only louder.

"BABY GET UP, THEM NIGGA'S TRYING TO STEAL PERCEY'S SHIT, WE GOTTA RIDE ON EM'!"

At this she jumped to her feet, grabbed her gun and followed Jay out.

Once they turned the corner Jay and Lulu saw them not only trying to get the Porsche, but her car and Jay's truck as well. That's when Lulu let off the first three shots, BOOM' BOOM' BOOM' it sounded like she was shooting from a small cannon. As one fell to the ground, the other two turned and tried to run. As Jay caught one in the back of the leg.

Car alarms, and house alarms the same where going off like crazy, the Police would be on the scene in a matter of seconds, Jay thought.

He's in his shorts and she's standing in a half shirt with thongs on.

"Baby! What are we going to do?" She spat.

"Go get dressed, get one bag and you know which one I'm talking about! And let's bounce." Jay screamed.

She runs and puts on a pair of sweats, some socks her A- one's, as she comes back out with the bag and the lap top. Jay kicks the body over in the driveway, as he sees it was the Leader of the bike gang. They get into her car and drive off

Lulu's up driving all night until Jay tells her where to go.

They pull into to WILLIAMS PORT, LOCK HAVEN. The center of P.A.

Jay telling her to go here, and turn here, like he knows the place.

"Okay pull into that drive way".

"Jay baby, who lives here?" She questioned.

"Nobody baby, don't you see the for sale sign?" He replies.

"But it's like four in the morning, don't you think we look a little crazy in a neighborhood we never been just rolling up in a driveway?", She asked.

"True , true, your right I tell you what, let's find a motel to lay our heads till morning."

"Now that's a plan Jay baby you know I'm with you right?"

"Hell I hope so baby don't even say it I know your scared, don't sweat it trust me all else fells I'll take that, it's me and you no truer two baby I'm gonna ride for us but let's not think like that we'll be cool I'm setting us up forever not just for tomorrow, baby forever!!! You feeling that!" Jay stated.

"Yeah boo I feel you".

"Then let's ride we'll throw them "bows" when we have to feel me? Meanwhile, what kinda old school jams you got up, in here".

She hits the C.D. changer, and Al Green comes through the speakers "Let's stay together" as Al Green's cooing "Let's stay together"

"All naw, that's my shit right there".

They drive for another ten minutes, until they find a place to lay their heads she pulls into the parking spot.

This old white guy is up front sitting on a milk crate, with some dirty cut off overalls.

Jay jumps out the passenger side, and asks the old aged white man for a room, just assuming it was his place.

"We only take cash! That's a fancy looking car you

got there little lady", as he smile showing his brown and yellow teeth with a tooth pick hangin' from the corner of his wide mouth, that's seen better days.

When he saw the stack of money Jay pulled out his pocket, he was in awe.

He called out to what looked to be his wife.
"May, May sweet heart! Get theses young people one of our best rooms, and make them some of your famous lemon aid, will ya?" He ordered.

"No please, don't go out of your way for us we don't want to put you through any trouble." Jay reasoned.

The short elderly woman, who looked like she couldn't hear waved Jay her way, as they got to the room. Jay went inside and sat down on a chair in the corner, thinking to himself this is pretty cozy. It had a small fire place, hard wood floors with a throw rug under the bed.

Lulu had stayed behind talking to the old man, about who knows what.

Jay's cell phone rang, he answered it and started getting excited as he talked into the receiver. He sat in the chair and continued his convo-

"Okay, okay, well my father was looking forward to this call, yes he can western union that amount tomorrow, about noon? Okay, okay yes well I'll be there to get the keys he's very, very busy this time of year okay, yes it was nice talking to you to okay, thank you good bye."

Jay ended the call. Feeling the best ever, the house was theirs. But just how was he to, tell Lulu? First things first, he had to get in touch with Megan.

He though of what to say to her then just dialed her number she answered, as if expecting his call that very minute.

"Well, well, well, if it aight "the most wanted" right now, on the phone where are you Jay babe, I was worried sick about you?"

" Look I'll call you back from the diner down the street this place is hot okay wait for my call, give me about twenty minutes cool?"

"No doubt! Smart thinking, hit me back a.s.a.p. one".

They hang –up

Just then Lulu comes into the room.

"Okay! I'm feeling this It feels personal that's cool, so you call Jason yet?"

"No, but I called Megan".

Lulu hearing this got a weird look, on her face.

"What was that look for Lulu baby, you think I'm just gonna leave the bikes, and my truck?"

"First of all Jay, the 600 I just won you is in the shop, so we can get that back no doubt but as far as the others shit! Jay baby, what are you thinking".

She said hitting herself up side her forehead, with her other hand on her hip.

"Jay, that's exactly what were gonna do, I won't let you take that chance of going back, we got too much to loose".

Her words, hit Jay like a ton of bricks. Just then he thought of the house he wanted to surprise her with, and it all fell into place her words alone with her movements and if he wasn't sure before he was now. He really had his "Bonnie," his ride or die bitch, no doubt.

"You know what! You are absolutely right, girl what would I do without you?"

"I'm gonna go run your water, so you can relax okay?" Jay stated.

"That's what's up?" Lulu answered.

Jay walked over to his Bag and thought damn! We gotta go shopping within' the next couple days. He was looking at three outfits they each had three outfits packed into their " get-out-of town-quick" bag Jay thought to himself, but now they were gonna not have to be on the run. And they would have their own closets damn most people waited most of their lives to get a house, here he was doing it big 17 going on 18.

He slid his gun under his pillow, as he undressed down to his boxers.

Lulu came out of the bathroom with just her boy shorts and half shirt.

As Jay went back to the scene of the shoot out, her standing there holding that big gun, looking sexy as all hell whew!!

"Girl if there's any women who looks as sexy as you, wearing that!"

He said looking her up and down as he walked passed her turning his head around looking at her ass.

"Let me tell you they would be hard pressed, damn baby! All that?"

"Would you stop and go and get in your bath?" She ordered.

"Will you come and wash my back?"

"Of course, just call me when your ready".

While Jay was in the tub, his cell phone rang, as he thought damn, that's Megan, what was he gonna tell her?

He pick-up an began to talk.

"What's up? Naw, there's been a change of plans, listen".

As Jay went down to a whisper, as for Lulu not to hear him

"Give me a week to get back to you cool, yeah but

it's still too hot okay, okay, yeah I know your down I know you wouldn't set me up, that's not the point".

They hang-up

Jay just lay there as a million and one thoughts, go through his head.

Lulu calls to Jay, as he snaps out of his thought.

"Baby! You want anything from the store?" She inquired, from the other side of the door.

She grabs the lap top and the money, she was gonna put it in the trunk.

Jay chilled in the tub, for a while longer as he though he heard a knock at the door.

As he stepped out of the tub and wrapped the towel around his waist. He went to answer the door he opened the door all he saw was police lights, and the back of what looked to be a sheriff walking away from the door. Jay almost went into shock, as he tried to close the door slowly he quickly put on his sweat pants, and his sneakers. and went to the bed and snatched his gun from under the pillow.

As he heard another rap at the door Jay was climbing out the side window, as he heard the door come crashing down behind him. He thought two things, as he ran with his shirt in his hand, one he grabbed his gun, and not the money or the lap top. And, thought about getting into a shoot out with them.

Cause without that, they had nothing. He was

jogging down the street he heard the sounds of sirens and ducked into a yard and hid behind a tree.

Jay's heart was in his ass, he couldn't seem to think as his phone rang. He quickly answered not looking to see who it was.

"Baby, what happened! Where are you?"
Her voice came across the phone, Jay was now at ease.

"I don't know".
"I'm riding down a well lit street".
Jay yells, "stop!"
As he came out, and jump into the car.
"Just drive, baby I fucked up I left the money and the lap top".

"No you didn't Jay, I got that in the trunk."
"Lu baby don't bullshit me?"
"I'm not I thought that if we were to get ran up on, hey! If one of us got to the car I know you wouldn't leave with out me and you know I'm not going no where, without my man, Right?"

"So what now, Jay?"
"We go put this car in storage and take a nice trip, relax, and regroup how's that sound?"

The following day, Jay got up early in some pain.
They slept in the car after Lulu got tired of driving. Jay walked down the street to a dollar store. Where

he went in, and grabbed a few things a bottle of water some tooth paste, and two wash clothes. He then went to the dunking' donuts, where he ordered two medium coffee's and a half a dozen donuts.

While the girl was getting his order, he dip into the bathroom where he washed up quickly, with the little bar of lever 2000, he washed under his arms, and around his neck. As he used the bottle of water he brushed his teeth as he rinsed out, with the bottle of water. He heard a rap at the door, he quickly got his stuff together, and walked passed and older man, as he went to the counter and got his order.

After he paid for his order, he put a five dollar bill, into the tip cup and he was gone.

He walked back to the car, and got in. As he closed the door Lulu woke up.

"Uhmm that coffee smells good, Jay baby."

"Damn baby! Here take a few sips of this coffee to help kill that dragon trying to get out of your mouth, whew! Ya breath is bangin"

"Fuck you nigga! You got jokes early in the morning, huh?"

"Oh I almost forgot I got you a wash cloth and some toothpaste so you can get yourself together, cool?"

"Jay, you must have bumped your mother fuckin' head, running from the cops last night, huh? I'm not stopping at some rest stop, and running in the bathroom like some nut ass nigga! We getting a room we gonna go shopping, so we can get ready to jet that way, we can pack chill and think, so just pump your brakes?"

"Okay, I feel you on that". He replies.

They sit in the car and drink their coffee, Lulu reaches into the box of donuts and grabs her favorite, "toasted coconut".

"Damn! Is this donut this good, or am I just that hungry?
Probably a combination of both, I know my neck is stiff as shit from sleeping in that car, no doubt".

"Well start this thing up, and let's roll out hey put that `Marvin Gaye` in again".

"So Jay tell me again, how you started listening to the oldies?"

"It's not how, it's more like why well at first it was because when I was in the foster home we would get money for doing different jobs and shit like that, and once a week we would be aloud to go shopping for whatever, well I use to get all the latest `rap shit,` but the kids who didn't do shit didn't have shit so they would steal other people stuff, or you would lone some one something and they would leave with it, but no one listen to that old shit, so I started listening to it and I fell in love with it, but mostly (Marvin Gaye, Sam Cooke, and Al Green) but I also like, different ones like (Lionel Richie, Luther Vandross, Ray, Goodman and Brown etc.)

Lulu just drove, as she leaned back (Marvin Gaye's) "troubled man" came through the speakers.

"Their you go! That's the shit right there."
Jay said as he took another sip of his coffee.
They went another few miles down the street, as they pulled into a Motel 6.
Jay hopped out to get them a room as he walked across the court yard of the hotel parking lot all Lulu could do was stare at his little ass.
She loved how her baby walked to be little. Jay had a swagger like a ball player walking like he was 6' 7," when in reality he was just big in the way he handled life. He was a go getter no doubt, and that's one thing that attracted not just Lulu, but a hand full of women, to him.

Jay came back with the card as they got their room they backed the car up to their room door, which was on the ground level. Jay popped the trunk and got the bags out, as he asked Lulu

"So, did you forget that the beetle's trunk is in the front or what?"
"Actually smart ass this that new shit, it's in the back".

She said, with a chuckle.

Lulu grabbed her stuff and made a beeline, towards the bathroom.

Jay turned on the lap top, and e-mailed Mrs. Jenkin's about getting the key's, before they left for their little "get a way".

Then Jay went on the net, and got them some tickets for the following day to go to Maine, he thought to himself where gonna have some fun.

Then Jay called the "Cream Squad" Face answered.

"What's up Face, how's everything going?"

There was a brief pause, on the other end of the phone.

"Well look, there's been a change of plans I'm fucked up right now, I just ran into some problems. Naw, naw nothing like that, do me a favor is Button's there? Let me, holla at that nigga right quick".

"Jay baby, what's crackin'! If you going through something, that my team can help you out with talk to me?"

" Button's that's good looking but, it's nothing like that. But what you can do is look me out, on another truck?"

"Say no more, when you need it by?"

"Next meeting, a week cool?"

"You got it baby boy, you got it. Big Paul get with you yet?"

"No not yet why, what's really good?"

"You, you got at least four hundred thousand coming to you Jay baby the streets is loving you, right now!"

Jay heart almost skipped a beat as he sat up from the bed.

"He's going up near State College, to take care of some property up there".

"Word! That aight that far from me, I'll hit him up I'll get the next list out to you cool?"

"Alright baby boy stay up I'll holla one"-

(they hang-up)

Lulu comes out of the bathroom, feeling like a new woman.

"Who was that, Jay?"

"That was face your not gonna believe how close, Big Paul is to us right now with our money."

Jay calls Big Paul...

He answers

"What's up big boy! I know you know who this is?" Jay spat.

"OF COURSE, THIS BIG MONEY ON THE

OTHER END OF THIS PHONE, WHAT'S HAPPENING PEOPLE? WHEN YOU GONNA GET ALL THIS MONEY OUT OF MY HAND?"

"That's the thing, Button's told me you was up near State college? I'm right near there myself, you want to meet?"

"JUST TELL ME WHEN AND WHERE, AND IT'S ON PEOPLE'S".
"You know where the Motel 6 is?"
"THERE'S ONLY TWO UP HERE, ONE WITH OUT A POOL"-
"That one!" Jay shouted.

"NO PROBLEM PIMPIN', I'LL SWING THROUGH THERE IN AN HOUR ONE"-
(they hang up)

An hour later on the D.O.T. big Paul was pulling up in his Hunter green sitting on 22" rims 300m.

Jay went to the car with the tinted windows knowing It could be no other than big Paul, cause he always had some "hot wheels".

Jay shook the big man's hand as it seemed to swallow his up.
"What's crackin' big boy? Damn I missed you".

"WELL THAT'S GOOD TO HEAR, JAY BUT

IT'S ALL YOU JAY BABY WE NEED TO GO SOME WHERE AND TALK".

" No problem, what's really good follow me".

Jay turns and walks into their room, big Paul follows behind.
"DAMN YOU STILL FUCKIN' WITH THESE ROOMS, HUH?"

"It aight even like that big boy, I'm makin' moves dogg, believe that".

"THAT'S GOOD TO HEAR, LOOK I'M GONNA HAVE TO TURN YOUR CREW AWAY, FOR A WHILE COOL?"

"Hold up! Naw that's not cool what's up?" Jay stated, looking at Big Paul uneasy.

"JAY BABY, "CREAM SQUAD" IS GETTING SLOPPY, YOU NEED TO TALK TO THEM THEIR ABOUT TO MESS UP ALL THIS BIG MONEY AND I DON'T WANT TO SEE IT GO, BUT I DON'T WANT TO GET SENT UP EITHER FEEL ME?"

"Jay I've never seen a young bol like yourself, bring in almost a million dollars in two months yeah, we all eating but you know how nigga's is, somebody was bound to fuck it up. Big Paul said as he took it down to a whisper".

"Okay! I feel you, I'll call the team tonight I'll holla at Smash and I'm gonna get outta here for about a week, and hopefully when I get back, we'll get back to this good money thing, no doubt".

"OKAY YOUNGSTER YOU TAKE CARE OF THAT SEXY LITTLE WOMAN OF YOURS AND HIT ME UP WHEN YOU COME BACK IN TOWN COOL?"
"I got you big boy stay safe, one love baby".

They give each other the "black hand shake", as they pull each other close, touch shoulders and break.
Big Paul hands Jay the bag.
"THAT'S ALL YOU, BIG PIMPIN' PUT THAT SOME WHERE SAFE YOUNGSTER".
No doubt, as Jay grabs the bag.
"Damn! That's heavy".

Chapter 28

Jay went back inside, and called the "Cream Squad".

Face answered.

"Yo! It's Jay what's up? Let me holla at Smash".

Face holla's into the back ground, not covering the phone.

Damn! What the fuck you screaming in my fuckin' ear for, man?" Jay spat, annoyed.

"Smash what's happening baby? Words out ya'll making it hot out there look we still cool but being, that's your team cool em' out for a week, get back to being hungry, and let's all eat without one nigga fuckin' it up for the rest of us you feel me?"

"Okay, okay, I understand that". Smash replied.

"But listen I'm putting together a nice list that could bring us in a lot of cheese, (money) but you gotta pull the chains on your dogs we can't have them calling the shots if you want this to go off smooth, so give me a week and I'll get back in touch with you, cool?" Jay reasoned.

(They hang up)

The whole time Jay was on the phone, Lulu was running around in her thongs putting thing away, Jay was talking on the phone. But his dick was hard as a brick, as he got up and made his way over to her. He got up behind her, she could feel his dick on her.

"Jay baby, your nasty".
As he started singing "next" too close.

"Step back your getting kinda close, I feel a little poke, from you." He cooed.

She started laughing.
"Awe, your crazy".
As they both strip down and fucked, until they could no more.
"Come on, lets get outta here".
"What do you mean, I thought we were sleeping here?"
"No! We'll get another room, down the street".

"Why, because big Paul was here?"
"Look stop asking all these questions, and let's just go you feel me?"
Jay cut her a look.
She quickly started getting everything together, then she turned to him and said.

"You don't trust, big Paul?"

"Baby I don't trust any one, but you! It's not even about that, look were on a whole different level now we just had a nigga drop off a little under a half million dollars, an how long ago did we meet "Big Paul" huh? Come on Lu baby do the math, it's dog eat dog on theses streets, you aight no stranger to danger you know, what it's hittin' for".

"Your just a little relaxed, cause the money that's coming in and you use to everybody doing you dirty but believe me theses boys we getting money for, even thou we all eating, jealousy is a motherfucker!! Don't think for a second, theses streets love us".

"You done! Naw I'm just fuckin' around no I feel you, and your right I did get a little comfortable, but that's only cause I got you and I never had anything, until you came and rescued me".

"Baby we rescued each other no doubt! And it's time we get them tattoos".

Chapter 29

XX-Rated

Meanwhile…

Noah runs into this guy Pete. They started just kickin' it after work a few times next thing you know their together all the time.

Pete's what you call a "Hack". He always had money, but not in hand money he used a credit card for everything. One day when they were coming out of the movies, Noah asked him what was it he did for money. Cause Noah worked, and Pete was up at his Job he had all the time in the world to play games hang out with girls you name it.

"Okay! You really think your ready for this, we boys right?"

"No doubt! Come on, don't play me like that".

Noah said giving Pete a slight punch, on the shoulder.

"Well I took a computer coarse at " Pennco tech" and let's just say I met up with this girl, who showed me a few things after I banged her back out a few times you see I can get into bank accounts, and move money around so I went to a bank with my last two hundred dollars put it in, and I just add to it from other peoples accounts, got me?"

"Get the fuck outta here! Are you serious?"

"Hell yeah! I'm serious It's sweet all you gotta do, is stick to the rules and it's all gravy baby".
They both share a laugh.

"Look I already broke one of my own rules, by letting you know what's up I mean you cool people and all, but I did just meet you".

"I feel you".

"But if we keep kickin' it, trust me I'll put you on, no doubt".
"That's what's real, I hear you but.. well uh?"
"What?"
Pete could tell by Noah's body language, that he was in need of some cash, right now.
" Look, let's meet up tonight about 7:oopm feel me?"

"Yeah, that's sounds cool why what's good?"

"I'm working on something, I'll put you "D" later cool?"

They give each other dap, and Pete steps off.

Later, that night…

Pete calls Noah's spot.
"Yo, what's good?"

"I'm just laid up, watching a little T.V. why what's crackin' wit you?"

"Look, I got something for you, you feel like going out? I got a couple "chicken heads" coming through the spot in a minute If you feel like getting your dick wet, tonight?"

"Oh! Hell yeah that's what I'm talking about, how mine look?"

"All shit! What you mean, "what mine look like?" Don't tell me you one of them, "get attached kids" huh? They just a couple of birds, what's good?"

There's a pause, on the other end of the phone.

"What's up? Yo! You there?"
"Yeah, I'm here."

"Look we gonna fuck these's bitches, and it's a wrap You wit it or what?"

"Look come scoop me in the " hoopdie" and I'll show you dog".

"That's my man, give me about ten minutes cool".

Pete came through within five minutes, and they rolled out.

They rode for about another 10 minutes, and they pulled into the P.J.'s (projects) Pete laid on the horn, as Two nice looking girls appeared in the dim door way.

Pete screamed out his half rolled down window.

"YO! WHAT THE FUCK ARE YA'LL WAITING FOR,COME ON".

He said with irritation in his voice.

As, the two girls hurried across the street.

The short thick one, opened the passenger door where Noah was sitting. Noah stepped out and pulled up the seat, as the two got in back.

Pete snapped.

"Come on Stacy, what the fuck I tell you about wearing all that shit! We fucking, or having a fashion show?" He spat.

Noah was shocked at how Pete was grillin' the girls, but more so cause they seem to like it.

"Can't teach a young bitch new tricks, but we gonna try tonight! Huh Noah?"

They both laughed out loud, as they drove back to Pete's spot.

As Pete pulled up to this Nice sized house. On a beautiful street, Noah quickly asked-

"Damn player, you balling hard huh?"

"Naw, this aight my spot". As he continued to drive around back. And parked, there was an in ground swimming pool, as they got out the car Pete pointed up. On the back top half of the house, you could see the light coming through these huge ceiling to floor windows.

"This my parents crib but up there, is all mine".

As they make their way up the side steps, to Pete's private entrance. They went inside Noah was in awe of the place, as he could see the look on the one girls face, she was never their either.

"Look Noah my man help yourself. "me-casa- sue-casa"

"You know anything about this, right here?", Pete said leaning on the billiard sized, pool table?

"Of course! We use to have one years ago". He stated, lying.

The girls were on the love seat, giggling.

As Pete pulled Noah to the side. "Here check this out." As Noah looked in the closet Pete had opened, it was then Noah knew they were in for a long night. Before him was shelf after shelf, of sex toys.

"Believe me when I tell you Noah, we gonna fuck these bitches tonight son, you ready?"

  Pete walked over to the girls, and told the one girl "Nina".

"Look, why don't you and your friend go get ready in there he said pointing to the bathroom?"

She nodded her head in agreement, as she got up from the love seat, her friend was close on her heals.

Pete went back to the closet and got this huge black double sided "dildo" and some K.Y. jelly as he rolled out this throw rug. He started to get undressed right, there.

"Noah, I can tell your a little nervous don't be, these "chicken head" bitches aight here to get impressed, they here to fuck so look, that bowel right there on the coffee table, has all the condoms we gonna need feel me?"

With that being said, Pete grabbed the remote to the stereo an put on some "Pac, he came through the clear speakers "shorty wanta be a thug" as the two girls came out both where looking like run way models. "Nina" had on some teal green boy shorts, with matching lace bra, and Samantha was wearing black see through French cut thongs, with a bra that showed off her, hard nipples.

Pete dimmed the lights, as Noah was helped with his clothes coming off, by Samantha. Once they both had the girls in the nude Pete, was ready to put on a show.

"Come here Nina, what's your girl's name?" He inquired.

"Sam, just call her Sam". She ordered.

"Sam! Come here".

She came like she was told, as Noah looked on at what was happing. Pete got both girls to get doggie style facing away from each other, as he put the K.Y. jelly on the huge "dildo" and handed it to "Nina."

"Baby, you know what to do with that".

As she put the one end in Samantha' pussy, she was getting hotter watching Noah jerk off in front of her. But "Nina" putting that fat "dildo" into her waiting pussy, turned her on more. She put the rest into her own pussy as Pete and Noah looked on Sam put her finger in her mouth, as her hair fell into her face.

Noah went over to her about the same time Pete went over to Nina. They both got on their knees, and put their dicks into the girls mouth. Within' a few minutes Sam was about to gag as Noah came in her mouth but instead she let the cum drip down her chin.

As he glanced at the large mirror across the floor, looking at both girls rocking back and forth fucking themselves with the Dildo Noah's erection quickly came back but now, he was ready to fuck.

But he stayed kneeling in front on Sam rocking back and forth getting fucked by the dildo, and sucking his dick.

Pete got up and went to the closet Nina got up, and sat on top of Sam facing the other way, sitting on her ass Noah went around as he now was fucking Sam from behind, as he sucked on Nina's titties and finger fucked her at the same time.

Pete's started the video camera, when Nina saw what he was doing she started fucking his fingers, like a pro. Noah pulled her down, now their both side by side "doggie style" Noah pulled off the condom he had on, and got another one. But now he entered Nina from behind, as he fingered Sam.

Pete mounted the camera, and slipped on a condom. And put his dick in Sam as he rode her hard and fast. She screamed louder as he pulled hard at her hair, and smacked her ass.

Noah and Nina had went and got in the recliner, she bounced up and down on him Noah pulled her hair as he felt her hot juices on his leg. He had to peel himself off the leather recliner. He and Nina looked on at Pete fucking Sam like he was a robot she was in obvious pain her face was red she asked him to stop but he went on it's when Nina and Noah started walking towards the refrigerator That's when they noticed, Pete had a huge dildo stuck in her ass, as he still with one hand pushed it deeper inside her with the other hand he had a hand full of hair.

Nina pulled Noah close and whispered in his ear, as Noah was standing there naked drinking a " Nestea" Nina grabbed his dick and started jerking him off, so he could go over there and give her friend some relief from the madness, Pete was inflicting on her.

Nina went and got on her knees behind Pete and pulled his dick out of Sam. As she almost fell to the floor, but Noah was there to catch her. Now were he had saw fear in her eye's, she now felt a little relief as he put on another condom and fucked her slow. She know it wasn't love, but it felt good. As Sam turned around and saw Nina picking up where Pete had left off with her but Nina just smiled and winked her eye at Sam, as the four of them fucked the night away as the tape rolled on.

Chapter 30

The next morning…

Sam was the first to get up, as she had awoke laying next to Noah.

Pete was on top of Nina, as Sam looked around for her before noticing. She gave Noah a peck on the cheek, he woke up.

"What was that for?"

"Saving my ass, last night I saw what you did, and I don't know what you think of me? But thank you pain is only pleasure, when it's something you kinda look forward too I mean I'm a big girl and all, but I thought he was trying to rip me a new asshole with that thing".

"Look you think you and I could hook up again soon, just us two?"

"Yeah! Why not, I would like that here I'll give you my cell number."

As she got up, and looked for a piece of paper. She found a piece on the counter, and wrote down her numbers.

"Look let's keep what happens with us, between you and I, cool?"

"Come on girl, that should go without say, I aight the kiss and tell type."

"No offense, but that's what they all say".

"Hold on a sec! Didn't you and your girl, just fuck me and my man all night with a camera rolling, and now you want to be discrete? Your getting a little beside yourself, just a little, don't you think?"

"Look Noah, yeah I just met you and your man"-

And you knew what it was hittin' for, So what are you better than me now?, No, no, let me guess you don't usually do that kinda stuff, huh?" Noah barked.

Cutting her off, with a sarcastic tone.

"Okay, okay maybe I deserve that but don't just think, you got me all figured out young pup! Cause you don't and before you realize what it's, hittin' for?

Maybe, I'll be at another party fucking who knows, but I'll tell you this much I don't wear masks, I'm real, what you see, is what you get, I don't feel sorry for what the streets got me doing, I'm playing the cards I was delt and far as I'm concerned, I'm gonna ride this life, till the mother fucking wheels fall off I'm not in a position to change my cards, so I'll play em' out, that sound good to you?"

"I hear you, but why don't you and I go get something to eat before theses two, wake up?"

"That sounds good but if you think, I'm leaving my girl here alone with your crazy ass boy shit! You got another thought coming".

"Okay, I feel you on that he did get a little crazy last night but it was fun, I had a good time". Noah reasoned.

He said, looking for a response from her.
"I was having a good time with you, but I wasn't feeling your boy at all".

Two day's later…

Noah and Pete met up at the mall. Pete walked up to Noah with a slight grin on his face as he took Noah's hand and shook it firm in his as he pat him on the back with the other.

"So what's really good dog, you was bout It a few

day's ago with them "chickens" you like that?" He stated, playfully hitting him on the shoulder.

"No doubt! Why you got something else jumpin' off soon, or what?"

"Of course, but if you liked that your gonna love what I got brewing, for tonight."

"Tonight, you said?"

"Yeah nigga! Why, you got a date or something? If so, cancel that shit pimp, and bounce wit a player here I got something for you."

He said as he reached in his pocket of his Armani button down shirt, and produced a new credit card "visa Gold" with Noah's name on it with a bogus, last name.

"That's for you pimp, it's got a 10,000 dollar limit, just let me know when you get close to that, cool".

"Oh shit! That's what's up damn "Visa Gold!" it's everywhere I want to be".

They both shared a laugh, as they walked through the mall.

Noah got a few outfits as they shopped without a worry, and before they were done. Pete got a call on his cell and told Noah he had to step off, but told him the time to be there and they parted ways.

Noah went back to the little one room apartment he was renting and got showered. And put on his new clothes and walked about ten blocks to the motorcycle shop.

When it was said and done he left on a yellow Kawasaki "Ninja" with a matching helmet.

Two hours later...
He was pulling up to Pete's spot, as a few girl's came around him Pete went to the window to see what the commotion was about, that's when he saw Noah.

"Yo, up here, Noah!"
He hollered out the window, when he got Noah's attention he waved him up stairs.
As they gave each other a brotherly hug and a firm hand shake. He pulled Noah to the side.
"Yo son! You see what we got, tonight?"
"What! All theses women, you can't be serious?"

"Hell yeah! I'm serious, it's on and poppin' baby."
"Yeah I see you got you a little sumtin' sumtin' I feel you with the bike thing, it's hot but me I don't fuck wit them things like that, I mean I like looking at em,' and seeing other people ride em', but it's not me." He repeated.

" Damn! Look at shorty right there".
Noah said, pointing to a little Italian jaun, with long black hair and a fat ass.

" Oh yeah! She's nice, that's Lori she is "like that" thou well the nights young, you do you son I'm about to get a few drinks in me and that Blonde girl, right there". He stated as he walked away.

As the girl was walking by Pete pulled her close, and they went to get something to drink.

Noah looked her up and down humm, nice he though to himself, as the two of them walked away.

Noah went back outside. He came across Lori, eyeing him up, so he decided to talk to her.

"Hey, hi you doing I'm Noah and your?"
He said extending, his hand.
She took it and gave him a smile, that sent him on a cloud.
"I'm Lori, is this your bike? Well, I know it's your bike cause I seen you pull up on it, can you ride good?"

"Yeah yes I can why, you want to go for a ride don't you?" He asked sounding cocky.
"Hell yeah! Let's go, before this party really starts cool?"

"Yeah I feel you on that don't want to miss no action, huh?"
"Why did you say it, like that? Why, how long have you known this guy for?"

"I should be asking you the same thing, but on the real I've only known him for about 3 weeks, but it's been and interesting 3 weeks no doubt! He's a cool dude, a little weird at times but none the less he's cool".

"Well I heard the total opposite, sorry I heard your boy's a straight up dog, no let me rephrase that, he's the "bit bull" of dogs, that's what I've heard."
As he gets on the motorcycle she follows his lead, and does the same.

"So where you taking me big boy?"

He just started up the bike and turned the throttle, as it screamed he popped the clutch as the bike took off, with the quickness.

As they rode through the neighborhood. She tapped him on the shoulder as he pulled over. They were near a park as she went and sat on a swing, Noah got off the bike and kicked down the kickstand, and went and stood in front of her.

"So let me guess, you saw me and thought humm, it's one of them party's, so all I gotta do is pick out who I want to fuck and they gonna be about it, huh Is that what you thought Noah? Tell me the truth". She questioned, with a slight grin.

Noah just laughs, as he turns around she swings and kicks him in the butt.

"Come on girl! Theses jeans are new".
He said, as he dusted off the back of em'

"Look what you did!" He spat

"Awe poor baby well you know what, truth is I've been feeling you for a little while now anyway, I wanted to talk to you a while back when I saw you with that kid Jay they call him "Jay-razor" I need to get in contact with him, no doubt."

"What would be your business with him?"

"Oh, I just heard he was into making big moves, and I'm feeling that on the real".

"Well it just so happens, we are going to be hooking up when he comes back whenever that is, maybe I'll introduce the two of you depends on how you, treat me thou".

"Oh now you really think you're getting the puss, now huh?"

They both laugh.

As she gets off the swing and grab's his hand, and leads him to the bench where they share in their first kiss of the night.

"You know what, I'm really feeling this vibe of yours and that's no lie, but let do each other the favor If were gonna get to know each other let's start by being straight up real with one another, cool.? Now, with that being said you gotta promise me this, from this moment on, everything that comes out of your mouth is your real thoughts, no bullshit now let's see how real you are".

"That's a bet boy you aight saying nothing but a word, but how's this Noah what if I said I want to fuck you right here, right now? How real is that?!"

"Are you serious! Girl, it isn't even dark out yet!"

She unzips his pants and pulls out his dick. She looks him right in the eye's, she jerks him off for about 5 minutes not kissing him or anything just staring at him.

He's " rock hard" looking back into her pretty brown eye's.

"Oh, somebody's ready for work."

She went down on him It's only twilight time, so anyone walking by could see right there.

What's going on, but she handle her business like it was just the two of them in the privacy, of their own bedroom. She's licking up and down as she puts it into her mouth then pulls it out again as she smacks herself in the face with his dick, he pulls her long black hair to the side so he could look into her eye's, as she took his manhood into her mouth like a porn star.

But Noah was really into it, but he was still nervous as he got up and lead her behind the jungle gym, were it was a little more discrete. That's when he took full advantage, as he pulled out a condom, an put it on. He had her up against the slide as he fingered her.

He felt her wetness, and showed no hesitation as he penetrated her he learned fast, she was a screamer.

She got a look of fear mixed with pain, that quickly went away, as he went in and out of her slowly. But they had to quickly put back on their clothes as they heard a group of kids approaching carrying a radio, and bouncing a basketball.

The radio was playing Cassidy's "I'm a hustler".

"I like that song, that's probably gonna be one of our songs huh?
Noah just laughed, as they made their way back to the bike, he popped the seat off and removed a hand towel that he wiped his hands on, he looked her up and down. They got on the bike and quickly, went back to the party.

Once they get back to the party it's in full swing, Noah thought as they walked in on Pete in a sex act, with three girls in the middle of the floor two Chinese girls were in the sixty nine position at the other side of the room as Lori looked, at what was going on.

"I know, you want to get into some of that, huh? Before you answer, remember what we promised each other the truth."

"Your right, and yeah I would like to get into that."

"Well at least go wash up, before you get one of them chicken heads". She spat.
"Wait, are you telling me, you don't mind?"

"That's exactly what I'm saying Noah, be real I came to this party knowing there was gonna be fucking, as you did so do you, but don't get angry when I do me". As she kissed him lightly on the cheek an lightly rubbed her hand on his other cheek.

Noah was thinking, what next? He made his way towards the bathroom.

He got a fresh wash cloth, and dropped his pants and began washing up right when he was about to dry off his hands, he heard a knock at the door. He was thinking it was Lori but was in for a surprise when this nice looking white girl came in followed by a black girl, he had thought them to be lesbians.

But here they were the black girl was grabbing at his dick, as the white girl was behind him sticking her tongue in his ear.
She whispered into his ear.
"I was wondering if you were coming back, but now that you're here, I just want to see you cum".

The black girl was real aggressive, as she pulled hungrily at his dick, she quickly undid his belt and pulled his pants down to his knee's, she got on hers and took his now hard manhood into her mouth.

The other girl, followed suit as she got on her knee's Noah was a bit taken back.

"Hold on a sec! Ladies how about we all take this in another room preferably one with a bed, Cause I'm going to have to stretch for this by the way, what's your name?"

He asked the black girl.

"What do you want my name, to be tonight?" She replies.

"Cool, that's how we doing things, alright well you'll be, thing one and you, he said turning to the white girl, you'll be thing two yeah, I love Dr. Seuss".

He said as he cracked, a wicked smile.

He lead them across the crowded room, as he looked on, every one was into their own world. As he saw Pete, his eye's almost popped out of his head.

There was Pete giving head to a Chinese girl, who was wearing a strap on. As the other girl with the strap on was fucking him from behind the shock was. The girl was Lori, and she looked like she was having a ball.

He continued to make his way across the room to the open door, with the two girls in tow.

Once in the room, the two girls started to dance in front of Noah.

But, as they danced they slowly stripped each other, Noah looked on as he became hard.

Thing one, (the black girl) saw this, and went over to Noah as she pulled at his pants until his dick was out. As she went to work sucking hungrily at it, while she's bent over Noah's lying on his back thing two (the white girl) was behind the first girl with her tongue in her ass.

Noah was getting hot. He had the black girl's head from behind, pushing her up and down on his dick, until he was about to nut as he got up, still jerking his dick he grabbed the white girl and pulled them both down on the bed, now their both sucking his dick he cum's in the black girl's mouth, she shared with the white girl, as they both played with his hot sticky cum. It was dripping from the black girl's chin as the white girl licked it off, and stuck her tongue in her mouth.

Noah gets up, and finds a towel.

(Thing one-) "No, no, don't tell me your done? We didn't even fuck yet!"

"Nobody said anything about me rolling yet, but why don't you two get into something, until I'm ready"

" Oh you would like that, huh?"

"You damn right! So what you waiting for? Make it happen".

The white girl at this being said, took charge as she pushed the black girl down, on the bed.

She told her to spread her legs,

Come on bitch!, turn over, you know what I like.

The girl turned over, as she started fingering her with two fingers she could feel her juices flowing as her finger slipped in and out with ease, she sucked on her left tit as the girl started to squirm.

317

Noah looked on as he felt she was about to climax, he slipped on a condom and quickly joined in. He mounted the white girl from behind. She was a tight fit, but once he was in, he road her long and hard, she was now eating the black girl out as he pounded her hard, from behind. Her face was red as Noah now had both of his thumbs up her ass doing his, "butter fly". He continue to pound her until he was about to fall out, from being tired.

He didn't know when he was going to get a chance to do this again, so he took full advantage of the situation.

She screamed out. "Awe! I'm Cumming, I'm cu, cumming awe, ohh shit!!!"

That's when Noah pulled out, she turned to him.

With a smile on her face.

"Damn! What was that? I never came, that long or that hard before ever."

"Let's just say, my "butterfly" technique never fails".

They share a laugh.

"Well no offense but we need to get back, to the party I'll see you around, don't be a stranger". The black girl(thing one) said.

———————————————

Meanwhile... back in "Lock Haven" Det. Jake and Ms. Roberts are hot on Jay's trail.

"This little bastard! Has a high body count, and he has no certain weapon or style. It's gonna be hard, but theses kids gotta go down."

"Let's just hope we catch up to them, before they get another body".

"The thing that gets me, is how are they getting this money I mean the truck we got impounded along with the motorcycles, that's about 60,000 worth of vehicles and their how old? And I'm pushing a fucking "95 Neon".

"Tell me about it! Well I guess nobody told them, crime don't pay".

Chapter 31

Jay gets up from his full body massage, he goes to their room he calls the operator, and she dials out for him. With minutes, he's connected to "Big Paul".

"WHAT'S UP KID? DAMN A WEEK TO THE DAY HUH, ANYWAY HOW'S YOUR LITTLE VACAITON?"

"How you know?"

"COME ON JAY BABY, THE STREETS ARE WATCHING. AND I STAY IN THE STREETS NO DOUBT, BUT LET'S CHANGE GEARS FOR A SEC THIS MIGHT STING A LITTLE, BUT I GOT WORD THESES "TWO JAKES" ARE ASKING AROUND ABOUT YOU AND THEIR SHOWING PICTURES".

"Word! Look it's nothing, that's just them trying

to catch up with me for running away from the foster home".

"HUMM.. MAYBE HOMIE, BUT RIDDLE ME THIS, DID YOU LEAVE BY YOURSELF?"

"Yeah why? What's up look "Big Paul" stop stalling. What's really good stop talking in rhyme, what's the deal?" Jay questioned nervously.

"THEY ALSO SHOWED A PICTURE OF THIS YOUNG GIRL WITH YOU AND IT WASN'T YOUR SHORTYTHIS GIRL HAD A DIFFERENT NAME".

(With this being said, a chill ran down Jay's spine)

"Was the name… Pam?"
He said slowly, as he swallowed hard.
"THAT'S IT! SO NOW YOU TELL ME, WHAT'S UP YOUNGSTER?"

"Yo! I got that list I'll be back in town in two days, I'll hook up with you and tell you everything cool?"

"I GOT YOU, ONE"-
(they hang up)

Jay got the look on his face, like he saw a ghost, Lulu asked.
"What's wrong, baby?"

"Listen, we need to talk well let me rephrases that, I need to talk, you need to listen okay remember Pam?"

"Of course, Jay babe what's wrong?"

"Well, something went down and she was getting raped, and to make a long story short, we got a body".

"What? Are you telling me, you killed someone?"

"Look, I'm not gonna lie to you we might of got a couple body's and I don't want you to be in for a surprise, if they come".

"When they come, not if Jay when it's homicide, the Jakes are coming and as far as I'm concerned, it's me and you baby".

"Are you sure about this? Cause I can just give you some money, and you'll be straight?"

"I tell you what! Let's get theses tattoo's while were here, and then we'll be straight". She replies.

"So your serious about this, huh?"

"What the fuck! Did you think Jay I was bullshitting, all this time?"

———————————————————

Mean while… back at Big Paul's

Big Paul just got off the phone with a cop, who's a "little dirty" who just gave him some info. About Face and Smash getting caught-up in two stolen cars.

"IT'S ALL THE SAME, I DIDN'T WANT TO FUCK WIT THEM ANYMORE ANY WAY. BUT JAY WHEW! I WONDER IF HE'S STILL GONNA WANT TO RUN WHEN I GET THIS, NEW CREW".

Paul said, talking to his man C.J.
"Well it's like this pimpin,' if he don't want to roll, fuck him!"

"SEE, THAT'S YOUR PROBLEM YOUR SO QUICK TO CUT OFF A GAREENTEED MONEY MAKER LIKE THIS YOUNG BOY JAY, AND TRUST ME HE'S GOOD AT WHAT HE DOES SO YES I'M CONSERNED THAT HE MIGHT NOT WANT TO ROLL WITH THIS NEW CREW".

"Okay Big Paul your right I feel you, I feel you".

Mean while… back in Lock Haven Ms. Roberts is talking to Noah.
Jake, was across the street, getting coffee for the two of them.

While Ms. Roberts asked him a few questions, Noah played his part, by telling them a bunch of lies. Noah began walking away as her partner, was coming back, across the street.

"Who was that kid, you were talking to?"

"Just some kid that looked about Jason's age, so I thought it wouldn't hurt to ask him a few questions but the truth is, I don't think were getting anywhere, with this little town".

No sooner than she said that, crack head Tay-Tay came up to them.

With his breath hotter than ever, he spoke.

"How you two cops doing, on this fine day?"

He said with a yellow teeth smile, trying to sound proper.

"Excuse me! Where detectives, not cops and who might, you be?"

"Well let's just say for a few dollars, I might bring some answers to some of your questions do you mind if I have a look, at them pictures your showing around?"

Ms. Roberts hands them to him.

As his body odor comes in contact with her nose, she takes a step back,.

"So! What are the crack head prices these days, huh?"

Det. Jake said, as he snatched the pictures from Tay-Tay's hand.

He never like drug addicts, one being because his

younger brother was one, and he saw how it destroyed, his family.

"I'm not giving this piece of shit anything, but his freedom and if he don't answer my questions, I'll take that! And he'll see how hard it is to detoxes, in jail".

As he spun him around, and slammed his limp body into a near by pick-up truck.

"Now, you fuckin' smart ass! Have you seen this kid or not? If you think your gonna shut down on me, you stinkin' fuck! Think again, now I asked you a question you better fuckin' give me an answer".

Tay-Tay looked over at Ms. Roberts for some sympathy, but none came, as he began to answer trembling, in the larger man's grasp.

"Okay big guy! Just please let me go, I'll tell you what I know". He spat.

As the huge Detective, unhanded the smaller man, he got his feet back on the ground.

"Alright, all I know is the kids got money the crew he's involved with, would do anything for him but the other picture the girl, is not the girl he's with I never seen her before, and that's all I know, but that kid you were just talking to, knows him and her".

With this being said, Ms. Roberts and Jake both

looked at each other, as she gave him a twenty dollar bill. They quickly went to their car in hopes of catching up to Noah, but he had rode off on a motorcycle and they hadn't seen witch way, he went.

The two of them talked, and agreed to get a hotel room. And stay in this town, until they could turn up something, on these two kids.

Meanwhile…

Up in Maine the tattoo guy, is finishing up with Lulu's tattoo which says LuLu a.k.a "bonnie" Jay got his first. His read J-Razor a.k.a "clyde" on and on.

Being that this was their last night in Maine, afterwards they went out to eat, at a place right off the water witch had the best lobster on the east coast. " Caught fresh off the boat."

They sat eating, and engaged in deep conversation.

"So baby, what's our next move?"

"Well the truth is, we gotta play it as it goes right now but first things first, I got a big surprise for you when we get back, no doubt".

"Oh yeah! I was hoping for a big surprise, tonight".

She said as she reached under the table and grabbed his dick.

"You know it's our last night, here?"

"Yeah so, we can do like "Keith Sweat" and make it last for ever"-

Jay sang out as. they both shared a laugh.

Jay ate the last of his shrimp, as he turned up, the last of his sprite. He dropped a nice tip, and they walked hand in hand down past the water front, back to their "love nest".

"So Jay, can I get a hint on the surprise?"
"Uh no! But thanks for asking".

"Oh! So you're a smart ass huh?"
"Yep, that I am! But might I add you have a nice ass, can I see what's in "those Jeans?"

He said, as he sang a bit of "Ginuwine's" (in those Jeans)

"You know what baby your all I need".
"That's what I like to hear, don't never get tired of telling me that cause I'll never get tired of hearing it".

As she starts to sing (your all I need) by "Method Man, and Mary J."

―――――――――――――――

Mean while…

Back in Scranton "Big Paul" was talking to Smash and Face who was "bailed out" from the county, earlier that day.

"SO LET ME ASK YOU TWO SOMETHING, I'VE KNOWN YA WHOLE CREW FOR A WHILE NOW, AM I WRONG?"

He said as he walked towards Smash.
"This is true, so "Big man" what are you getting at?"

"IF YOU WOULD SHUT THE FUCK UP! AND LET ME TALK I'LL TELL YOU JUST WHAT THE FUCK, I'M TALKING ABOUT".

At that being said Face pulled his gun, and shot "big Paul" in the gut. As the huge man grabbed his wound, he slowly fell over blood leaking everywhere.

Smash screamed out.
"Man! What the fuck, did you just do?"

"You think I'm just gonna let this fat piece of shit, just talk to us just anyway he wants? Fuck that nigga! Come on, let's get this money and get outta here".

They both scrambled around tearing the place apart. Looking for money, by the time they came across some. It wasn't that much as They grabbed it, and went back pass "Big Paul" lying on the floor, in a pool of his own blood. Smash went for the door, as Face leaned over the body to make sure Paul was dead, and that's when Paul shot him in the head. Smash heard the gun shot, as he turned around to see his boy " Face" body slummed over Big Paul's.

He cursed Face, as he continued out the door.

Chapter 32

C.J. went over to Big Paul's shop, as he went in he almost passed out from the scene. There was blood everywhere, as C.J. went farther into the shop. That's where he saw "Face's" body, laying over top of Big Paul.

At this, C.J. dropped his head as he saw his friend laying there, dead.

Then C.J. quickly went through the place until he found Big Paul's books. Then he leaned over and kissed big Paul, on the cheek.

"Good bye old friend, I hate to do this to you. But I know you would understand".

As he poured gas all over the place, he walked out with a trail of gas behind him. Then he dropped a match, and ran as the place went up in flames.

C.J. jumped into his car, and left the scene.

—————————————————

Jay and Lulu were on their way to what she didn't know, would be their new house.

"Jay baby, this is a nice little quite town, and the house are so pretty they almost look fake but this is like the third time you brought me this way, what's up? Are you stashing another woman here, or what?"

Jay pulled into a driveway, of one of the houses.

"That's not funny, girl."
He said with a blank look, on his face.
As he opened the door and jumped out
He looked over at her.
"Come on, she said she would leave a key in the mail box".
Lulu quickly got out the car, and followed behind.
He checked in the mail box, until he came out with a key, as he put it into the door.

He pushed open the door, Lulu's face had the look of awe all across it.
"Wow Jay! Baby, is this another one of big Paul's houses?"

Jay didn't answer, as he Grabbed her hand and lead her through the rest of the house.
They walked into the Living room, which had thick cream colored carpet that felt like you were walking, in

slow motion. It had a sunkin' rock look, Tile in front of the fireplace.

Through the dinning room, were sliding glass doors, that went out to a beautiful deck, over looking a "nice size" kidney shaped, swimming pool.

While they were taking in the view, they heard the door bell ring.

Jay went to the door, Lulu stayed out back, still in awe.

"Let me go see, who's at the door". Jay reasoned.

Once Jay got to the door, he saw two kid's, maybe two years younger than him.

"Hey! Can I help you?"

"Hi, is your mother or father home?"

"Not at the moment, why is there something I can help you with?"

"No, we didn't know they had a son we cut grass around here, and we were wondering?"-

Before they could get anymore, out their mouths.

"Sure! How much do you two, charge?"

"Well for this yard, front and back and cause we have to cover the pool, ask them how's $45.00 sound?"

"I tell you what, come back tomorrow about this time cool."

"You got it, we'll be here". The two boys replied.

Jay goes back into the house, just as Lulu was coming inside.
"Jay, baby I think I'm in love with this house".

" What! You haven't even seen the rest".
She follows him into the back room.

Her eyes open wide, as she looks at the Jacuzzi on the other side of the room, with the thick windows behind it, that only let in light.

 "Oh my God Jay! He has a Jacuzzi, in the master bed room?"
She walks over to it, as she looks at the bathroom, cause the doors open.

"Look Jay, he's got his and her sinks".

Jay walks over and puts his arms around her, as she stands in the door way, he opens her hand and drops the key in it.

"No baby we got his and her sinks. Surprise!"

She's screaming and jumping up and down, like crazy.

"Ho, ho, baby you can't be screaming that loud in this neighborhood, theses people might think I'm killing you, or something".

"Jay, Jay baby are you serious? Come on Jay, tell the truth cause I'm really feeling this house, are you saying this house, is ours on the real?"

"Baby, what I'm telling you is no more hotels, Motels and the truth is, your getting fucked in the living room, in front of the fire place, in the bedroom, in the Jacuzzi, in the back on the lounge chair, on the deck etc".

They both started laughing, as Jay's phone rang.

"Hello, who's this? C.J. who? He's what! Awe man, let me call you back, can I reach you at this number? Cool".
(Jay hangs up)

He leans against the wall.
"Jay! What's wrong? Who's C.J.?"
"Bad news! Lulu baby, big Paul's dead".

"WHAT!!! Oh my God, how did it happen?"
"I don't know but he found them dead, and burned the place".

"Them?"
"Yeah them, it was Face body, laying over top of big Paul's".
"Shit Jay! What do you think went down?"
"Well, I'm sure big Paul knew, but he, he aight talking right now".

"Jay, stay focused we got to find the angle, and see who's working it, we gotta think what happed and who was with Face when he went over there cause it sounds like a robbery gone bad, and I'm willing to bet it was Smash. Cause usually it's "Buttons" and "First come" together, and "Face and Smash," what's your take?"

" I think you're onto something, but we gotta get in touch with this C.J. guy he got the books outta there, so we might be still in business."

"That's what's up, cause that's our cash cow, right there no doubt!

Meanwhile...

Ms. Roberts went to the bar. And ordered her "favorite drink" a apple Martini she took out a cigarette, the bartender came over, and lit it for her cause when she was in any room, it was hard for men not to look at her. She was a tall sexy woman, who's beautiful blonde hair and facial features, demanded attention.

She got her drink and turned around, looking at no one in particular as she sipped on her drink, she took a long pull of her cigarette and exhaled, as she tried, to get her thoughts together.

What if, they were going in the wrong direction? What if this kid "Jason Banks" is the son, she gave up years ago how would she tell Jake?

Theses are just some of the thoughts, that ran through her head as she finished off her drink, and ordered another, as she finished her cigarette.

Meanwhile....

Jay went to the store, to get a blunt and something to drink, while he was gone. Lulu just sits back on the floor cause they have no furniture yet, as she leans against the wall she closes her eye's as she takes a deep breath, she opens them again.

"Wow! I'm really here this is not, a dream".
As she runs her hands over the thick, new carpet.
She gets up and walks around the house again, still not really believing, this house is their's.

Jay comes back inside.

"Hey baby, put on your shoes they got a nice diner down the street, come on let's go".

She puts on her sneakers, and they both leave.
As they pull up to the diner, Jay gets out, Lulu does the same as he holds the door open for her, she walks in.

"Wow! This place sure is clean, for a diner".

"Yeah I was thinking the same thing

but we out the hood now, so it's all good now!"
Jay said, as they both shared a laugh.

"HELLO, HOW ARE YOU TWO THIS EVENING? IS IT JUST THE TWO OF YOU?"

"Yes! It is".
"FOLLOW ME, PLEASE".
She lead them to a booth, near a window.

"SOME ONE WILL BE WITH YOU, SHORTLY".

As their waitress came out, Jay couldn't believe his eye's.

It was Debra (the older woman) Jay had slepted with.
She showed no sign of knowing him, as Lulu ordered and excused Herself, while she went to the bathroom.

"So Mr. when did you get in town? Better yet, I get off in another three hours If you come and get me, we can got to my place and you can give me some more of that young dick, how's that sound?"

Jay got a big smile on his face. He thought he would never see her again, but he had dreamed of her, from the first time he fucked her. This older lady knew how to touch Jay, and he loved the fact that a older woman, wanted him, for sex.

"I'll be here". He spat

She began to walk away, as Lulu was coming back from the bathroom.
"Damn! Jay the bathroom's are cleaner than most people's, house".

They sat ordered and talked until the food arrived, then they ate and talked, some more.

All Lulu was concerned with was getting the house furnished. So Jay knew she wouldn't mind him slipping out, and also she wouldn't think nothing anyway, with them being in a new town.

Once they got back to the house, Lulu was telling Jay were she thought things, should go.

"How about the big screen, over here".
She said standing near the corner, with her arms stretched out.

As she continued to talk, and walk around Jay opened the dime bag of weed, as he split the blunt and picked out the seeds, he held it up to his nose, and inhaled.

"Damn! I know "Redman" said everything light

green aight the bomb, but this shit smells, strong as hell".

" Well what you gonna do, just keep smelling it! Or are you rolling?"
"Anyway, just keep talking about hooking up the crib, I got this!"

There's a knock, at the door.

"Who do you think, that is?" Lulu questioned.
"Humm, let me guess being that you and I just moved here, and don't know anybody? My guess would be my long lost friend? Girl how the hell! Am I suppose, to know?"
Jay said, with sarcasm dripping from his words.

"I'll get it". She yelled back.
She walked over to the door, and opened it.

There was a nice looking Puerto Rican Jaun, standing at the door.
Jay could see her from the living room, as he got up and put the bag from the store over the fresh rolled blunt.

"Hello! I just wanted to be the first to welcome you to the neighborhood
I'm Anette, I live across the street in the blue house".
Jay put out his hand, and introduce himself.

She was beautiful. Long black hair, not that much ass, but enough to get his juices flowing.

"Well I'm glad you came by, and maybe I can have you and your husband over, once we get this place furnished". Lulu reasoned.

"Oh! It's just me I'm divorced, I have a son every other weekend you'll see him, riding up and down the street on his skate board well I won't hold you two up, I'll be seeing you around, bye".

Lulu walked her outside, Jay just looked on as the door closed behind them.

"Damn! That's what neighbors look like in the burbs, I'm feeling that, no doubt!"

He said to himself.
Lulu comes back in.
"Well, she seemed nice but this could be one of those, "Desperate House wife's" neighborhood's so, only time will tell".

"I'm RICK JAMES, BITCH!! COME SMOKE WITH YA BOY, IT'S THE STICKYEST OF THE ICKY"

"Your crazy, come on we got all the time in the world."

"Speaking of time, I need to run out for a while, is that cool?"

"What am I, your mom now? You never ask me before, hey handle your business your not gonna be that long, are you?"

"No I shouldn't be, why?"

"Well Jay, it's gonna be getting dark soon and I don't want to be in a big empty new house, by myself."

"I got you, Yo! I won't be that long okay?"

He kisses her passionately, as he grabs her ass while pulling her close.

She pulls back.

"Don't start with this, if your leaving."

"My bad, I'm outta here, Here let me hit that one more time".

She passes him the blunt, as she exhales the thick smoke.

"That's some good shit right there but we aight gonna be smoking in here, anymore".

Jay closes the door behind him, as he walks over to the car. He sees out of the corner of his eye, his new neighbor peeking out of her window. Jay just smiles, as he closes the door an starts the car, he throws his arm over the seat, and backs out of the driveway.

Ten minutes later he's pulling up the same Diner

he and Lulu just left about an hour ago. Debra waved at him from her car, he jumped out and went over.

"Hey baby! I was hoping you came oh Jay damn, come on get in your car and follow me hurry up, you got my panties wet, waiting for that young dick".

Jay quickly went back to the car, an followed her as told, he was open over this older women, she knew exactly how to make love to him. She taught him things, he still think about and have tried with Pam, not Lulu.

She pulled into the parking lot that had a Cvs in it, Jay parked and got out with her.

"I just had to stop and get some water, cause I remember how you put it on me, last time".

" Oh that's cool! Cause I gotta get some condoms, anyway".
They walked in looking more like mother and Son, than lovers.

When they got what they needed, they went to the counter together.
Jay's behind her holding the box of condoms, as she put the 1 liter bottle of water on the counter, she told him to put them up there.

"It's together?" The clerk questioned.

The woman behind the counter got a smirk on her face, as she went from Jay to Debra a couple times.

She paid.
As she put it in a bag, they left.
Jay got into his car and followed behind eagerly.

About ten minutes later their pulling up to her apartment, outside it looked poor and ran down, however once inside. Jay was a bit taken back.

"Wow! This is a nice place, you have here".
"Yeah, you like huh?"

"No doubt, no doubt".
He said as he looked around, nodding his head in approval.

"Good, I'm glad you like it maybe you'll come over again and again, but enough with the small talk you've been in here all but five minutes, that's five minutes to long, for you to still be dressed".

At this, she's in front of him on her knees undoing his shorts as she pulls them down in one motion, shorts and boxers.

"jackpot!!" She let's out.

With his dick in her face, she pushes Jay back against the entertainment unit, she sucks on his nuts, as she aggressively jerks him off.

Jays trying to hold his balance, as he stumbles trying to get his sneakers out of his shorts. He's getting hotter by the minute, as he grabs a hand full of her hair and gives it a twist, as he forcefully fucks her mouth.

She reaches behind him and turns on the stereo.

Lauren Hill's, "Can't take my eye's off of you" comes through the speakers.

Jay let's go her hair, as he pulls off her bra her titties pop out, and Jay takes over.

He plays the aggressor, and pulls her skirt up and pulls her thong to the side almost forgetting about the condom. He quickly rips open the box, and bites one open and throws the rest down, he mounts her from behind, he has her skirt up on her hips, as he pumps faster and an faster, then slows down as she rocks back, he smacks her on her ass.

"Damn!" She said almost out of breath, "baby fuck this pussy oh shit!"

Her talking, just made Jay ride her harder, as he reached under and Pinched her nipples, she let out a loud, scream.

Jay turned her over, as he looked her in her face "Oh! You want to scream, huh?"

Jay takes her legs, and put them over his shoulders as he enters her he looking in her eyes he can see her turning red, as he pounded his dick harder, and deeper in her.

"This what you wanted, right! You want this dick right?"

"Yes baby! Awe please Jay, stop, baby stop".

Jay pounded her a few more times, then pulled out.

"I thought you said you wanted to fuck! What's this stop shit bitch? I know you didn't bring me here, to waste my time." Jay snapped.

"Jay, wait listen! I haven't been with anyone in four months, it's just a little too much to go from nothing, to all that! In one night. Damn I'm saying I'll take care of you! Just go get, washed up."

She said, pointing to the bathroom.

———————————————

Meanwhile back in Scranton...

Tyrone and Tamela was just walking through the park Tamela was thinking about this Detective asking all these questions about Jay.

"Hey, let me ask you something do you think Jay did all that stuff the two cops, were talking about?"

"Humm, well let me put it to you like this, I grew up with a lot of friends that I thought was incapable of doing what they did to get life in prison, but their there so just think about that for awhile, I mean sure Jay seems cool, but we just met him."

"Yeah, I feel you on that for his sake I hope it's not the same guy".

"What the fuck! Are you talking about didn't you see the picture? That's Jay all day everyday, trust me! It's him you might not want it to be him, but I saw the flick (pictures) it's him babe".

———————————————

Meanwhile...

C.J.'s putting the final touches, on Big Paul's funeral.

He just got a call from one of Big Paul's contacts, who's coming through, for the viewing.

Then he thinks damn! I'll hook up Jay, with this guy.

Jay's phone rings. while he's laid back on the couch getting head from Debra.

He answers.

"Hey baby! What's up?"

"Yeah, yeah, I'll be home soon, what? Who? Okay, okay well do ya thing, no, no, that's cool yeah, okay bye"

While he was on the phone, Debra was working over time, to get his voice to change. Jay noticed this, as he took his dick out of her mouth he started jerking

346

off while, she was still on her knees her face about two inches from his dick,

She tried to move, but Jay grabbed the back of her head and held her there, as he shot his hot cum all over her face. Jay stood up over her as he continued to cum it was dripping down the side of her face on her chin, Jay just slowly fucked her mouth what she didn't swallow, dripped down her chin and on to the floor.

" Look, I can't stay It's been fun! But I gotta bounce, but trust me I'll hit you off again this week, cool?"

As she wiped her face, and tried to straighten up. "You promise?" She replied.

"Hell no! I don't promise, look I'll do what I can do is that cool?"

"Yeah baby, that's good. Look I'm sorry, give me a little while to get back use to you, and I'll be better, trust me".

"Alright, well I'm gonna jump in your shower and rinse off, cool?"
"Oh I'm in there with you, please believe me".

Chapter 33

Jay gets back to the house
    As he's talking to Lulu, his phone rings.
    Jay looks at the number, like he seen a Ghost.

    He shows the phone to Lulu, now she got the same look, on her face.
    Jay answers.

    "Yo! What's up? Smash, what's really good son? Naw, naw, not right now haven't you heard?" (there's was a long pause) as Jay wanted to see if he, was gonna go first.

    "Yeah, there's a couple Detectives on my ass right now but look, I'll keep you posted no doubt."
    (They hang-up)

    "Shit Jay! So it was that nigga, in there with him, that shot big Paul that's some foul shit so how you gonna play this?"

"We gotta kill em' or they gonna kill us!" Jay spat.

"So babe! What do you have, in mind?"

"Remember that kid "Noah" said he wanted, to get down?"

PREVIEW TO: TRUST NO ONE THE "JAY-RAZOR" STORY STILL RUNNING.

Okay so where cool now we still getting money we got a nice house out in the "burbs" your still the realist bitch I know so what's next you say huh?"

" No Jay! I know what needs to be next this "Cream Squad" thing is gonna get us jammed- up I mean Jay, this mother fuckers talking shit now on the streets, telling everybody this, that, And the other thing but giving us a whole different story, so you tell me are we fools?"

"Look, I understand were your coming from but we gotta let this boy Noah do this"-

"No Jay! This time your wrong, fuck! That boy Noah".

She stated putting emphsis on the word fuck.

"If he was gonna do it, he would have done it already shit! It's been almost two weeks can't you see he's bullshitting!?" She stated holding up two fingers.

"Well, sense I'm wrong! What should we do?"
Jay said with a little sarcasm, dripping from his words.

"Your not gonna do shit but tell him what's really good, have him meet you at that dirty motel around the hood and I'll handle that nigga! Once and for all, for the streets start thinking we sweet the street will respect me, or respect my gangster, no doubt!"

"You sure, you want to go through with this?"
"Jay, I'm as sure as the Tattoo, on my arm".

She said pointing to the name "Bonnie" on her arm.
"You got it! I'll call him, right now."

Jay takes out his cell phone, and dials Smash's number.
He answers.

"What's really good? yeah, yeah, well that's what I was calling you for tomorrow? Tonight".
Jay covers the phone, and looks at Lulu.
She shakes her head, in agreement.

"That's cool, well look meet me at that dirty motel-yeah, yeah where all the hoes be at that one In the back near the dumpster, cool?"

Lulu's already putting on her sweatpants, and her running shoes, as she grabs her gun, she empty out all the bullets.

Then puts on a pair of latex gloves, and loads it again, as she cocks it back, an evil grin goes across her face.

"So you really ready, to take this man outta here, huh?"

"No doubt! Jay we worked to hard to get all this shit but were young, and if we get caught we do life are you ready for that?"

"Shit, I don't even want to go back to living the way I was, before I met you let alone prison! Look it's either him or me, so it is, what it is".

"Trust me, I feel you there I'll hold court in the streets before I go back!"

This book is dedicated to all the writers out there doing their thing, keeping it real, and following their hearts. One#1 Love

Deon Hayes.

This book is dedicated to my mom Mamie P. Hayes who passed away in October 25ᵗʰ 2006. Mom your always in my heart, and all the talks we had I still listen to your "Words of wisdom" every time I'm going through something, I get it now you were always right.

Also to my Father-in law Robert "Bob" Moyer. Pop-pop you'll be forever missed R.I.P.

To my wife: Kelly Hayes, I'll love you forever and 2 days!! Congrats to my son for getting into College, My Daughters Chelcie, Alexis, and Lauren I love you all…

To my Family: My Dad John C. Hayes, My big sister Desiree, Renae, Pam, Tracey. My brother Mark.

Special thanks to my cousin Adrianne. Thanks for everything, and helping me put out a better book. My man K'wan new facebook friend thanks for keeping it real. Love your book's.

To my man I.M.D. the award winning poet. Thanks for always showing love. GOD bless, my Man Alpha doing his thing on the music tip, I love your music keep doing your thing.

To my old friends and new. Dominic and Vanessa congrats on your new beautiful baby girl. Norma, Zenaida, Annette, Lourdes, dedria, Carlos, Lenard etc. Thanks for the picture Norma!

To my Target family: TSC Rachael thanks for the picture, Chris, Keep listening to your Snoop Dogg and Lil Kim. Julie, Chandra, Barbra, John, Ki, Danielle.
Food ave: Laura thanks for the picture and the fresh cookies. Jamie, Linda.

Starbucks: George "you don't do any work, where are the toilet seat covers?" Chloe, Ally, Venessa, Stefan, Brian, Helen.
Backroom: Dave, Rich, Nekesha, Jeff, Matt, Bill, Ryan, Mike.
Phar: Kristy, Anthony
Market: Norman, Mike, Cory, Sandy, Kevin, Allison, Shawn.

Soft lines: Kenya, Holly, Kim, M.L, Chrissy, Barbra, Amiee, Carrie
Front end: connie, Jessica, Paola, Penny, Katie, Jennifer, Ashely
Cashiers: Kelly- "pretty ricky's sister" Lindsay, Julia, Lizz, Katelyn, Jamal, Patrick, Chris, Gina
Security: Joe, and Diane.
Floor: Janet, Karol, Margret, Isaias, Suok, Eva, Megan, Tina, Larry
Eletronics: Brian 'Pretty Ricky' Ralph, Brandon, Evelyn, Colleen, Dawn, Joe, Tom, Chris, Carol, Ian.

and last, but not least the Lod's :Marc, Daneda, Laura, Mike, Steve, Blair and my long lost friend -Melinda! Can't forget Liz.

God bless our New President and his family the Obama's congrats on your first year, hope the next 7 is even better.

If I forgot anyone, I'll get you next book peace!! Keep it real and keep it moving...One love~
Pictures: Derrick, Norma, Laura, Rachael, Emily, Talia.

And for all those people Hating on my old High school Pennsbury, Neshaminy etc.

HARRY S. TRUMAN...BITCHES!!!

DeonHayes/Facebook.com
DeonHayes/Myspace.com
Dnice24flawless/blackplanet.com